A TRAITOR'S

GEOFF CARTHY

THE CROWN AND THE ARROW SAGA

PART 1

Also by Geoff Carthy:

A Traitor's Son Vol 2

Forthcoming:

The Thegn Vol 1

The Thegn Vol 2

GEOFF CARTHY

A Traitor's Son

Volume I

Part One of The Crown and The Arrow Saga

STORIES*into*LIGHT Publishing

A Traitor's Son Vol I

ISBN of paperback edition
978-1-7392612-2-1

Geoff Carthy

First edition 2025

Published by Stories into Light 2025

In memory of

RON CARTER

1927 - 2023

CONTENTS

Prologue: The Fourteenth Day of October, in the Year of Our Lord One Thousand and Six

(Wulfnoth Cild)

"Fuck all thanks I'll get for it."

The Thegn of Comtyn and Bosham stood proudly on the tiny foredeck, holding tight to the wolf's ear. He called his vessel Sea Wolf for his own name, Wulfnoth, and had paid good silver to get the beast's head sculpted and pegged in place.

The carver had chiselled the wolf's fur thick and wavy, rippled by the wind as it leapt at its prey. He'd carved bared fangs and wild eyes, but failed to match the savagery in Wulfnoth's own.

For the enemy was in sight. Three drekkars sailed abreast, heading straight for them. Probably Danish, not Norse, come from Normandy and targeting Cicaestr, but Cicaestr had its walls, unlike Bosham and the villages around the mouths of the Ems and the Lavant. Should they land here, it was a short way up the vale to Walderton, the Mardens, and Comtyn.

The Sea Wolf was the point of an arrow, with the Sea Lynx and the Sea Boar to one side, and the Sea Bull and the Sea Fox to the other. The Danes probably assumed that, too big to be Saxon boats, they were friendly, returning from a plunder of Cicaestr. Too late to get more than the dregs of wealth from the berh, they'd definitely be thinking of turning aside to fall on the coastal villages.

Cicaestr could go hang, but Wulfnoth would protect his

own lands. The Sea Wolf and four others would guard the place they'd been littered. Thanks be to Hemming the Dane.

The drekkars were in for a shock. Sea Wolf was crewed by Comtyn men, save the skipper Ham, but the other crews were mostly from the coastal villages. They would defend to the death their homes, their farms, their families. They'd defend their Thegn and each other, bound by kinship, loyalty and honour woven into their veins and sinews through lifetimes of song and story.

On land, summer was dying its annual death. Trees were still in leaf, but the next gale would strip them bare. Harvests were in, and it was the time for storing, pickling and smoking food. October was called winter-month, with its full moon marking the start of the year's long while of hardship.

Out at sea, the clouds were light, the air clear, and the breeze biting. The Sea Wolf, beam to the wind, rolled and yawed into each trough. The planks creaked. Hemming had assured him they were meant to, that the boat's flexibility gave it strength to survive a long voyage. Wulfnoth considered strength to ram a drekkar amidships would be more valuable. He'd have to talk to Hemming about that.

Hemming remained in Bosham. His skills were too rare to risk, and it was true that, were he captured by his countrymen, his fate would be cruel beyond contemplation.

The bow slapped into each wave, sending up a spume of spray that blew over Wulfnoth. Salt dried into his beard, disguising the strands of white that had appeared of late. He'd come to relish the sea. He'd make a good Viking, he decided. But he was born into a non-seafaring race whose fishermen had no need to venture beyond sight of land.

We have the numbers here, he thought. But the Danes have the experience. Or do they? Unchallenged for so many years, how many of the Vikings on those boats had actually fought at sea?

How big were those longships? How many men? They were prow-on, so he could not guess their length. The sails were big, but how big?

He signalled to Ham at the stern to veer closer to the Sea Bull to the west, and beckoned its skipper Londfreth to sail alongside. Wulfnoth chuckled, for 'Londfreth' meant 'peace on land'. But battles at sea. When the Bull was in shouting distance, he called "You and Tabbut take the western boat!" He pointed at his two boats, then at the rightmost of the three Danish vessels. Londfreth raised his fist in understanding.

However big the enemy's boat, it would struggle to defend itself once trapped between the pair.

He waved Ham to veer east, and shouted a similar instruction to Othi.

The crew were hunkered down, tense and fearful. Those who had puked over the side blamed the waves and the boat's roll. No-one jeered them. The Sea Wolf was the biggest of the five, with twenty oar on each side, and room for twenty more men who currently crouched along the centre with wet feet and sore arses. Each had three bows ready to hand out, and countless arrows, throwing-spears and glaives; and swords to wield when they climb aboard to finish the Danes off. Or for when the Danes board us, Wulfnoth thought. First they'd need to get past Cudbert, his chief husceorl, a giant of a man yet swift of arm, with a face like a huge flint fallen from a chalk cliff.

It was Cudbert who had captured Hemming a few years back, knocking him unconscious during a random Vikingr raid. Cudbert refrained from killing him only because he'd had to defend himself against three others. He beat them off, and the raiders left Hemming for dead. When he was pulled before Wulfnoth it was discovered he spoke some English, from time spent in the North. He claimed to be a Christian. He did not beg, but swore an oath of service and loyalty to Wulfnoth if his life was spared. "I am not a fighter," he said. "I'm a boatwright." And Cudbert said "It's true he's no fighter."

Wulfnoth put Hemming to making new boats for the fishermen, and took most of the price they paid, be it in coin or a share of the fish. All knew that the Danes were enviable boatwrights, and Wulfnoth prospered as news of Hemming's prowess spread along the coast. Hemming took a second baptism to show his faith, married a Bosham girl, and had two children. Then, when Wulfnoth hatched his plan to defend his realm at sea, he supervised the construction of these five new boats, proving his loyalty to his new Saxon friends.

The Danish boats came on. The central one had a carved prow, some kind of serpent by the look. Beside it stood his foe, a big man, whose long hair blew sideways. His beard was fair. Young, then. *When he realises he's in for a fight, he won't flee. Such a shame if he does.*

Wulfnoth's flanking boats pulled away, as if to skirt the Danes altogether. He checked Ham, who nodded, knowing he must keep straight on.

The Danish chief raised an arm in greeting. Wulfnoth returned it. The Dane spoke to his steersman, and his boat veered closer to the wind, inviting Wulfnoth to pass by on the easier leeward side.

He looked back at Ham once more. Using his body to hide the gesture from the Dane, he waved Ham to spurn the invitation, and follow the longship into the wind. *How long before the Danes realise this is not bad seamanship, but an attack? Will we be close enough to shoot a volley of arrows before they raise their shields?*

The closer they came, the more hits they'd make. Just get as many arrows off as they could, hard and low. At sea there was no point aiming at targets, not till you're close enough that you don't need to. His men knew this.

The *Sea Wolf* closed in, tight to the wind. The Bosham

boats weren't as fast as a good Danish drekkar, Hemming had said, not with a following wind. But they'd be better into the wind, and more manoeuvrable.

The more the drekkar veered into the wind, the slower it went.

To each side, the two pairs of English boats were each forcing their target between them. Then their fates were their own, for the Danes ahead were moving on their boat, standing, looking at the Sea Wolf in puzzlement. The drekkar was indeed bigger than the Sea Wolf, but not so tightly crewed. Wulfnoth wanted to be closer, but now was the time for arrows. A standing man is a bigger target. He nodded at Cudbert

"Bows," Cudbert called.

The men of Comtyn knew what to do. They had practiced this score of times on land, then again on the boats in the shallow estuary. They swiftly notched their arrows below the bulwarks. When Cudbert saw they were set, he called "Shoot!", and they rose, loosed their arrows, and knelt again to notch a second. First the rank of fighters, then the oarsmen on the left, shooting over their heads, then the oarsmen on the right. Then again. Sixscore arrows in all. Many passed above the Danes' heads, or pierced the sail, or thunked into timbers, or uselessly speared the sea. But one in ten found a mark even as the panicking Danes raised their shields. They were just yards away, close enough now that their cries carried across the waves. Fools. They'd not hear their leader calling vainly from the prow.

They left gaps between their shields, and these were the spaces into which his men threw their spears. They did little damage, but that wasn't the point.

The Danes picked up the spears to hurl them back. Archers were ready, and as they stood another volley was loosed. Now it was easy to make a hit. Three men tipped forward into the sea, two fell backwards, four more dropped into the hull, while another four stared uncomprehendingly at the arrows embedded in shoulders, ribs, arms, and guts.

The Danish leader strode into the midst of them, shouting. His men ducked down, leaving him standing alone. Brave, for sure. Wulfnoth wanted a bow of his own. At this range he'd not miss, even at sea. As twenty Wessexmen rose with their bows, the chieftain ducked below the shields.

He'd come up with his men, wielding axes and swords. Counter-attack was the only way they knew.

The gap between the boats was too large for them to jump. "Keep us apart" he yelled at Ham. Ham leaned on the steer-oar.

"Glaives," Cudbert called.

The men at the side of the boat each took a glaive, a short sharp blade at the end of a long and heavy pole. They chopped down on the shields. Some of the Danes lifted them to protect their heads, leaving bellies exposed to spears and arrows.

Two pairs were charged with the billhooks. They must get the hook with its sharpened inner curve behind the ropes of the other ship, and pull. If the ropes were cut, the sail would be left flapping, and even if not, it was dragged out of line.

An axe whirled across the gap, taking Lineker full in the chest. Comtyn's bridle-maker pitched forward into the sea. Most of the Danes seemed unwilling to part with their favoured weapon, for only a few axes followed. While a couple of his men took deep wounds, most managed to duck out of sight.

Wulfnoth had a choice. To close in, and let the Danes try to board the Sea Wolf, hoping to stab many of them with spears or pierce them with arrows before the hand-to-hand fighting started. One boat or the other would be captured and its crew killed. Or to pull away, and let the Danes limp back to

Wihtware if they could.

There were many enraged Danes still alive. His mission was to protect his villages, not to lead his best men to death.

The Racton brothers had a rope hooked, and were pulling it, stretching the Danes' sail out of shape. Wulfnoth picked up his sword and shield, and went to them. "Closer," he shouted, and the brothers heaved.

His shield felt the thud of an axe, and was suddenly heavier. He ignored it, and lifted his sword-arm to slash at the rope. Scissored between two blades, the rope severed, and the Danish squaresail flapped loose in the wind. "Now, go," he called to Ham. Ham pulled at the steer-oar, and immediately the gap between the two boats widened.

The Danes stood and jeered. "Ragr!" they called. "Ergi!"

He'd shared mead with Hemming, and asked what words would most insult a Dane. Ragr was one, and ergi another. They both meant much the same: a man who is a girl, who opens his only hole to other men. A ragr does it for coin, ergis do it for free, for some unfathomable demeaning pleasure.

Call me either at your peril. Call me both and watch your fate unfurl. "Back at them!" he shouted to Ham.

Cudbert look up.

"Kill them all!"

Cudbert's flint face was expressionless. He knew this was not the plan. But the men cheered. English and Danes made noises across the water, knowing only that their manhoods were being ridiculed. Until Cudbert called "Archers!"

The row of Englishmen armed only with insults hid the rank of archers who rose behind them. Six fewer Danes would resist them when they came alongside. "Jump when I say," Cudbert called.

The two boats juddered against each other. Spears and glaives did more work as the Sea Wolf made a pass alongside the Danish longboat with its half crew and half sail. Then when the Sea Wolf's higher stern matched the Serpent's midships, Cudbert led the men of Comtyn over the side, six abreast, roaring, wielding swords and axes over their heads with such wild force that they were as like to brain a comrade as a foe. Wulfnoth had to shoulder his way through from the prow to join another six, and more, and yet another wave onto the Danish foredeck as Ham steered the Sea Wolf past.

The Danes were outnumbered on their own boat. Their shields were useless when they were being attacked from behind as well as in front. The Saxons hacked and stabbed, pushing the Danes back by weight of numbers, forcing them overboard.

Cudbert was a goliath, but Wulfnoth was worse, for he had a rage in him. He knew what it was to be a berserker. His shield felt like a leaf on his arm, his sword like a feather. His own roar filled his head. An enemy's shield dropped, and Wulfnoth swung at his exposed neck. Another turned to face Arculf. Wulfnoth's sword pierced his jerkin and skewered his ribcage. It was harder pulling the blade out than thrusting it in.

The smell of human blood inspired him. He wanted the bearded chieftain, who had been pushed to the prow and was stood with his back to the serpent, held at bay by the Racton brothers, each with a glaive. They jabbed in unison at his body so he had to hide behind his shield. They slashed at his feet. He could not hop clear of both blades, and one smashed into his left ankle. He roared his pain, and stumbled but did not fall. He looked over the side into the dark sea, then back at the Ractons. He gripped his axe tighter. He wanted a warrior's death. He was going to charge.

Wulfnoth shouldered between them. "Ergi," he snarled, and the Dane flew at him. He feinted to his right as if wanting the two shields to smash together. If they were as close as that, the Danish silver-sharp axe would be deadlier than the English sword. Wulfnoth dodged back left, and before the axe could start its swing he thrust his blade inside the shield to slice the shoulder of the young man's axe-arm. The axe fell to the deck as the hand holding it lost all strength. One of the Ractons' glaive blades smashed the Dane's knee but still he stood. His shield was too small as he tried to protect himself from the three blades that assaulted him. When Wulfnoth swiped to cut his left shoulder to the bone, his last defence fell.

The Dane held his head up, baring his throat white between the brown beard and his waxed leather jerkin shiny with blood. He was asking for a swift death. The pulse in his neck beat fast. It would not do so for long. Wulfnoth stabbed him in the gut and turned away to join the last of the fighting behind. The Ractons might show him mercy with a swift death, but Wulfnoth felt no compunction. The Vikingr were themselves merciless.

The Danish dead, they pitched into the sea. The wounded, they pitched into the sea.

Their own dead – just four of them – they laid out for burial at home. Their own wounded, seven of whom would lose limbs, never to fight again, and thirteen who had gained scars to boast of, were tended as best they could be. You shall have the pick of the captured weapons, Wulfnoth told the twenty, and if you can no longer fight, then by Bevis, you'll have valuable trophies.

He gave Ham one of the few Danish swords. Ham patted the steer-oar lashed in place for the voyage home, and said "If you think I'm a better fighter than a sailor, throw yourself into the waves right now."

Wulfnoth laughed as loudly as he'd roared, for the tension had ebbed. "For your boy then. May he grow up strong." Ham had a son of ten years, called Arni, and a younger daughter. Wulfnoth had taken his own son, Godwin, down to Hemming's boatyard, and told the boys to play and not get into any trouble. Godwin seemed not to have taken to Arni as a pal, which was unusual, for Godwin usually liked everyone, and was popular across the thegnship.

The villages around the mouths of the Ems and the Lavant were never attacked again, not for a decade, and then not by Danes. Cicaestr was too rich a target to escape entirely, but the raiders chose to march from the beaches at Pagham and Aldwick, so the attacks were lighter and less frequent.

All of Wessex knew the reason for the terrors that beset them through those years. Sveyn Forkbeard, King of the Danes and ruler of northern England, was exacting his ruinous revenge for the St Brice's Day edict. In 1002, King Aethelred had commanded his people to put to death all the Danes who lived among them. The day chosen for the massacre was the thirteenth day of November, St Brice's Day.

Wulfnoth was not alone in ignoring his King. To kill Hemming, so valuable to himself and the all the fishermen? Unthinkable. Wulfnoth set Cudbert and others to guard him.

Only the King's loyal subjects in Oxenford took the command remotely seriously, perhaps because as the most northerly town of Wessex they had the most to fear. Oxenford's Danes were Christians who took refuge in the church. They should have fled. Their Saxon brothers and sisters in the sight of the Lord barred the church doors and set the building alight. No-one counted how many men, women and children were immolated there; but all of Wessex soon knew that one of the victims was King Sveyn's own sister Gunhilde.

Oxenford's shame and Gunhilde's tragedy brought years of suffering. In his rage, Sveyn ordered attacks on Escancaestr and southern Defenas, on Dorcaestr and Wilton, Suthamtun, Wintancaestr, Cicaestr and Haestings along the south coast, on Cantware, and on numberless villages. Readingam, Lunden, Wallingford, and of course Oxenford were attacked overland; East Anglia too, though Ealdorman Ulfcytel had forbidden his people to follow the St Brice's Day order.

Aethelred agreed on a gafol payment of twenty-four thousand pounds of silver to stop the attacks, but Sveyn didn't honour it, and a semblance of peace only descended on the payment of a further twelve thousand pounds.

Wessex was impoverished and endebted by the gafol taxes. Sveyn and the north were vastly enriched, so it was only a matter of time before the attacks resumed. Danish concern swung from vengeance to extortion.

A few years on, word reached Wulfnoth that Aethelred had conceived a grand plan to protect Lunden and the coast. The information came through his wife's family, for Saehild was a second cousin to Wessex's Ealdorman Aelfric. Aethelred was to issue another edict: every coastal village, town, berh or thegnship must build one boat for every fifty adults in its bounds, and provide fifteen men for each boat.

It was something of a surprise that Aelfric himself wished to come to Comtyn, for Wulfnoth was not well liked or respected by the nobles of Wessex. Saehild was judged to have bought discredit to the family by marrying one so wild and rough. Wulfnoth suspected that Saehild had come to agree with them. But she was as proud as she was tempestuous, and she loved her surviving children, Godwin and little Saewin. In Comtyn she remained.

Wulfnoth and Saehild threw a great feast for Aelfric. There were fishes fresh and smoked, sweet pigmeat and salted hams, a calf roasted for succulent veal, hard cheeses, soft cheeses, breads. Mead and ale flowed, and cider and wine – Soussex wine was the best in the land, everyone knew; and Soussex would fight any from the western scires over their claims to brew the best cider.

Every man, woman and child of Comtyn had a share of the food and drink, though not all could fit into Wulfnoth's hall.

Saehild began the evening graciously, then as the drinking progressed became her blunt and outspoken self. "Bring Godwin," she called, and the boy was presented to Aelfric.

He inspected the dark hair, the brown eyes with their level gaze, the confident half-smile even facing his Ealdorman. Godwin stood tall for a fourteen-year old, and his shoulders were already broad. "He'll grow up stronger than you," Aelfric said to Wulfnoth.

"Twice as strong!" Saehild said. "Because he has me for a mother."

"Are you teaching him well?"

"He learns sword skills," Wulfnoth responded. "And archery. He's already the most accurate in these parts, and soon he'll have range too. And Snell, our priest, is good with words and numbers. I say priest – he's an old fool of a monk who seems to prefer our village to the monastery." He winked at Godwin. "Give us some Latin, boy."

"Honorati sumus per turam praesentium, domini."

Aelfric burst out laughing. Wiping tears from his cheeks, he said "I'm grateful that you're honoured at my visit, but you put us both of risk of blasphemy. Domini is 'lord', but it is the One Lord, and not even the King is that mighty. Best you stick with your sword and your bow. The King may need them."

"Off you go, Godwin, and tomorrow, ask Brother Snell about titles," Saehild said.

The boy shrugged, and left.

Wulfnoth turned to Aelfric. "So the King, as well as ordering these boats-"

Aelfric interrupted. "How are you getting on with that?"

"We are ahead of schedule. We had a head start, of course, with the drekkars we captured. They are twice the size of the average English boat so I'm counting them as two. And

Hemming is leading the building work on more, and they are larger too. The King will not be disappointed."

Aelfric stroked his grey beard. "I'm sure that's so. Your feats between here and Wihtware are famed. Wessex is grateful. Others have been inspired. It may be-" and he lowered his voice as he leaned close to Wulfnoth. "It may be that you were the seed of this grand plan."

"Fuck all thanks I'll get for it," Wulfnoth said, knowing he should keep quiet. Aelfric was leading up to something, and it was unwise to utter words that could be taken as hostages.

Saehild saw it too. "Uncle. Say what is on your mind."

Aelfric had a goose's drumstick in his left hand and a mug of wine in his right. He bit off a large mouthful of meat and put down the mutilated leg. He chewed slowly, and swallowed. He took two mouthfuls of wine, and placed the cup onto the table, holding the wine in his mouth before downing it. "The King is in Wintancaestr. So are the Mercian brothers."

Eadric and Brihtric. The older brother, Eadric, was Ealdorman of Mercia, and as close to the King, if not closer, than Aelfric himself. The younger was nearly as powerful in Mercia, although not as well respected.

"Eadric has wormed his way into the King's ear. I think he wishes to place his brother at the head of the King's fleet."

Wulfnoth was amazed. "Brihtric? He knows shit about boats and the sea. Mercia is landlocked! Brihtric can be in charge of river-skiffs."

"Precisely. I want you to return with me to Wintancaestr. It is you who should be in command. You have experience. You have success. The boats will be mostly built in Wessex, and crewed by Wessex men. The fighting will be done by Wessex men. Some from Cantware, maybe from Eassex too. But they need a Wessex man in charge. Not a damned Mercian."

Wulfnoth was happy to stay in Aelfric's lodge a mile south of Wintancaestr, and avoid its inns and ale halls. Anywhere but here, he'd love nothing better than to drink and roister. But he knew Wintancaestr, and hated the place. It was where weak men gathered like rats to chew at each other's wealth and power. He had shed no tears at each report of another Danish raid on the place in previous years, save for the knowledge that the result would be higher gafol taxes. Or boats, which came to the same thing as far as Wulfnoth's riches were concerned.

At least boats had a purpose.

It took two days before a messenger came to say that the King would see them on the morrow at noon. "He'll keep us waiting until after he's lunched," Aelfric told him. "No doubt he'll be eating with Eadric. The bastard."

Wulfnoth couldn't tell if his Ealdorman was referring to the King or to Eadric.

They rode through rain into Wintancaestr, and were let into the royal compound. At least the gateguards were Wessex men who recognised their Ealdorman. Their horses were led to a stable, their cloaks were taken to dry before a fire, and their weapons were taken for safe keeping until they had left the King's presence. They were greeted by Reeve Wilmaer, a short round man with florid cheeks, who had a habit of interlacing his fingers under his paunch whenever he stopped his bustling. Wilmaer led them to the small hall where the King received nobles, clerics, envoys and ambassadors. A fire burned in a stone hearth, and thin smoke rose up to lick at soot-black rafters and shiny reeds of the inner thatch. He showed them benches to sit on, whose waxed wood was polished from thousands of hopeful arses.

The King and the Queen were seated on heavy chairs of carved oak. They were on a platform so their heads were higher than the Mercian brothers Eadric and Brihtric's, who sat before him explaining something about the troublesome Waelas.

Aethelred leaned back, appearing all the stouter for the mass of furs draped around him. He regarded the world with a disapproving frown, which Wulfnoth suspected had been cultivated to direct at all those before him. He ignored their entrance, and made no gesture of recognition, although Wulfnoth had met him at several Witangemots. Wulfnoth didn't take this personally, because it must be easier for the King to frown than to recall every thegn in the land.

He had never met the Queen before, neither at feasts nor at the Witans. But then, he hadn't been to Witan for several years, for it was as like to be held in Lunden these days, and he had no urge to endure eight days of travel just to listen to old men bickering. "Is Queen Emma trying to involve herself in affairs?" he whispered to Aelfric. "More than before?"

"She is," he replied.

"But who is the affair with?"

Aelfric glared at him for his joke.

It would have to be with someone who liked tall, skinny, small-titted, sharp faced women, Wulfnoth decided. Someone, in fact, who really preferred boys. But to her credit, she had avoided running to fat after bearing – what was it? – three children. Saehild couldn't boast as much. But Seahild would best Emma in a fight, be it of words or weapons. She'd probably best the King, Eadric and Brihtric too. Especially if words were the weapon.

The King ended the matter of the Waelas by saying "Yes, yes. Do what you must."

Wilmaer cleared his throat and leaned between the King and Queen to whisper to them. A reminder of the next matter to be dealt with, no doubt.

The King shifted his arse to sit straighter in his chair. The Queen was already sitting like a building post. "So, Aelfric, you are here to force my decision," he said

No welcome? No enquiry after Ealdorman Aelfric's family? No introductions for politeness' sake? Wulfnoth knew his own rustic reputation, but even he had more couth than the King.

"We need to do what is best for Wessex and England," Aelfric said.

"Especially Wessex," Brihtric muttered. He was a square-faced man, whose dark eyes glared at the world from under the thickest black eyebrows Wulfnoth had ever seen. Like two furry caterpillars they were, brought together by their owner's frown as if about to mate.

"My Lord, have you met Wulfnoth Cild, the Thegn of Comtyn?" Aelfric put his hand on Wulfnoth's shoulder.

"Heard his name, that's all."

Wulfnoth had bowed to the King three or four times. Wulfnoth made a point of remembering people's names, where they met, what their position was, and if possible their family's wellbeing. Make people think they are important to you, and you will be important to them.

"Wulfnoth here began to build boats for battle some six years ago. He has captured three Danish boats, burned several more, and-"

"Burned them? Why in heavens name burn them?"

Wulfnoth looked up. "Because I didn't have the crews to take them home, my Lord."

Aethelred hmphed.

"He knows the southern waters," Aelfric continued. "He has mastered the tactics of fighting at sea. He knows how to train men. The Danes fear him – they have kept clear of his villages for years now. He is respected along the coast from Escancaestr to Dofras."

An exaggeration, but Aethelred had no knowledge to counter the point, and the Mercians certainly didn't.

Brihtric could barely keep his seat. "Are you saying that I am not?"

Wulfnoth shifted sideways to stare at him. "I can't tell you what Ealdorman Aelfric is saying. But I can say that along the coast – and I live there – your name is hardly known."

"It will be soon!" Brihtric thumped the carved arm of his chair.

"Tell me this," Aelfric said to him. "How many sea battles have you commanded? How many have you been in?"

"Which end of an oar goes in the water?" Wulfnoth muttered.

"This fleet will be our fyrd at sea. I know how to command a fyrd, and I know how to make a shieldwall."

"Build a shieldwall of boats across the Tamys," Wulfnoth said, "and Lunden may be protected, from the sea at least. What of Dofras, Cicaestr, and Suthamtun? We need to be as swift on the water as mackerel are under it. We need more big boats like the drekkars." He turned back to the King. "We need to sail across the east sea, to plunder Denmark like they have been plundering us!"

"Then who protects the south coast?" Eadric spoke for the first time. He was smiling, or at least, pulling back his cheeks. Perhaps it was a snarl. Wulfnoth never wished to see it again. "You may be good at seafaring tactics, Thegn Wulfnoth, but you lack a strategic head. Or so it appears to me."

"It's only to be expected," Brihtric added. "He has a village or two, and cannot see beyond them. It's not his fault – he has never needed to." He looked up at the King. "My Lord. If Ealdorman Aelfric was arguing that he himself should command the fleet, I would at least respect the point. But what would it say about the esteem in which Mercia is held, if a mere thegn was appointed over an Ealdorman?"

Any thought Wulfnoth had had about the possibility of being the real commander of the fleet, with Brihtric as figurehead, disappeared like morning dew. Brihtric would not allow it, and Wulfnoth decided he could not abide it, not with this man.

"Consider his record!" Aelfric appealed. "Who do you put into a field as your champion? A man who has fought and won bouts before, or a-" Aelfric hesitated. Wulfnoth thought he was weighing the insult he was about to deliver.

He didn't get the chance to fling it. Eadric began to speak, and his voice was as smooth as snakeskin. "My Lord. You have sent my brother and I as your envoys to King Sveyn. You have trusted us with delivering may thousands of pounds of silver to him, which has brought us peace for more years than we had war."

War, Wulfnoth thought. War is when two sides fight battles, not when a stronger force hammers at a weaker until the weaker pays them to go away.

"We have been in Northumbria, we have spoken with Danish chieftains, the very men who Ealdorman Aelfric believes – and I'm sure it's a genuine belief – command their boats in abject fear of Thegn Wulfnoth Cild."

He had King Aethelred's full attention. Queen Emma looked expectantly down her narrow nose at him. Brihtric reclined like a cat onto which the sun had suddenly shone from behind a cloud. Wulfnoth sensed an ambush.

"Brother?" Eadric said.

Brihtric stood. He walked in front of Eadric, and circled behind him, past Aelfric, until he stood where Wulfnoth could not see him. Brihtric's hands fell like lead onto his shoulders. "Here is the sad kernel," he said, speaking over Wulfnoth's head to the King.

Wulfnoth wanted to stand and punch him on his smug nose.

"We learned that Wulfnoth indeed has a few decent boats. One day, three Danish drekkars approached Cicaestr, and spying five ships in their way, decided to turn back to Wihtware."

Brihtric's hands pressed down as Wulfnoth began to rise. "And there's no shame to Wulfnoth in that little success. But no glory either. And the reason they did not return to those waters? Because Thegn Wulfnoth followed them to Wihtware and promised them such silver as he had, and food from his lands, if they would take their attacks elsewhere. Bold, you may say. I say this – he fed the enemy that attacked his own Wessex – your Wessex, Ealdorman."

Brihtric released Wulfnoth's shoulders and stepped to where all could see him. He pointed a bony finger at Wulfnoth. "This man is not a fighter, he is a traitor!"

"Lies!" Wulfnoth wrestled his way to his feet, and his hand went to his sword-hilt. But it wasn't there. Eadric was up, blocking his path to Brihtric.

Aelfric had risen too. "Sit down, Wulfnoth."

Armed husceorls, the King's own guard, stepped from the fire's shadows. They were as big as Wulfnoth, and carried their naked blades lightly. Wulfnoth didn't sit, he just backed away.

Brihtric's accusation wasn't true. Yes, he had sent Hemming to open a negotiation. But that was only when the King had made his second gafol payment. This must be what Eadric and Brihtric had heard rumours of. The negotiation came to nothing – probably on Sveyn's word, or in the knowledge that he'd disapprove.

Only the English King is allowed to pay off the Danes; only the Danish King may receive.

Wulfnoth left Aelfric, and marched out, retrieved his sword and seax, stomped past the guards.

He did not betray the King. The King betrayed him.

1. The Voyage East

(Godwin)

"A sword'll get you into trouble it can't get you out of."

One oddity, his father had told him, and it's a joke. Two things awry, that's a curiosity. But three thing-

Godwin's belly cramped as the snake uncoiled again in his stomach, stretched his gullet, and slithered up his throat. He clung to the bulwark once more, leaned out, and the thought disappeared overboard alongside another portion of undigested mutton barley stew. Surely there was no more to be brought up?

"Look at the horizon," Hemming the Dane said from next to him. "It helps." The foreign lilt to his accent was a strangely soothing song. Godwin wiped vomit from his chin with a wet hand, for once content not to have a thick beard like his father's. He kept it trimmed to disguise the sparse growth. He concentrated on the horizon.

Godwin had pulled oar when they left Bosham, and the movement had fooled his belly into thinking he was pitching hay or chopping logs, or any chore that demanded firm soil underfoot. He pulled till his blisters bled, and for a while kept pace. But strapping lad as he was, he did not yet have the hard muscle to match the oarsmen for long. Oars had clashed, and the captain ordered him off the bench to sit on one of the narrow thwarts that tortured his arse-bones, to bail with Eg and Selferth. Then his guts recognised the boat's roll, and protested.

That was earlier. No-one rowed now. Once past Seolsey

they took advantage of the westerly, and the sail filled, bracing the boat against the swell. The breeze blew cold through Godwin's spray-soaked jerkin, adding to his misery. The seasoned fishermen who made up most of the crew had sealskin capes against the spray, or leather heavy with stinking fish-oil. He could have had leathers rubbed with lard, but his father had neglected to prepare him.

The captain took the Sea Wolf and the nineteen other Bosham boats far from shore. Land was no more than a distant smudge. If the chalk downs did not rise so near to the coast, England would not be visible at all.

With no features to provide a bearing, Godwin did not know where he was; and not knowing where he was, he felt he could be anywhere. He was a mere mote on a huge sheet, watched over by no deity, not the great One in the sky, nor by Wada of the sea.

I'm no mariner, he thought.

The captain's son Arni came and sat facing him, holding out a waterskin. Godwin waved it away. "Might as well pour it straight over the side," he said.

"You don't want to dry out," Hemming told him.

"Aye," said Arni. "And when you retch it's best your belly has something to grip."

Godwin took the skin and drank not water but weak beer, fresh and yeasty enough to have made him feel like vomiting even on solid ground. He forced himself to hold it down, and handed the skin on to Sel. "I'll walk to Sanwic, thank you. Wait for me there." Sanwic's wide beaches and the sheltered inlet made it a stade known to Saxon and Dane alike, as it had been to the Jutes and the Romans before. Beyond Dofras, it was their ultimate destination.

"You can't walk all that way!" Eg protested.

"You're right," Godwin conceded. "I'll walk back to Comtyn."

Arni snorted down his trowel-like nose. Funny how lanky boys – Arni wasn't a man, though he had two years on Godwin – all have big noses. "I've never been sick, never a once lost my meal, and I've been on boats all my life."

Godwin had no will to point out that one might arise from the other. How would Arni fare on horseback? Riding never made Godwin sore, nor did he ever feel lost, even when he ventured into unfamiliar forest. He at least knew he was somewhere.

"You've no stomach for sea, boy, nor for adventure."

Gret at home knew he was no boy.

"He's got no stomach, that's true," said Sel.

"You've got enough for the both of you," said Arni.

With his flab, Sel had not even been asked to pull oar, though Hemming said there was nothing like rowing to turn fat to muscle. Selferth ignored the insult, and merely patted his round belly. Lardyarse, Loafhead, Wobbler, he'd heard them all. He even answered to Pigbelly from friends, but Godwin wanted to punch Arni on his behalf. Not here, but later, maybe.

Eg took Sel's side, in his own sly way. "Why you wearing that sword?"

Arni had a sword buckled at his hip. He was proud of it, and lovingly sharpened it at every opportunity, as if its edge would dull not from use but from lack of it. It banged the thwarts as he moved along the boat, and men growled as they fended it away with oar handles or their own weapons. Those who owned swords had them wrapped in oilcloth lying across their laps, as Godwin did, not belted at their sides. "Capsize, and that'll drag you down," Eg said.

"Ain't goin' to capsize."

"A sword'll get you into trouble it can't get you out of."

Godwin looked miserably at his two best friends, Eagbert, scrawny and quick to smile, and Selferth, as quiet as his father Cudbert and as slow to anger. Sel would one day be as big as

Cudbert, too, and with a bit of rowing, who knew how strong?

Cudbert was not with them. That was strange, for Cudbert was Wulfnoth's husceorl, tasked with keeping Godwin safe.

Surely today's ordeal was at least half over. "Your dad said five hours to Scorham after Seolsey," he said to Arni. He looked at the sun, low enough now to warm the western horizon. "I don't know about navigation, but by that reckoning, we should turn back to land soon."

The Bosham boats, all twenty of them, sailed furthest out to sea. There were near two hundred vessels in all, it was said – too many for him to count. The Dertemuthe fleet with their rust-red sails were swiftest, and were already ahead to the northeast, although they had been the last to leave Bosham. Good boatbuilders in Dertemuthe.

In fact, the Bosham fleet seemed to be the slowest of all. Maybe that was why the captain had brought them further out, seeking stronger winds. He hadn't found them. Now, with more sea to cross, Bosham would come in last. They were not racing, but the Sou' Saxons had their pride. The redsails were turning to shore already. The Escancaestr, Suthamtun and Portlanda fleets would follow, and all the rest. Would there be food left? Godwin assumed his appetite would one day return.

"Aye, turn we should, if we is going to Scorham," said Arni.

"We are." Godwin repeated what he knew from his father. "We overnight there. And sail on tomorrow with the Scorham boats, as the others came on with us from Bosham." But plans change. Perhaps Scorham was too small for two hundred boats and their crews.

"We go where the captain says," said Arni. "My father."

No, we go where my father says, Godwin thought. Wulfnoth Cild, Thegn of Comtyn and Bosham, was seated with Ham the captain in the prow. Arni's sister Odylia was huddled next to Ham under a sheepskin. For all that she was the captain's daughter, wasn't it strange to bring a girl on a war mission?

Wasn't it strange too that Hemming would come to fight Danes? To venture out sword in hand against his own people? If he was captured he'd face horrible tortures. Surely this was madness?

Hemming there, and the girl Odylia. But Cudbert absent. What was it his father said? One oddity is a joke. Two, a curiosity. But three things out of place? Son, that's a warning.

2. Dragonhead

(Walt)

"Don't want nothin' unholy sniffin' round us..."

Seems it takes all night to get warm, then you have to get up.

The leather flap that served as a door, nailed at the top and weighed down with two stones at the threshold, had kept out the overnight wind. Vipers and svartels had been warded away by charms arrayed over the entrance, the sprig of rowan, the willow cross, the cord noose, and the dried fish that prevented Black Shuck from smelling the shepherd boy and his dog. "Don't want nothin' unholy sniffin' round us, do we lad?"

Stories told well that never was nighttime free from fear; but daytime fears were worse. Blighted crops, sick sheep, plague, storms at sea, cousins called to Ulfcytel's fyrd never to return, the theft of what little silver his mother owned. Worst of all was the terror of seaborne raiders and heathen armies with their swords and axes, and the madness that came upon them. They were immune to charms. Only God himself could save the village if the Vikingr came, and why would God bother to look at Croming?

Jack wagged his tail. Jack lent warmth, but would run from monsters, wolves and axes. He needed to be let out, so Walt shoved aside one of the stones with his foot, and Jack nosed his way into dawn's mist.

The bothy was the size of a coracle, formed of low stone walls into which branches were wedged and bound to a ridgepole. They were stout enough to bear the weight of turves, and with bracken and heather woven in a thin thatch and pegged down, the shelter was mostly rain-proof. Helped by its location in a small hollow, it cut the wind that could howl in off the big eastern sea. This morning, all was calm.

Walt twisted and, on his knees, looked out of the entrance. He couldn't see more than a few of the sheep in his care, but an occasional bored baa told him the flock was content. Jack returned to lie outside, white chin on black paws, ears twitching, eyes wide open. "I don't s'pose we got a rabbit overnight, but we'll go look right soon."

Jack's tail flapped feebly. He didn't s'pose, either, Walt thought.

He couldn't have slept too bad, because he remembered the frayed rope-end of a dream. There wasn't much more left of it than a face, or the memory of one. Bodil? The girl who lived at the far end of Croming, who spoke with an accent learned from her parents, whose hips had suddenly and mysteriously widened? Had he dreamed of her? Why?

He shook his head clear of such puzzlement, wiped his face with cold dew from the grass, and crawled outside. He stood and stretched, and swigged streamwater from an earthenware flask. He delved into a leather bag, and broke off a piece of loaf, putting the remnant back inside and thinking that this afternoon he'd have to walk a path down to Croming for more. Chewing, he stood in his hollow as two sheep grazing on the lip watched him. Jack paused his snuffling around the remains of the fire to eye them disdainfully.

Walt could not see beyond the sheep to the sea, but he knew he'd not be able to sight the horizon yet, even if he stood on higher ground. The sky above was blue, but wisps of a sea fret rolled inland having surmounted the cliffs. So he clambered out of the hollow and walked to the snares.

Empty, as he'd predicted. Stay clear of them all day, maybe there'd be coney to spit or stew later, and another paw to hang inside his shelter. Coney was good, near as tasty as young lamb, and lending wisdom to the eater because rabbits live underground and hear the dead.

He went down the slope towards the clifftop with Jack trotting beside him. Sure enough, the sea was covered with a flat blanket of white. It would flivver away soon enough. He counted the sheep as he went, recognising most of them, greeting a few by name, knowing he would neither spot them all, nor avoid counting some twice. Still, the animals who normally grazed closer to his shelter seemed to be all there, and the more adventurous wanderers could look after themselves for now.

Maybe tomorrow he'd get Jack to round them up into the stone-walled pen, then let them out one by one for a proper count. He'd do it knowing they'd all be there, but he'd be able to report to Thegn Elferic without lying.

Gulls cried "cah cah cah cah," and the sea swashed onto the beach below with a gentle swell, for there was no wind now. He sat on a stone between two large clumps of gorse, close to the very edge of the cliff, and peered over at the waves and the white gulls and cormorants diving out from their nests in the cliffside.

He could see maybe quarter a mile out to sea, or half – it was hard to judge distance into the fog. The sun would not be much higher before the mist was gone and he'd be able to see to the horizon. He'd wait here until then.

He chewed his bread, and threw the last scrap to Jack. "What say we do them yards there?" he said, gesturing at the gap between gorse bushes. Digging up gorse from inland to transplant to the cliff-edge was a horrible job which Walt hated, but the evil needles dealt trivial scratches compared to the flogging he'd receive from Elferic if a sheep should fall to the rocks below. It had happened once, not to him, but to his cousin Elbert. Then, still bloody from his beating, Elbert had been lowered down the cliff-face on a rope, which he tied to the dead ewe so she could be hauled up before the tide came in. Nothing must go to waste. Walt wondered what would have happened if the rope had slipped. Would someone else have climbed down for Elbert? Or just for the sheep, while Elbert was left to be washed away for the fish? But no, they'd have got his body back. Nothing must go to waste, specially not a soul.

He petted Jack's moleskin ears, and stroked the black and white patches oof his back. The sun was warmer on his face. No wisps of cloud made it to the shore now, still less over the clifftop. The white was not uniform. Where it thinned the dark sea began to show through in different shapeless shades. One small area of grey was somehow darker, and, strangely, almost square.

Walt watched it. Save the sun, the vague shape was the only thing to look at now that the waves and gulls were crested by the cliffedge. Was it darkening? Was it getting bigger?

His skin prickled, his heartbeat quickened. Jack became aware of Walt's heightened attention and sat up, looking in the same direction, seeing even less than his master.

A triangle appeared vaguely below the square. Walt stood. So did Jack, and looked up at the boy, ears up and tail down.

Walt realised he was not breathing. He took in air, hearing his own gasp. The blurred square and the triangle took form. A sail. A hull. A head rising above the sea to peer through the cloud. A dragon head, looking straight at him.

The helmed devils, the Vikingr, near enough now that he could hear the splash of their oars, more ordered and remorseless than the quiet waves. Coming closer. Aiming to run their longship up onto the beach and bring death and terror to Croming, to his mother, his sisters, his brother, Bodil, Elbert, Elferic, and all he had ever known.

He turned and ran up the hill, scattering the sheep whose baas turned urgent. He ignored them as he sprinted past his shelter. He abandoned his charms. The gnarled oak cudgel that his mother had given him against Black Shuck and dogs and foxes, he left sleeping beside his sheepskins. It was a mere twig against Vikingr with their axes, and his job now was to race down the path through the woods to warn the village.

Had anyone seen the ship? Probably not. The sea mist would have filled the valley, it probably lingered there still. Walt ran over the crest and down towards the treeline. Jack ran ahead of him, and he chased the dog for all he was worth, glad to be outpaced.

He charged as fast as he could down the hill, and faster, his body swifter than his legs until he fell on his belly. He got up straight away and ran to the trees. He must pace himself.

Then he was on a path more used by foxes than men, following Jack, beating aside ferns that overgrew his way, and brambles that grabbed his clothes.

Others were in the wood, away down the slope where there were no paths, crashing through the undergrowth and shouting words he did not understand but which sounded like curses.

The path widened and cleared. Running was easier, but his lungs were emptied. His muscles burned, and a dagger of pain stabbed his side.

He followed Jack around a thick bush and charged straight into a huge bearded man standing in the path, facing away from him, pissing.

The Viking barely moved as Walt bounced off him and fell onto his back. The pissing ceased mid-stream as the huge man stooped and swiftly rose holding a mighty axe, long in the haft and with a gleaming blade curving back towards the wood.

Walt stared up into the glowering face. He would never forget the thick beard the colour of a ripe cobnut shell, the blue eyes as cold as ice, or the sneer as the man tucked the axe under his arm, lifted his mallet-handle of a pintle, and released the last of his piss over Walt's legs. He pulled up his leggings, knotted his waistcord and hefted his axe, as behind him Jack stood with his forelegs planted wide, growling, hackles raised. Jack wouldn't run after all, Walt thought proudly as he shuffled on his back away from the Viking, who took a step forward. Jack followed, growling louder, and the Viking looked over his shoulder at the dog.

He started to swing his axe, and as he swung he turned his body. The axe scythed in a long arc through the air, and Jack stopped growling as his head was split horizontally at the line of his ears. The legs crumpled instantly, and the Viking put his foot on Jack's snout to hold his head firmly down as he levered the blade free from Jack's skull.

Still on his back, Walt cried "No!" even as he realised that he had missed his one chance to rise and flee. The Viking turned from Jack's corpse to Walt, and raised the bloodred-dripping axe.

A voice come from nearby, "Ralf! Vi ga!"

The Viking looked around, then stepped forward and planted his legs astride Walt. He said something, and his tone sounded oddly melodic to Walt's ears. He seemed amused at this encounter. For him it was more sport than war. Yet I shall die from this game, as swiftly as Jack.

Walt looked at the dog's one intact loyal eye staring at him from between the Viking's legs. The man saw where he was looking, and turned, and hacked through Jack's neck like he was pollarding a tree. He hooked his fingers into the broken skull and lifted Jack's head. The jaw was attached by scraps of flesh, and the mouth unfolded.

Laughing, he placed the bloody mess onto Walt's chest so the boy had to look into his own dog's dead eye.

Then the jovial Viking reversed his grip on the axe, and punched the end of the wooden shaft to the side of Walt's head.

3. Archbishop Lupus

(Edward)

"Is he not England's saviour?"

Edward entered the Cathedral of Saint Paul in a state of great fervour. This was going to be the high point of the year, even more so than the coming Witangemot. At last he was to hear Archbishop Wulfstan speak!

He loved the Cathedral. He loved the strength and solidity of one of the very few stone buildings in Lunden. He loved the Lord's presence. But he had to admit that it was too small for a town growing so rapidly. Why, at any of the rebuilds after Viking attacks, had no-one stood back to say "This time, make space for a church that shouts out our praise"? Who would give that order? Wulfstan himself, because he'd been Archbishop here before taking the northern sees? Dunstan before him? Archbishop Elfhun, the incumbent?

The King would not. His father preferred to pray alone.

His mother had already attended the Terce service with Ecfrida, his father was not inclined to come at all, and Fulton would attend his own family's church. His little sister Goda was recovering, to everyone's relief, from a pox. So it was just the three Princes representing the Crown at Sext today: himself, Alfred his brother, and Edmund his half-brother. Prince Edmund was the King's son by his previous wife, ten years older than Edward, twelve more than Alfred. Dubbed Edmund Ironside by the folk, he was the Atheling, heir to the throne of England. Of all people, Edmund absolutely must hear the Archbishop's message.

Wulfstan was famed for his fiery sermons. His missives and homilies were read out by priests from pulpits across the land, or cribbed for their own sermons. Folk called him Lupus, the Wolf, less as a wordplay on his name than a description of the savagery with which he ripped into England in its descent.

Edward settled through the service, offered his own prayer that Goda would fully recover and not have poxmarks on her face, and waited for the sermon to begin.

The great and holy man spoke slowly and mildly, his voice clear and sonorous. None would miss a single word. "One thousand years ago, Our Saviour walked in Galilee. One thousand years ago, He showed mankind the meaning of His Father's purpose. He was still a youth, but already He had cleansed the temple of profiteers and usurers."

Wulfstan had a round pink face, and a broad high forehead curving onto his bald pate. His hair, where it grew, grew thick, like a grey wool ruff over his ears and neck. His smile was as warm as a kindly grandmother's. His eyes were hard as flints.

Edward moved his hand onto Alfred's thigh to still him, for his brother had barely stopped jiffling since sitting down. They were terribly exposed at the front, and Edward didn't want Alfred to draw the priest's glare. Wulfstan had paused to look around the hushed Cathedral, and Edward's movement caught those dark eyes, which swung to fix upon him as if to shine a light on his sins for all to see.

Edward looked down, awaiting an unfair scolding, but the voice rose and passed over. "Soon will be the thousandth year since Our Lord Jesus' sacrifice for all mankind's sins, and since his resurrection and ascent to heaven. One thousand years!"

The words boomed through the nave, then the voice fell again. Wulfstan's sermons were thunder one minute and the chanting of angels the next. "A millennium God has given us, a thousand years to learn the lesson of His son's teaching, and of His sacrifice. But do we live lives of rightfulness? Are we free of lust and greed? Are we free of anger and envy? Do we worship and praise our Lord Jesus not only on Sundays, and not only with prayer, but always, and in our hearts?"

Wulfstan did not just speak, he declaimed, and used his stance dramatically, one moment crouching like a cat ready to pounce, the next standing tall; one moment with sternly folded arms, the next sweeping his hands around the nave, choosing another poor exposed soul to point at.

"One thousand years!" he shouted. "Why do we test His patience? No-one can know the mind of God, but it is not just of a man that we can say 'By his deeds ye shall know him.' Look at God's deeds. Look at the wrath He visits upon us. The heathen horde! Demons of the Antichrist's vanguard. They prepare the way for Satan in the thousandth year after Our Saviour's crucifixion. Be not mistaken: we have brought this terror upon ourselves, for these demons are our warning of what is to come if we do not heal our ways. God warns us with famine, with pestilence, with the blood of war and conquest. Three horsemen we know. The fourth is coming. Death! Death, and eternity in the Dark One's fires of Hell!"

His voice fell and made music. Once more he was the patient teacher. "You ask: How may a good man save himself in this life, and heal himself so that God will protect his soul in the next? There are but two things he must do. First, he must live in holiness and righteousness, showing humility and charity under God's warm light which shines eternally behind the clouds. If you seek with your hearts, the clouds will part. And secondly, he must fight Satan's footsoldiers with all his might and muscle. Be not deceived by those who purport to worship Christ, as some of the heathens claim to. He is no Christian who smites his brother so! We alone are Christ's true servants in this Christian land. We have been so since blessed Columba, since blessed Cuthbert, since blessed Dunstan."

Wulfstan laced his fingers together, closed his eyes, and

bowed his head. "Let us pray."

When they stepped outside into the sunshine, Edward looked to Edmund. "Is he not England's saviour?"

Edmund laughed. "Me, I'd have him ignite my men before every battle. And those not in battle? Well, scared folk are more willing to cough up their taxes. So our father leaves Lupus be." Edmund strode on towards the royal compound, then stopped and turned, and leaned with his palms on his knees as Edward caught up. "But mark this, Edward: the howl of the holy Wolf was the same in the nine-nineties. Only then, the message was that the year one thousand marks the end of days. After the world woke up on New Year's Day in the year of Our Lord one thousand and one, people were less inclined to hear his message."

"The Antichrist will come a thousand years after the crucifixion, not after the nativity."

Edmund winked. "Of course he will. So best you be good."

They walked on, with the young Princes' guards Theo and Wendel close by, one ahead and one behind.

"I must tell father the Archbishop's message," Edward said.

Edmund halted, and stilled him with a hand on his shoulder. He bent his lean body and stooped once more. He pulled Edward front-on, to look close into his eyes. How did he stare so hard without blinking? Why did he shape his black beard to such a sharp spearpoint?

"Don't do that, Edward. Your father knows this message, and he will not like hearing it again."

They walked on. Then Edward stalled of his own volition.

Fight Satan's footsoldiers with all your might and muscle, the Archbishop had said. The King had not sanctioned any major offence against the Danes for years, not since the failed St Brice's Day assaults.

Edward realised: Archbishop Wulfstan's sermon had been nothing less than an attack on his father the King.

4. Marketplace

(Eadric)

"What is the right decision the King must make?"

Barrows, tables and marketstall shelters jostled each other's shoulders. The ground was a patchwork of pitches defined by spread cloths. So many competing traders barely left room for customers, for women weighing quality against value and men duelling on price. Meanwhile children ran between the pitches until they were told to fetch this chicken or lift that cheese, or simply to sod off on pain of the stick.

The merchants were clustered to sell wares to all who gathered in Lunden for the Witangemot. Not to the ealdormen, thegns and bishops themselves, of course, but to their stewards, pages, cooks and dokksies. And as the Witan drew traders, so traders drew locals seeking dried meat and fish, salt, flax and wool, pots and jewellery, and journeymen for hire; then came jugglers and clowns in motley; tricksters, acrobats and scops; fighting bears, dogs and cockerels; gamblers, whores and footpads. And so Lunden prospered.

Not that its prosperity benefited Eadric. Once, Lunden had been part of Mercia, and the taxes flowed north alongside the tributes paid by local reeves, coiners and thegns for their favoured positions. Now, Lunden was part of Wessex. The King spent more time here than in Wintancaestr or Suthamton, and Lunden's wealth went west.

Eadric half scowled and half smiled at himself, so anyone watching might think he had a bad itch on the sole of his foot that he could not be bothered to take his boot off to scratch.

The silver did not end its journey in Wintancaestr but made its way north again, past Mercia to be sure, but Mercia got its slice. And some had made its way back to Lunden, in his purse.

The mayhem of the market square spilled along crooked streets formed of merchants' cruck-frame cottages each with its own stall outside. Eadric picked a way through the crowds and the dung piles, walking between burly Nothman and lean Leofric. Reeve Terning, a surly and dour fellow whose double chin was almost the size of his belly, waddled half a pace behind. Marton trailed them, but Eadric knew that his eyes were several steps ahead, and that his strong hand was poised on his sword hilt. Marton was a full head taller than most men, so all could see him coming. No-one stepped into their path.

A man stood outside one small house, behind a small table draped with black cloth, on which lay an assortment of rings, clasps, armbands and small brooches. Eadric knew that the cloth was in fact a bag, ready to be closed and snatched away at any sign of trouble. A hefty man holding a long stave with an iron head stood to the side. That metal would smash a thief's skull before he took two paces.

"Gorfman!" Eadric called.

"Lord Eadric! How fare you? I had hoped to see you."

"I'm sure you did." Many of the clasps, rings, and chains Eadric wore had come from Gorfman the jeweller. He was famed not only for his craft but also for his connections. The Judaics and the Vikings worked trade routes to Byzantium and beyond, to bring the rarest stones for his craft. He waved his hands over the assortment of shiny pieces before him.

"Trinkets," Edric said. "Show me what you dare not show the street. Brooches, I think."

Gorfman gathered up his cloth and retreated into his little house, to emerge after a short while with two brooches. He handed them over in turn for Eadric's inspection.

One was wrought of silver, a circle of writhing dragons interlocked, around a centrepiece of garnet. The other was a garland of flowers woven in gold, circling a large stone. The petals and the stone were a colour between a duck's egg and weathered copper, deeper than one, paler and more lustrous than the other.

"Firouzeh," Gorfman said. "All the way from Persia. You'll not see its like anywhere else in England."

Eadric pretended to be more interested in the garnet, but Gorfman was too experienced to be fooled. He reduced the price enough to let Eadric save face, but no more.

Eadric handed the brooches back. "Excellent as they are, my friend, you drive too hard a bargain for this poor Ealdorman."

He would send Marton back later, and Gorfman knew it. He'd done it before.

A voice with a western accent spoke from behind him. "Eadric, if you cain't affard them, no-one can."

He turned to see a well-dressed older man, smiling from behind a neatly trimmed beard. "Then Master Gorfman will be out of business," Eadric said, before making introductions. "Ealdorman Smerdon of the Defenas. These are Ledwyn's boys, Nothman and Leofric."

They clasped hands and walked together, exchanging complaints about how hard it was to travel to Lunden. "The King should never have stopped meeting at Wintancaestr," Smerdon complained. "'At's what the place was farr! 'At's in the name, 'at is."

"I could not agree more," Eadric said, although he could. The Witan being in Lunden meant that he, Eadgyth his wife, and all their retinue had been able to travel smoothly down the river from Oxenford. Ideally, Eadgyth would have been left in Coventre, but that would have been a slight to her father the King.

Aelfgifu his Goddaughter didn't need to be here – he had plans for her – but it was always useful to see whose ambitions flared at the sight of her flashing eyes and golden locks. These last few days it had been, quite predictably, Nothman, Ledwyn's son. Big, brash, twinkling of eye and of tongue, loose with his coins, Nothman was rarely refused by girls. Eadric wondered if refusal made any difference to him. Well, it will do with Aelfgifu, because the refusal will come from himself, not from the girl. Let Nothman dream, let him fret. Today's task was to ensure that he and his brother Leofric were in step for the Witan. Though he was the younger, Leofric had good instincts and needed the lightest of touches. Nothman required a firmer hand, so if his mind was on Aelfgifu he was less likely to notice or resent Eadric's steer.

After they parted ways, Eadric told Nothman and Leofric to greet Smerdon like a respected uncle when they met him again at the Witan. The brothers had both attended before, standing behind their father. Now Ledwyn of Hwicce stayed in Hereford, hunted down by agony in his hips, gout in his innards, and a seized, unbendable back. Ledwyn was handing over to his sons, and Eadric intended to ensure that unity was still spoken from his domain.

"Every man has his strength, and every man his weaknesses," he told his two young ealdormen. "Those to fear are not the men with the greatest strengths, but those with fewest weaknesses. Or the best disguised."

"What is your weakness?" said Nothman.

Eadric did not rise to his impertinence, nor even pretend to. "I'll tell you what it's not," he said. "It's not giving itself away."

"What about Aethelred's?" said Leofric, moving the conversation to safer ground.

"How long is your scroll?" laughed Eadric. "Let us count. He's indecisive. He vacillates like my sausage swings when I run."

"Never seen you run," Nothman said with a grin. "No-one has."

Eadric ignored him. "He listens to others like you listen to the dawn chorus from your bed, but you don't try to pick out the best song. He hates to be thought less of, and everyone thinks less of him for that. Your thoughts?"

Before either brother could answer, the folk ahead of them hushed and moved aside to allow a gaggle of monks to pass through the marketplace. They were almost upon them before Eadric recognised Archbishop Aelfheah at their head. He dressed simply, with a faded brown habit and open sandals, and was distinguishable from the others only by his stoop, his thin white beard that needed a trim, and the smiling blessings he bestowed on all he passed. Some of the other monks wore more gold and jewellery than he. The one glint of gold from Aelfheah was on his finger. Eadric knew this heavy ring came with the pallium from the Pope, on the Archbishop's investiture; and he knew Aelfheah's little secret.

Once Eadric had been contemptuous of him, seeing his humble attire as at best an affectation of fake modesty, and at worst as a cunning disguise to make him popular with the lowest ceorls and thuws. But more recently he had come to wonder if it was a simple expression of genuine faith. "Your Grace," he said, bowing. "It is an honour and pleasure."

Whether cynical or holy, the Archbishop smiled, and looked up with pale green eyes as he rotated the gold ring on his finger to reveal an emerald the size of a gooseberry. Gorfman's lovely firouzeh brooch was indeed a trinket by comparison. He offered it for Eadric's kiss before twisting the jewel back into hiding. Eadric found this inexplicably irritating, but he smiled back.

He introduced the Hwiccans, and Aelfheah promised to offer a prayer for their father's health, before taking Eadric's hand to pull him close. "I thank you for your letter," he said.

"I am glad it found you," Eadric said. "I have not received a reply, so I was not sure..."

"You will hear my reply at the Witan," Aelfheah said.

His voice was low and gentle, and Eadric could not tell whether it conveyed comfort or threat. Before Eadric had time to form a query that would not ruffle his calm – for that was no way to work with the old man – the Lundeners behind were disturbed, and made loud complaints as another cluster of monks tried to pass. They were a smaller group than Aelfheah's, headed by six men unashamed of showing off their wealth. Their leader was bedecked with more gold, jewellery and ornament than Eadric himself. He wore finer furs, and boots of stouter leather. Wulfstan, called Lupus, Archbishop of Jorvik and Weogorna, bowed courteously to his superior, Aelfheah of Cantenberh. "Your Grace."

"Your Grace."

If there had been puddles on the ground, they would have frozen over.

"My goodness," Eadric said. "You wait all year for an Archbishop, then two come along."

"Rejoice," said Aelfheah in a flat tone that showed an enviable level of sarcasm.

"And we will see you both again at the Witan?"

"I am in Lunden to preach, but yes, I will attend the Witan," Lupus said to the crowd.

"He is in Lunden for the Witan," Aelfheah said to no-one in particular. "But yes, he will sermonise."

"We must never cease to spread God's word," Lupus announced.

Aelfheah turned to his followers. "We are beset by problems. If only we humble Archbishops truly knew what His word is on these problems." He turned back to Lupus. "God be with you."

"And with you," Lupus said. No keener than Aelfheah to extend the conversation, he led his retinue onward. They had to pass Aelfheah's monks. Neither group would give way, so there was much pushing and jostling before Lupus's entourage got clear. One monk was helped up from the dungpile into which he had been shoved.

"Bah," Aelfheah said to his flock. "Let us go onward to the Cathedral, since we know it will be peaceful." Before he moved off, he came close again to Eadric. "My reply, Eadric? All I can say is that my holy brother will not like it."

"Ahhh…" Eadric understood.

"Blessings upon you." Aelfheah departed.

"A happy meet?" Leafric asked.

"Indeed," Eadric said. "Let us pray that they never learn to respect each other."

"Why?" Nothman asked.

"Because if they spoke with one voice, the King might listen to them instead of to me. Now, where were we?" He led them as before, in the direction of the King's halls where they were staying.

"You were asking what we think of the King," Leofric said.

"So I was. And..?"

"He is no military tactician," said Nothman. "He botched his invasion of Cotentin."

"He didn't botch it," Leofric said. "It was doomed from the start. At least he has learned to let others lead men in battle, such as Edmund." He considered matters further. "What Aethelred truly lacks is any sense of strategy. Or geography."

"Geography?" said Eadric. He was coming to respect Leofric's brain.

"He failed to support Ulfcytel in the East. He abandoned Uhtred in the North. He let your brother lead the fleet from the Wessex ports, which really pissed off Aelfric and Athelmar."

Eadric laughed out loud. Getting the King to agree to Brihtric taking charge of the fleet, over that upstart thegn chosen by the ageing Ealdormen of Wessex, was an achievement that still delighted him. And Mercia a landlocked province!

"He thinks he can still be king of the North," Leofric continued. "So he invaded Strathclyde."

"It was Uhtred did most of the invading," Nothman said.

"And what did Uhtred get? Abandoned, that's what, and not so much as a Princess to wed."

Princesses were overrated. Can't trust them, and can't get rid of them. The one he'd been given couldn't even make an heir. Couldn't even make him hard any more. Ah, but Thyra his dokkse was fine consolation, and trustworthy too. He looked forward to being back with her.

Nothman snorted. "He shouldn't be King anyway, not after his mother's villainy."

"Hush brother," Leofric warned. "We do not speak of this."

"Why not? Everyone else does."

"One, they don't. And two, everyone else is not the King's closest friend."

"Thank you, Leofric," Eadric said, in a tone that put an end to the topic.

They skirted the market's densest chaos, and he moved the talk forward. "Our King, when he finally makes a decision, spends all his energy wondering if it was right, if it will succeed, and if others will laugh if it fails. While I, I listen to opinions as he does, I hear advice. But when I make a decision, I put all my effort into making damn sure it was the right one. And I know who to punish if it fails. So, boys, in this coming Witan, what is the right decision the King must take?"

"More payments to Sveyn," said Nothman.

"Yes," said Reeve Terning from behind, for this was his business, and he was keen to be heard by his lords. "More gafol. To keep Mercia safe."

"Indeed," said Eadric. "But with no talk of Mercia. Impress on our lord the importance of Wessex and Cantware. And be not greedy. Appear modest."

"What's the point of wealth if we can't enjoy it?" asked Nothman.

"If Sveyn rampages across the Trehynt," said Eadric. "All your wealth will be whisked from under your feet. Your feet will be whisked from under your body, and your body from under your neck." He paused to let the reminder embed. "You think we are just here to talk to Aethelred? We're also sending messages to Sveyn. The more he believes that Wessex is the jewel of England, the less he cares about Mercia. Rest assured that Sveyn will have a sparrow here to report proceedings to him."

The brothers looked at Eadric, but said nothing.

He knew their thought. "I don't mean me, I mean someone he trusts."

5. The Maid of Jorvik

(Fleada)

"I am next to the Queen!"

They had been given a small cold room, bare of wall-hangings, and with ill-fitting shutters. But the King was generous with blankets and sheepskins, and the thick feather mattress was not as damp now as when they first arrived. A maid brought a pan of hot embers every night to help with the mattress, and a boy kept the fire tended. Fleada had set two stools in front of it and, with difficulty, draped the mattress over them to dry it through the day. But it would take the fire a week or more to draw the chill out of the stone walls, by which time they'd be gone, returned to Lyccidfield or Coventre.

She hoped it was the former, because her mistress's room there was lovely, hung with tapestries of cream and purple linens, golden light entering through its yellow glass windows even in the cold of winter, and Jesus painted on the limewashed walls, protecting them day and night. The room was scented with rose petals on the table, and thyme by the bed.

Fleada's memories of her own family home were fading. Yes, she would love to see her mother and father, and Nothryth and Ozzie who had probably forgotten her, but their hut had been dark, dank and draught-ridden, especially through those long Northumbria winters. Her father was Headman, but this endowed little in such an unnoteworthy village. She would visit if she could – perhaps if her mistress ever wished to return to Jorvik, her own hometown – but she wasn't sure she'd enjoy sleeping there.

Life as Aelfgifu's handmaid was making her soft.

The mattress was back on the bed, and Aelfgifu was seated on the chair in front of the fire. Fleada stood behind, braiding her mistress's thick golden hair into two long plaits. She wasn't jealous of her beauty, and wanted to make her more beautiful. She wasn't jealous of her bearing, and admired the way she could comport herself in so womanly a fashion when only one year Fleada's senior. But she was envious of Aelfgifu's hair, the colour of ripe corn, and wished she too was so blessed. Why do boys like yellow, but tease her for her equally eye-catching crown of burnished copper?

Fleada bound off the end of Aelfgifu's locks, and rolled them up loosely behind her ears. "Do you wish them tied up my lady? I have ribbons, blue like your eyes." Her mistress's eyes were as green as they were blue, but Aelfgifu hated to be told this. "Or hung down?"

Aelfgifu looked in the polished silver plate, holding it up and moving it as Fleada held the rolled braids in place. "Leave it loose," she said.

Fleada released the braids. They fell below Aelfgifu's waist. "Men prefer hair bound up," she pointed out.

"Only so they can unbind it."

The two girls giggled.

"Now, your hair we should brush out," Aelfgifu continued, "To draw the eyes. We shall find you the very best husband!"

"I shall wear my cap, thank you." Fleada had a sudden fright, the same fear that had been troubling her for months. When she married and had babies, she would have to leave Aelfgifu; this she could accept. But what would happen when Aelfgifu married? It was surely a looming prospect. Maybe she shouldn't help her look more beautiful. Ah, but Aelfgifu's husband would be found by Eadric, her Godfather and guardian. Beauty had little bearing on the matter.

"I shall have Nothman, you can have Leofric," said Aelfgifu. Nothman was by far the more attractive of the two Hwiccan brothers, with his rough energy and informal, sometimes common manner. Dark eyes, set in a handsomely chiselled face, and such strong shoulders and thighs! The girls had watched him in practice melees, and seen him in the saddle, each aware of their breathing becoming shallower. Leofric by contrast stood remote, his thoughts obscure, his eye judgemental, with ugly fat lips always pressed tightly together.

"I think I'd rather die a spinster," Fleada said, as if there was any prospect of her marrying to such high rank.

"Me too," said Aelfgifu with a shudder, as if she had a say.

"Do you know where you will be sitting tonight?"

"I am next to the Queen!" Aelfgifu whispered. "And Nothman and Leofric aren't even at the top table!"

"Oh my!"

"And they could be there, if it was to be set on both sides. But it won't be. We shall be looking down over them and all the ceorls!"

"Shh!" The brothers were roomed in a distant hut, but would be angered by such an insult if word got to them.

"Actually, I'm not next to the Queen. The Princes, Edward and Alfred, will be between us. But they don't count. Too young."

"A pity it's not Prince Edmund Ironside there."

Aelfgifu was silent. She rotated the gold ring around her left index finger. The ring was a gift from her godparents on her last birthday, replacing an old silver ring become too tight. Silver or gold, it was Aelfgifu's habit to turn it when she was deep in thought.

Fleada wondered if she was thinking about Edmund. And if so, what her thoughts might be. "Does it mean anything, that you are at the high table where Edmund will sit?'

'He will be at the other end.'

'But Nothman and Leofric won't be at that table at all. They are nobles. Their father is an Ealdorman, as yours was. Aren't they at least equal in rank to you? What does it mean that you are at the high table with the Queen and the Princes?"

"It means the King has a short high table!"

6. The Death of Croming

(Walt)

"God don't let us be nothing, that's his blessing and his curse.'

When Walt recovered consciousness the woods around him were peaceful. Crusted blood had caked onto his neck. His shirt was stuck to his chest with Jack's blood. The dog's head lay in the leaf mulch beside him.

His head throbbed. In one ear, he heard screams and thuds and roars from the direction of the village. In the other, silence. He staggered to his feet, nearly fell, and stumbled onwards down the hill. The sounds grew more distinct, but the screams fewer, until the village of Croming resisted no more. He found a large holly bush on the edge of the village clearing, and, ignoring the scratches, crawled between its branches into the dark middle, and peered out through the leaves.

Mutilated bodies of men, women and children lay on the ground. There was Welan the drunk, who could harm no-one. There was Lissa who played with Benna. His friend Piggy Thom, his round belly sliced open with his guts more out than in. There was the head of Wyn, the best spearman in the hunt, and his muscled arm lying alongside but his body nowhere to be seen. He counted just two helmed bodies. Beyond, huts blazed, and Vikings were now setting light to the village's long hut. Why? For their two fallen comrades? A woman screamed, a fresh wail with every breath, screams that Walt was only aware of when they were suddenly cut short.

A group of five Norsemen led a naked man limping into

the centre of the village. Walt did not at first recognise Elferic, so bloody and dirtied was he. Other Vikings clustered around. Walt saw among them the man who had killed Jack. Ralf. The largest weighted his axe and began to swing it. Walt knew from those terrifying fireside tales of instruction that for Elferic to show fear, to cower or to beg, would invite slow death by torture. Beheading was, to a Viking, merciful. Walt heard the ripple of melody in their voices as they spoke, then the Viking treated Walt's thegn to as contemptuous an execution as Ralf had treated his dog.

The woman's screams still rang inside his head. Tears flowed freely down Walt's face, but he remained silent and still as Vikings herded a group of villagers together, and tied them neck and wrist to each other. Milktop Merritt whose nickname was justified, Farty Farly whose nickname wasn't, and, stumbling in their midst, his big sister Djorka. The dirt on her face was smudged with tears, her feet were naked, her skirt torn.

Footsteps and the grunts of a struggling woman came from behind him, louder, closer. Walt feared his legs protruded from below the bush, but did not dare move to pull them in. The footfall passed the bush. An older Viking whose grey plaited hair emerged from under his helm dragged a woman into the clearing. Djorka lifted her hand to her open mouth, and Walt realised that the woman was their own mother. She was pushed to the leader, who said something to the older man, who in turn gestured towards the tethered prisoners, the slaves who would be taken across the sea. The leader spoke again, more curtly, and others laughed. Walt's hopeful guess was that the older man's wish to take her as his slave, his personal prize, had been denied. Angrily, he hauled her back to the edge of the clearing, near to Walt's bush.

Walt and his sister gazed on, as the greybeard Norseman threw their mother to the ground, pushed up her skirt, and mounted her. She turned her head aside and was looking straight at the bush hiding Walt. He wanted the leaves thicker and bigger, he wanted to be hidden or swallowed, but she saw him, he knew, because her eyes widened and her head lifted from the ground. She shook her head at him, briefly but urgently, instructing him not to move or to cry out. Then she turned her face from him, instructing him to do the same. Walt needed no command, and reopened his eyes long after the rapist finished with a groan.

The grey Viking stood over his ravaged victim. He saw something, the silver amulet she always wore, the one with the five-petalled flower design that had come from her husband's mother and thence from Walt's great-grandmother. The amulet she had promised Walt would one day be given to his bride.

The Viking pulled at it, but it was hung on a leather thong around her neck, that would have to be unknotted or cut if she would not yield it. She tried to hold on to it, but she saw his glaring eyes and heard his snarl. She began to free the thong from her tangled hair, to lift it over her head. The old Viking would not wait. He lifted his axe high, and swung it down on her bare throat. He needed a second blow and a third, as the other Vikings jeered, to sever her head completely. He lifted the blood-spattered amulet from Walt's mother's headless torso, held it up to them, and put around his own neck the last thing of value that might save Walt's family when all else was lost.

The others were getting ready to leave. Some carried barrels and sacks, some led cattle and pigs. Walt's cousin Elbert who had been lowered down the cliff, and his friend, Croming's other Walt, were forced with whips at their backs to pull a cart. On the cart were the swords and bows and daggers that had proved so useless in Anglian hands, and jugs, platters and knives of copper and pewter and iron. The tethered captives, the young and the fit who would make good slaves for sale or for service were whipped down the path to the beach and the dragon ship.

They passed close to Walt. He wanted to shout "Djorka, I will come for you," but he knew must not, and that crossing the sea was beyond him.

There were no more screams, no more yells. Never had Croming been so silent. No laughter and shouts from children at their games, no conversations of men and woman, no grunting and lowing and clucking from the livestock. All who had not fled, the demons had killed or taken.

Walt crawled out from his bush, aching and thirsty. He walked past razed huts to his own home, now little more than a scorched platform on smouldering posts. A man lay outside, Chetwynd, his guts exposed to flies. Their buzzing was the first sound Walt heard. Then came the cruel cawing of crows now gathering for carrion.

On the black floor of the hut lay the burned body of his brother Portheof. A small seax lay in his lifeless palm. Walt took it, and went to the back of the hut where two naked legs protruded from under the charred floor. Half underneath the hut, where she had surely been told to hide, was the body of Benna. What cruelty made these devils cut the throat and stab the stomach of a six year old girl? One hand held the doll he'd made for her last Michaelmas from folded and knotted cloth.

Walt fell to his knees and vomited, but he had no more tears.

He heard a rustle of footsteps and looked up. Elders, and some children and babes, trudged back into Croming from out of the woods. No-one spoke.

Walt rose, and searched two of the intact huts for food of any type. He saw little, but what he did see he stuffed into a bag he picked up. He got to the far end of the village where Bodil lived with her family among the other Danish speakers.

Some had fled, but some had stayed and yet were spared. Their pleas in Danish must have saved them. Bodil came out and put her hand on Walt's shoulder. He punched her on her arms, her head, her tits, anywhere, shouting incoherently "You… You…" and "They… They…"

You should be dead like Benna. You should be enslaved like Djorka your friend. They should have killed your family, but they didn't because You Are Them.

Bodil's father pulled him away from her, but didn't hit him.

An old man came up and led Walt back to his end of the village. He made bread so he was called Baker, but Walt knew it wasn't his given name. "Walt," he said, patting the full bag, "we all need this food. That's not yours to take."

"There's sheep on the hill."

"You must bring them down for us," Baker said.

"Grandfather, go slaughter what you need. I'm no shepherd no more."

"Well what are you?" Baker sounded outraged.

"I'm nothing." Walt walked away, between bodies still on the ground. He must bury his mother, Portheof, Benna with her doll, and then Jack too, up in the woods.

Baker stood immobile, and Walt thought he would not reply. Then he spoke softly, regretfully. "No-one's nothing, boy. God don't let us be nothing, that's his blessing and his curse."

"I'll fight. For the King. I'll kill Danes."

Baker spat. "The King has no will to fight, and if he did you'd die quick."

"What does God want?"

"If'n I knew God's will, Walt, I'd be Pope."

Walt was about to turn away when Baker spoke again. "Your best bet maybe? Go find your ma's family."

7. Brimclif

(Godwin)

"Crows'll peck his eyes out first."

The beer in his stomach churned. The snake uncoiled once more, and before he could lean over the side it slithered out through his throat, and smaller worms squirmed down his nose. Vomit coated the curved inside of the hull.

"Oi you, boy, you dare puke in my new ship?" The captain was angry, or pretended to be. "Now my crew's got to paddle in your churn! I'll have you thrown over!"

The Sea Wolf wasn't new, it just had a few replacement planks, yellow and clean. And it wasn't Ham's ship. And his regurgitated beer was lost in the bilgewater. And the crew would sit in their places. Ham was an idiot. Godwin wiped his sleeve across his face. "The other boats! They're turning back to land. Why don't we? The wind…"

Ham looked at Wulfnoth. Wulfnoth looked at the rest of the fleet. "I don't think they can see now," he said to the captain, who nodded. Both ignored Godwin. Wulfnoth said something to Hemming, who stood and turned to face the other boats. He raised two flags of pale sunbleached linen from waist height to high above his head, several times, keeping his arms stiff. Godwin looked across the white-tops. One by one flags were waved back, and Hemming did not sit down until every boat had acknowledged his signal.

The crews were from around Comtyn, Bosham and the neighbouring villages under his father's Thegnship. Aiden the Chin, who really should let his beard grow, Nothelm, Garwig the moon-bald, Hemming the Dane, the boatbuilder, now trusted to fight against his countrymen. Men known to each other, a tribe, bound in collective loyalty to their Thegn by oath, by debt, by pride and by belonging. Near half were thuws, landless, property-less, indentured, little more than slaves, but better a slave than a vagrant or outlaw, and better still a fighter with a hope of loot to buy freedom.

Ham stood. He shouted at the oarsmen "Now row, you lazy bastards. Row like your lives depend on it!"

The crew were clearly confused. They reached for the oars, but with no sense of urgency.

Wulfnoth stood, tall and craggy. His furs rippled in the wind, his hair blew wild around his face. He put his hand on Ham's shoulder and pressed him down to the bench. "Your lives don't depend on it," he called. "But we will cross the wind now, and we need both oar and sail if we're to make our new landfall before dark."

One of the men stood "Well why didn't we row earlier and more steady? Not in panic and rush at end o' day." He was no mariner either, even Godwin could tell.

Ham stood angrily, but Wulfnoth pressed him down again. "Wait until we land, boy," he said, although the man's hair and beard was flecked with silver. "Then I will say."

Godwin moved back to his bench seat to unship an oar.

"Not you," Ham shouted. "You can take that bucket and sluice down where you puked, then start bailing."

He worked between the growling oarsmen, thinking that their separation from the main fleet was now the day's fourth out of place event.

Godwin was proud of his father, proud and frightened in equal measure. Ah, being honest with himself, he was more frightened than proud. Arni's dad was in charge of the seafaring, but Wulfnoth was commander of the twenty boats of Bosham and Comtyn. He took orders from Brihtric of

Mercia alone, as willingly as a ferret from a fox. Brihtric was brother of Ealdorman Eadric Streona himself, said to be the most powerful lord in England.

His father was big, with the shoulders of a boar and the legs of a horse. His mother told Godwin that he, her only son, would be bigger still. That much was obvious to all, but she did not always state the obvious. She must have said it on one of her good days.

His father was brave. His mother told Godwin that he would be braver still, she knew it. That too was a good day.

His father was wild and cruel and evil. Godwin would be wilder and crueller and more evil, there was no doubt, the way he cared less than an oat-grain for his poor mother. She could see it in his eyes, she could penetrate Godwin's wicked soul. "You take after him," she screamed. "Your devil father, whyever did I take into me the seed of such a demon?"

A bad day. One of many.

A demon? He'd seen his father clout his mother many times, and clung to the vow made to himself on the heart of Nertha that he would never raise his hand at a woman.

His father lashed at her after announcing that he would take Godwin to sea and to war, as she screamed and pleaded that her son was too young and would come back skewered and drowned. Then, on a good day, she argued calmly: Godwin had responsibilities, he'd be better off learning the ways of the village and its people, and this would be better for Comtyn because one day Godwin would take Wulfnoth's place as Thegn. Again he silenced her with his knuckles.

She never argued that Wulfnoth himself should stay at home.

The day before they left was a bad day. She raved, and cursed her husband and her son alike, and vowed to pray for neither to return. Yet the next morning, she slipped Godwin a purse of coins.

After two hours of steady rowing, the men pulled the boats up a pebble beach where chalk cliffs dipped to nothing. Stretching eastwards, England's vertical white chest grew higher than any height Godwin had ever seen, then fell, and then grew again, loftier still, sheer and forbidding. Clearly this was the last landfall for many leagues.

When the boats were safely above the high-tide mark, the crews swung their arms to flex their aching shoulders. Godwin, Eg and Sel tramped past a small and poorly cared-for squadron of fishing skiffs, and up a track towards a threadbare hamlet.

The meagre thatching on the cottage roofs was more weed than reed, the chickens were listless, the pigs skinny. Lime kilns had fallen out of repair. Charred skeletons of three cottages stood up like rusted nails, signifying that Vikings had once visited. Godwin wondered if the village had been too poor for the Vikingr to bother with complete razure, and the villagers too depressed to tidy up the casual damage. Perhaps, so exposed and isolated here, they thought that improving their dilapidated homes was nothing more than an invitation to the Vikingr to visit again.

Suddenly Selferth started running to the centre of the village, as fast as Godwin had ever seen him move. He was lumbering towards a handsome grey horse. Why was Ash here? Sel wasn't running to the stallion, but to the man who held him.

Cudbert had to steady himself against his son's impact. As they embraced, Ash stepped sideways, and his hindquarters nearly toppled a lean old man who also stood there. Gaunt he was, with a thin beard and sallow face, tall and bony but with a paunch like an inflated ox bladder.

Wulfnoth strode to the man, who held up a flagon and welcomed him like an old friend, with open arms and a grin fashioned somehow while turning down the corners of his mouth. He was clearly the village's Headman, or perhaps – for his clothes were good wool and leather, and he wore gold around his neck and on his fingers – the local thegn. "Wulfnoth Cild! Welcome to Brimclif," he said.

"Gewis Cild, by Bevis!" Wulfnoth said. "It is an honour," He took the horse's tether from Cudbert, and handed it to Gewis with some formal words of thanks that Godwin could not hear. Godwin strongly suspected that Gewis's "Cild" was an honorific added by Wulfnoth to flatter this old chief of such a tiny, remote, rumpled and wrecked place.

Cudbert's absence from the boat was explained – he had brought the horse overland, evidently as a gift to Gewis. Ash was sired by Wulfnoth's own Whitebeam, and Godwin had always felt the horse to be his. The saddle definitely was – a gift from his father on his thirteenth birthday.

It was not obvious what welcome Brimclif could offer, nor what honour. There was no hall, and the visitors were herded under a large wattle canopy covered with turves and sagging between its supporting poles. It had a hole at the centre so it wouldn't burn from the fire. Two sweating women turned a roasting a pig twice the size of the others in the village. It dripped fat generously onto the fire. "That pig ain't from round here," Eg said.

"I'll have yours Godwin, if you can't eat," added Sel, now returned from Cudbert's side.

The smell was making Godwin salivate. He was ravenous now that his voided stomach was steady on land. "Don't you worry about me."

The men settled themselves on the ground, and received bread and slices of meat from the village's womenfolk. The locals joined the meal, and two of them sang badly to a tuneless lute, but raised a cheer for their efforts.

Godwin sat between Arni and Eg and chewed his food.

"Better than I was expecting," Eg said.

"Me too," said Arni. "Them what put in to Scorham be lucky to get dried fish."

Wulfnoth and Ham sat with Headman Gewis, who was as happy as he was deferential. Rewarded like a servant, thought Godwin. He rose and left his friends, to sit with the important men by the fire. Being the Thegn's son had its privileges.

Wulfnoth sat on a hefty log that had done much service as a chopping block; Gewis, Ham, Hemming and others were in a row on a felled bough a handspan's diameter, a good size for children but not for men, yet better than squatting on the ground. Wulfnoth ordered them to disappear for a moment – "I want to talk to my son," – and continued the lazy work of sharpening his sword. Godwin unsheathed his, found the whetstone in his shoulderbag, and sat on the vacated branch.

Ham's daughter Odylia came with a pitcher, and they held out their mugs for her to fill with beer. She was short, skinny and sharp-nosed, with wayward black hair cropped short and spiky and left unbound. She had an impish smile that she shone onto Godwin as she poured. "I hope you feelin' better now, my lord."

"Not a lord," said Godwin. "But it's a kind thought. I'm much better. I thank you."

"Sweet girl," Wulfnoth said to him as she left.

"Seems so," said Godwin.

"Don't be fooled. She's wild, and it's her own father told me. Wild is trouble."

Godwin knew he was thinking about Mother.

"Save yourself for better. Don't be tempted. You'll piss off two men I don't want pissed off."

Two? Ham, the captain, Odylia's father, yes. Naturally Wulfnoth didn't want him angered. Who was the other? He put his mug on the ground to resume stroking his sword with the stone.

"I hope the fighting never gets so close you need use of

that," Wulfnoth said.

"I may not be strong yet, Father. But I'm fast."

"Not many places to run to on a boat. Get behind Cudbert, there's no shame, not at your age." So Cudbert would be coming with them. "He'll protect you as long as he breathes. He pledged that to me. More important, he pledged that to your mother."

Godwin had to chuckle.

"Do you miss her?"

Godwin's chuckle stopped. "No!" he lied, half insulted, and half just plain surprised that his father would ask him such a question.

"Me neither," Wulfnoth said.

"I do miss Rabbit though." His sister Saewin had been called Rabbit from the age she first jumped into people's laps. With her energy, her joy in running and prancing, and her affectionate soul – come from where? – the name had stuck. His mother had birthed two other girls and a boy between Godwin and Saewin, but none had survived infancy. It was as if Godwin had garnered all the strength due to them. Saewin found some, though, and she was the precious one.

"Yes," was all his father said.

"Father, have you given Ash away? What about my saddle?"

Now it was Wulfnoth's turn to chuckle. "Don't need horse and saddle at sea."

"But the saddle's mine." He tried not to whine but to speak a simple truth, and mostly succeeded.

"And costly it was. I'll get you better."

"Why did we not go to Scorham with the other boats?"

"Go back to your mates. You'll find out soon enough."

Godwin rose and sheathed his sword, and returned to Eg and Sel and Cudbert. He wondered if Eg was missing his father at this time. The man had died three years back, after his ox bolted when being unyoked, and the plough blade had cut through his foot. Neither prayers nor potions could unlock his jaw and resist the blackening of his flesh, and Eg's da' had not survived the amputation. Fatherless Eg and motherless Sel had been bound like brothers since. He punched Eg lightly on his shoulder to move him along, and sat in the space between the two, an arm around each until the flagon of beer reappeared.

Eg drank, and nudged him, nodding towards the fire. Wulfnoth had stood, and was stepping up onto the chopping block so all could see him clearly in the rippling glow of the flames.

He raised his hands in a priestly fashion, and the songs and hubbub quelled as the men turned to listen.

"Hard times," said Wulfnoth, and he spoke quietly to make them strain to hear. "Hard times for us, hard times for England. When were they not?" He looked sternly at his men, and nodded slowly. More than one nodded back, unaware that they mirrored their leader. This is how it's done, Godwin thought.

Wulfnoth went on. "Your King," he said. "Your King, Aethelred, guided by the counsel of Lord Eadric, has selected us, we men of Comtyn and Bosham, for a special task. This is why we did not stay with the rest of the fleet. The King wishes our role to be secret, and that marks our importance to him."

He paused as the men absorbed this information, and watched them sit up straighter. They knew how Wulfnoth had been passed over for the Mercian, so it must be good that their Thegn was still esteemed by the King. "And what is that role, you ask? What is our role if it is not to fight the Dane? And ask you might. And fight we shall!"

A cheer rose.

"But ours is not to join with the Mercian farmer to face Sveyn Forkbeard's fleet directly as they sail around our shores.

Ours, my boys, is to harry single Viking ships, be they Danish or Norse, wherever we find them. If they sail towards these shores, we sink 'em. If they sail away, we stop them and retrieve the plunder. And then we sink 'em."

A bigger cheer, and fists lifted, and shouts of "Yes" raised.

Wulfnoth took Hemming's arm, and made him stand. "For we have one who understands how the Viking fights, and how he sails. Most of you know Hemming, who was once a Dane. You know that he has sworn oaths to me, with his hand on the holy bible and Lord Jesus in his heart. I trust him, and so will you. And if you don't, remember this: he will fight or sink with us. When swords are drawn and arrows fired, Danes won't know where he was born. And if they do, they will mark him a traitor, and fight each other to be first to open his belly."

Most of the men cheered for Hemming. Some cheered at the image of his demise.

"And meantimes," Wulfnoth continued, "we have such a fleet! Enough to outnumber one, two or three Viking longboats as normally sail together. Their boats are built for speed with the wind. Ours are better against it. We can't outrun them, but we can go directions they can't. We have slings and bows in our armoury. Aye, and fire arrows. We can cripple them from a distance. And when we come close, we shall have pikes and spears. They will be defeated even before we are close enough for swords and axes. I tell you this: we prepare to attack at sea. They do not prepare to be attacked."

Wulfnoth looked at his men, and lowered his voice again. "And you will have another thought. You will wonder how, once we have relieved them of the plunder they stole from our brethren, how we will ever know from which town or village it came? Then how are we to return it? Well, those boats that have captured slaves, we shall simply ask the prisoners when we free them. But for the others, the answer is, we shall not know. We retrieve England's riches for the

King, and he will distribute it among those villages and towns that have been attacked.'

"More like give it back to Sveyn as gafol," one of the men shouted from the back, and the others laughed.

"That is the King's affair. It's his business to decide what to do with it. It is ours to get it to him." Wulfnoth lowered his voice, again forcing them to listen carefully. "But he won't know how much the longship held. His Reeve won't know how much we took."

He let the thought enfold the men, then put wide his arms again. "That's right, m'boys. There's wealth to be taken and shared amongst those that have the strength and the will to take it. This venture, this plan, this mission granted us by the King himself, will make us rich, lads. And when it's done these riches will make us masters of wherever we want to settle!"

"Ain't we going back home then?" asked one of the younger men.

"We go where we will. But our homes may not be big enough for the throng of us and all the gold we shall carry. We may find better places where our booty will go further, if we spread ourselves. Maybe Flandra, or Normandy, or Eirinn. In good time we can choose where to go with our wealth."

There was a murmur of discussion.

"And you thuws among us, you will have your shares too, and you will be free."

The thuws cheered mightily, save a few who just smiled and waited on events.

"I tell you all, we hold our destinies in our own hands. We choose who we strike, we choose the where and the when. We sail together, and lone longboats will not dare attack us. We will not be played by that lying worm Brihtric who thinks he can use our boats like merels on a board, to be placed and moved at his whim. This way we protect England, harry the Dane, and make riches for ourselves. We will return as heroes, with bounty to dispense. Oh it's a great future for us, my boys."

And he yelled: "Are you with me?"

And the men stood with their flagons and mugs, and lifted them so the beer splashed up to the canopy, and they cheered Godwin's father, and yelled back "Aye" at him, and "We're with you," and "Wulf-noth, Wulf-noth, Wulf-noth," ever faster, until it was "Wulfnothwulfnothwulfnoth," accelerating to a single roar.

Godwin's heart swelled with pride as he stood too, as his father with blood in his cheeks and fire in his eye looked down over his men, his crew, his force.

Later, when the men had drunk their fill and caroused until the day at sea caught up with them, Godwin huddled down between Sel and Eg. Their blankets were shared over them and their waxed capes spread under.

"It's a grand plan, is it not," said Eg.

"Did you know the King set us this task?" Sel asked.

"No," said Godwin. "But I saw the way my father planned the voyage. I saw the stores loaded, and I did wonder why we had so much if we were sailing to Sandwic, because there we could re-stock. And I saw the weapons stowed, and braziers."

"We need weapons," said Eg.

"From what I heard, the ships would be armed mostly at Sandwic, same as getting supplies. And ours was all loaded at night, in secret." Yes, his father had had an air of conspiracy about him, something he wasn't saying.

"No boat needs a brazier," Sel said slowly. "That's playing with fire."

"Did Selferth just make a joke?" Eg said.

"No. I was serious."

"Oh good. You had me worried for a moment."

The thought of being special, of being secret, excited Godwin. And the way of fighting that Wulfnoth had spoken of, he loved that. The planning, doing what the enemy was not prepared for, using Hemming to anticipate the Dane's moves in advance, somehow that roused his blood more than the idea of simply swinging a sword. Fighting first with the head, and only then with the arm.

"I want to shoot them fire arrows," Eg said. "Aim for them Danish sails."

"Shame about any slaves and hostages," said Sel. "They'll be mainly women and young 'uns."

"Well, we can't set fire to ships if we see English slaves on board, obviously," said Eg.

Arni's voice came from the darkness beside them. "Hah, won't make no difference. First, the Danes will threaten to cut their throats if we come close."

"Oh God, they'd do it too," said Sel. "Quick as blinking."

"They won't," said Arni. "They'll throw them into the sea instead, so they can sail off while we stop to rescue them. Well, rescue the ones as can swim, which won't be many."

"Father won't stop," said Godwin.

"What?"

"Our job is to attack the Danes. Hostages, slaves, they're as good as dead already." He tried to decide how his father would think it through, and when he did, he didn't know whether to be proud or shamed. "If we stop, we look weak, and the Dane just can't wait to come back for more. Father's a tough bastard. He'll say, best let 'em drown."

"You got it," said Arni. "Or let the Dane take their heads off and sling 'em at us, so we can sling 'em right back." He laughed.

Godwin stared up at the clear starry sky. Did this adventure, this mission to be led by his own father at the King's command, rest on so dishonourable a foundation as bringing death to scores of enslaved women and children? Wulfnoth would say "The Vikingr are hard, we must be harder." He'd tell Godwin that the Vikingr must come to know that the boats leaving the fjords may not return, so Saxons must have the cold will to sacrifice those stolen slaves thrown into the water or tied to the oars of a burning boat, to reduce future kidnappings. But, but… Who has the right to put those poor people's lives into a balance against others who may or may not be taken in the future? God? The King? Not his father, surely?

It was deeply troubling, for if Wulfnoth, Thegn of some few hundreds of the South Saxons, was commanded to determine those destinies, then it seemed that one day he, Godwin, might also be called upon to decide who may live and who must die.

He couldn't sleep, such was the weight.

He needed to talk to his father.

He lifted the blankets, crawled from the bed, and slowly stood. Three pairs of eyes looked up at him.

"Couldn't you have gone before we layed down?" said Eg. "Like the rest of us? Don't think you're coming back into the middle."

Godwin picked his way around snoring bodies to the remains of the fire. He could see his father's broad back. Wulfnoth now shared the narrow log with Ham and Gewis the Headman. Seated at the end, next to Gewis, was Odylia, huddled again in furs. Slowly he came closer, not wanting to interrupt.

Ham was speaking in a low growl. "About a week," he said. "When we get a westerly we must go to Flandra, for when the wind changes and blows us back to England…"

"We can steer south," said Wulfnoth. "Normandy will suffice. Or Brittony. All will provision us if we have gold."

"And if we do not?"

"Oh, we will. But if we don't, we find a small place, and just take what we need."

Godwin was by now in the dark shadow right behind his father, close enough to tap his shoulder. He stretched out his arm as Ham said "The men will want to come back to England eventually."

Godwin paused. Eventually?

Wulfnoth laughed. "You think?" He leaned forward to look at Odylia. "Girl, go find your bed."

Odylia stood and came in front of them to kiss her father. She could plainly see Godwin behind them, and she stared at him, but her elfin face was shaded from the firelight and Ham had no glimpse of her expression. Godwin shook his head, and she did nothing to reveal his presence. As she walked away Gewis patted her behind. So it was fine for some men to piss off her father.

Wulfnoth resumed, in a low voice that Godwin had to strain to hear. "When we tell the men they have a choice, to share these riches between us, or to hand all but a sackful to the King, what will they say? Hah! They will choose to be rich in Flandra. Those that wish to sneak back for their families may do so, but the mass of 'em, they'll opt for flaxen Flandish maids. That's what I'll do. I recommend you do the same."

Godwin froze. His father would not return to Comtyn. That meant Godwin would not return to Comtyn, to his mother or his sister, to Gret with her thick hair, full breasts and her soft thighs. Eg would not return to his mother. Sel – he had no mother, and his father Cudbert was here. Did Cudbert know?

"Those as do want to reclaim their families in England…" Gewis lowered his voice. "If they are caught… they'll be hung."

Hung? For doing the King's work?

"Better pray they don't say we landed at Brimclif," said Ham. "Or you'll be strung right up with them."

"He's not staying here," said Wulfnoth. "Are you, Gewis? You're off with your new horse and your little new wife."

New wife? Odylia?

Wulfnoth laughed, and leaned closer to Gewis. "Better go somewhere very safe, because you won't be hung. You'll be tortured a week, and sliced, and you'll die watching crows peck out your own entrails."

"Nah," said Ham. "Crows'll peck out his eyes first."

All three laughed.

8. Swordplay

(Edward)

"Launch a surprise attack when your enemy least expects it."

Edward jerked his hand away from himself when Ellin came in as bold as a thunderclap to announce that the Queen wanted them at the table to break their fast with her.

She retreated, banging shut the door, and Edward sat up on his feather mattress wondering again if the maid's manner was deliberately rude, or if she was equally curt to her own children. Worse, did she somehow know what he'd been up to? He wanted to tell his mother to scold Ellin, but he feared his mother would see straight through to his sacrificial offering to Onan.

Perhaps he was just being over-sensitive. He wished he could talk to Alfred about Ellin, but his brother was under-sensitive and would not understand. That was at best. At worst, he would mock Edward, for all that Edward was the older, and then decide to tell their mother just to see Ellin punished. Edward didn't want her punished, he just wanted due – what was the word? – deference. And to see her smile for once.

He looked at the mess laying siege to Alfred's bed: skittles and balls, wooden practice swords, clothes, half-eaten apples, chicken bones on a wooden plate, an overturned clay beaker, broken quills and spilt wax. Someone should tell Ellin to tidy it up. Better, tell Alfred not to make a mess in the first place. Alfred rolled under his blankets to face the tapestry that warmed the walls of their room. Another bloody hunt scene.

"Alfie, time to get up," he said, but Alfred merely muttered "Don't call me Alfie" into his pillow and stayed motionless.

Edward swung his feet out onto the spotless woven wool rug on his side of the room, well clear of Alfred's mess. Before putting on his day clothes he crossed to the corner, where his bible lay open on a lectern. The chill air withered the bone in his pintle and eased his conscience.

Pride was a sin, but how could it fail to please God that his most treasured possessions were his biblical books? God's words were scribed onto finest vellum, each chapter had an illustrated initial, the bindings were shiny leather tooled with designs inlaid with gold leaf, with brass corners and clasps that Edward polished assiduously. The Gospels had been a baptismal gift from the Archbishop Aelfheah, no less. The Pentateuch followed; and every year on his baptism-day the great man presented him with a further book. He was up to Job.

His reading had taken him halfway through the Book of Esther, second time around. First time, it was priests who had read to him. Now, he was trying not just to know God's word, but to understand it. The Commandments had been clear enough. The words of Our Lord and the parables, these too were simple messages that a child could understand. But Edward knew that the tales of The Fall, of Abraham and Isaac, of Joseph, and David, held meanings too subtle for that child. He was growing now, and on a quest to find the full import of these stories for Christians. Surely they were more than the history of the Judaics, or why would they be in Christ's Bible?

Already he thought it unfair that Xerxes should banish Queen Vashti simply because she refused to be paraded like some fine pony in front of guests at his feast. But he understood too the argument of Xerxes' counsellors, that to allow Vashti to get away with contumation would encourage all wives to disobey their husbands. Then again, wasn't the problem of Xerxes' own making? If husbands did not make unreasonable requests of their wives, there would be no cause for disobedience… It was very complicated. What is God trying to say?

No, God does not try to say anything. God speaks. It is up to mankind to try to understand him, to follow his rules.

This he had discussed with his mother. She had smiled and said that Vashti was a fool. What did her pride matter, compared to the goal of securing position and influence for herself and, most importantly, for her children? Edward understood his mother's message, that she, the Queen, would always do what she must, for him and for Alfie. He was not too young to sense that in a court seething with whispers and plots, with new faces appearing and old ones vanishing, his mother's protection was a reassuring constant in his life.

All the same, her interpretation hadn't really helped. The Book of Esther was after all not about Vashti, but about Esther saving her people from the evil Haman. Haman wanted to slaughter all the Jews, just like Edward's father when he'd told Saxons to slaughter all Danish settlers on Saint Brice's Day.

"Alfred," he said. "We're on Esther, remember? The Book of Esther. She fears for Mordechai. Alfred? Are you listening?"

"Pox on Esther."

Edward was on the point of giving up with Alfred. If priests and bishops, and even archbishops, couldn't make him listen, what chance did an older brother have?

The brothers took their breakfast in one of King Aethelred's smaller halls in Lunden, watched by Queen Emma. Edward was old enough to know that their mother was counted a beauty, and old enough too to recognise that she had to be so counted, for she was Queen. Her features were hard, and not greatly softened by her small smile as she watched her sons. Edward took after her. Square-faced Alfred took after his father, as did Goda who sat with her little friend Hendi debating the colouring and character of each of the kittens one of the cats had littered. The Lord had looked kindly upon Goda, who seemed to be making a full recovery.

His half-sister Ecfrida sat alone at the table nibbling cobnuts one at a time. She too took after their father: plain, mousy-haired and round of face; but with big wide eyes that drew you in, and pale skin smooth as cream. He liked Ecfrida, and felt sorry for her. She and her older sister Aelfrith were his father's last unmarried daughters from his first marriage, but with Aelfrith recently gone to the Abbey at Wherwell that their grandmother founded, poor Ecfrida was lonely.

Fulton served him meat, bread and a quartered apple, then leaned forward to pour his posset. Edward felt the warmth of Fulton's torso on his shoulder. He wondered if Fulton would help him extract Esther's true message. Fulton was a ceorl's son, an illiterate serving boy, but was Edward's best friend in spite of his station. His curiosity and insight matched Edward's. He too preferred wordplay to swordplay, reflection to riding, calm to competition.

They would talk together, discussing Edward's recounting of biblical tales, and mulling over the threats to the Kingdom posed by the Wealas and the Cernwaelas, the Scots, the Norse and the Danes. Edward could talk about Alfred and Goda, and could hear of Fulton's family too, his crippled father and toiling mother, and the sister, pregnant yet again. Fulton saw his little nephews daily. Edward was not an uncle, nor even a half-uncle.

Alfred was served by Wilf, his friend and companion. The

boys weren't needed to serve; their presence was a concession for which the Princes would soon be too old. Cynethe, Ecfrida's handmaid, hadn't been privileged to join them at meals for a year now, excepting great feasts when she would attend as a mark of Ecfrida's rank, as Arsindis stood behind Queen Emma.

Prince Edmund strode into the hall and helped himself to a slice of pigmeat already cut from the ham. While Queen Emma's smile stayed on her lips, Edward noticed it leave her eyes.

Edmund never ruffled Edward's hair like he ruffled Alfred's. "Big week, Alfie Atheling. First Witan!" Alfred didn't mind Edmund calling him Alfie. Even in so simple an act as bending to kiss his sister Ecfrida, Edmund's lean body held an energy that Alfred seemed in awe of.

Alfred didn't warrant the title Atheling. That was for Edmund himself, the oldest Prince, the heir. If Edmund was to hold anyone else up as Atheling, even in jest, it should be he, Edward.

Alfred said "Edward has told me all about it."

"But has he told you about the Forkbeard?"

"I know about the Danes. They take our gold."

"Then you will know what to speak for!"

Emma cleared her throat. "They are there to watch and to listen. If they are asked for their views they are to support their King." She spoke slowly, because people had trouble with her accent. Sometimes she talked quickly to her sons so only they understood what she said. She had of course ensured that their French was fluent, but speaking to them in her native tongue risked being thought overtly rude to Aethelred, Edmund and others whose French was more limited.

The door to the hall was opening as Emma continued. "They will not speak. Nor should you, Edmund, save for the same purpose: to stand with your father."

Edmund turned away from the door and snorted to himself, as Aethelred came to the table. The King of England was ageing and careworn, but he managed to summon some jollity. "Of course they'll stand with their father. Everyone stands with their father!"

Emma suppressed her sigh, and even Edmund's lips were held firmly together. Ecfrida offered to pour more posset into Alfred's cup although he hadn't asked, and had even placed it upside down on the table and wouldn't let her turn it right way up. Anyway, pouring his drink was Wilf's job. She just wanted to be doing something. Edward looked from face to face, not quite sure how or why the mood had changed.

Goda and Hendi continued their whisperings.

Alfred slid his overturned cup to the edge of the table, and as it reached the edge he put the palm of his hand flat underneath it. Alfred had something hidden in the cup, and Edward could guess what. He should say something, but this had happened often enough before, and his father had told him not to intervene. "She has to learn," Aethelred said.

Alfred walked behind the girls with the cup pressed to his chest. His free hand kept the wooden practice sword hanging through a belt loop from tapping the floorboards. He held the cup over Goda's head, turned and shook it to let fall two spiders the size of coins. She felt something but barely reacted, merely brushing at her hair. Then she realised it was Alfred behind her, saw his wicked grin, and knew what he'd done. She stood and screamed and slapped at her hair. The spiders hung on their strands of silk, and Hendi tried to brush them clear. Goda, not knowing how many Alfred had dropped, continued to squeal and shake her hair out long after the spiders had disappeared, as their father chortled merrily.

Emma spoke sternly. "Alfred!" She would surely tell him to go to his room, and that was the least he deserved. Goda was still frail from her illness, and Alfred as her older brother should show her kindness.

Aethelred stood. "Come Alfred," he said. "Draw your sword!"

Emma glared at him. Alfred grinned again, rescued by his father and predictably eager to show off. The birch sword was over three feet long, heavy, straight-grained and unlikely to split. He pulled it from the bawdrick and took stance with a two-handed grip. Aethelred lifted a similar weapon from a rack that stood near the fireplace, and adopted his own casual stance.

Goda did not run off, but settled down again to whisper with Hendi. The topic was surely now that of horrid brothers. Edward wanted to say something to her, but what could he say when he'd stayed silent just before? He'd eaten his fill, so he slid along the bench to the far end of the table and motioned for Fulton to come next to him. He quietly began to tell Fulton the story so far of Esther and Xerxes, Mordechai and Haman.

He was only vaguely aware of Aethelred's gentle attack on Alfred, easily parried. Alfred retreated, defending, backing over a bench. Aethelred's attacks grew faster and fiercer, and the clack of wood on wood was distracting Fulton from the scriptural tale. Alfred emitted a nervous laugh, but still parried successfully.

"You've taught him well, Edmund." Aethelred called.

"It's Bullward you need to thank," said Edmund.

Edward squeezed Fulton's arm to keep his attention, and continued whispering about Esther.

Aethelred told Alfred to attack, and the boy advanced, swinging the stick, swipes which Aethelred saw early and blocked easily.

"Remember, when you have the light sword," Edmund called, "it is the thrust that will kill."

So Alfred tried, and Aethelred deflected his thrusts, and countered, and soon had the rounded nose of his wooden sword at Alfred's throat.

Edmund stood up. "I think it is time to dispense with birch." Edmund took off his sword, the ancient relic that only the Atheling could wear and must never use, and stepped to the rack of steel swords next to the wooden ones. He selected the two lightest, proffered one to Alfred, and placed himself where Aethelred had stood.

Alfred laughed at the clash of steel ringing out in place of the clack of timber, but it was nervous laughter that soon abated. Aethelred clapped and cheered as Alfred blocked each of Edmund's well-signalled attacks. The girls looked up, then returned to their discussions, immune to the noise.

"Come on, attack me," Edmund said to Alfred.

Alfred tried two-handed swings, which Edmund blocked nonchalantly. He let Alfred's blade slide down to hit his cross-guard, and jumped back crying "Ow!" He dropped the sword with a clang onto the floor, then held up his right hand. "You've taken off my finger!". His little finger was missing. There was no blood. Alfred giggled. Edmund had lost that finger in a real fight several years ago. "I shall have to fight left-handed," Edmund said, picking up the sword. "Maybe that will even things up a bit."

Edward abandoned Esther. Edmund's left hand fighting was the same as his right, as far as he could see. Edmund was famed for his skills with weapons.

He attacked Alfred again, more vigorously, and Alfred concentrated hard on Edmund's blade, his brow sweating, and fear now illuminating his eyes as Edmund's swings and jabs grow fiercer. Alfred's moves were desperate and panicked, until one sharp stroke from Edmund freed Alfred's weapon from his slippery palms. He stood there, undefended, his hands apart in a gesture of helplessness. Edmund pulled his blade back behind his shoulder and swung it level. It whistled through the air and stopped with the blade turned vertical a single inch from Alfred's left ear. Edmund swung from the other side and stopped the blade again with its flat an inch from the right ear. Alfred stood rabbitlike, fearing for his life but unable to flee, or to duck, or even to flinch.

"Edmund!" Emma called, and her voice was sharper even than his sword.

"What?" he said, turning to her, all wide-eyed innocence. "It's just an exercise."

"If you were my son…" Her voice was colder too.

Edmund picked up Alfred's sword and returned it to the rack. Aethelred looked from one to the other, smiling uncertainly, unsure which son to support or scold, or both, or neither.

Edmund turned back to Alfred. "You are disarmed." Edmund dropped his sword to the floor with a clang. "You either retreat…" He stepped backwards. "…or you take your next weapon…" He stepped forward and drew the seax from its sheath on Alfred's belt. "…and you launch a surprise attack when your enemy least expects it!" He attacked himself with Alfred's little dagger, miming jabs at his own heart and stomach, groaning "Arghh! Arghh!" He plunged the blade under his armpit, and fell to the floor with a dying groan. He writhed, and stilled. Alfred laughed uncertainly. Edmund jerked his final throes. He lay dead, as Alfred giggled again.

Edmund lifted his head. "See? Surprise attack. Surprisingly effective. I even caught myself out." He winked and stood up, went to Alfred and bent to kiss his cheek. "Sometimes it is necessary to defend, and sometimes it is necessary to run. Do not be ashamed of running, my brother, because when a Prince runs, he runs with his men, and for their sake, not for himself. Just remember, Alfie, one day you must stop running. Victory can come only after attack."

Prince Edward wondered if Edmund would ever call him brother. Or even Eddie.

"Come on then Edward," said Aethelred. "Have you finished eating? Have you finished conspiring with Fulton there? Let's see how well you've progressed."

Edward wanted to tell him he was up to the Book of Esther, but he reluctantly drew himself to his feet as Aethelred picked up the two wooden swords.

He took guard against Alfred.

Emma said "Alfred has been tired by you two."

"No I haven't," Alfred insisted.

Edward had the advantage of age and size, but Alfred's blood was up, he was competitive, and having been killed thrice this morning, he had a point to prove. Edward found himself under attack, and realised that this year or next, Alfred would have the beating of him, age and size notwithstanding. Edward did not try to deliver his young brother to his maker for the fourth time the morning, he just defended. Then he was backed against a bench, almost touching Fulton. Distracted, he allowed Alfred's stick to glance off his own and catch him hard across the cheekbone. He gasped, and suddenly he couldn't see properly for the tears in his eyes. They sprung not just from the pain, but from the unfairness. He hadn't wanted to fight, and he'd been careful not to hurt Alfred. Now he was cut, and looked inadequate. He knew he cried too often – at thirteen years, he shouldn't cry at all – but he couldn't control it.

Anger flared. Why were you cruel to Goda, he thought? You know how scared she is of little crawling things. He advanced on Alfred, swinging hard, and Alfred dropped his sword as he stepped back, but Edward kept swinging, beating his brother on his shoulders and forearms as Alfred lifted his hands in fear.

Sounds came in a rush. Alfred's "Ow! Ow!" Edmund's

"Know when to run, Alfie, it's all right." Aethelred's "Never drop your weapon boy."

And Emma's loud "Assez!" that cut through everything.

He stopped and saw his little brother cowering and crying too. He looked at the others. Ecfrida glared at him as much in surprise as accusation. There was no ambiguity to his mother's glare. Goda blinked back tears – even she didn't want her brother hurt. Edward dropped the practice sword and stooped to put his arm around Alfred. "I'm sorry, I'm sorry, I didn't mean-"

Alfred shook him off and ran out to their room, with Wilf quick to follow.

Edward looked up in shame. His cheek throbbed. On a different day he'd have gone to his mother for an embrace, but her angry eyes forbade approach. His father, surprised at the sudden loss of temper he'd witnessed, emitted a laugh like a hiccup, then frowned, then hiccupped again. Edmund nodded and tapped fingers into his other palm in unwanted appreciation of Edward's attack. Only Ecfrida reflected his upset and confusion.

Fulton's thoughts were hidden behind a face like the surface of a frozen lake on a grey winter's day. But Edward knew them, all the same.

Ellin offered a salve for the swollen cut to his cheek, but he refused her, and went to find Fulton as soon as he judged his friend would be finished with his kitchen duties. He was too soon, but when he said "Come with me," fat Frethi the steward could not overrule him. Fulton followed with a slow step that said he wished the steward could.

Edward led the way to the millpond. It was a favourite place. The still water was calming, while the rush of the stream's fall over the wheel drowned the sound of their conversation to anyone more than a few paces away. Confidences shared here were safe.

They sat on the grass, and Fulton was silent. Normally Edward liked Fulton's silence. He could listen to it as he gazed at the water. Today his silence was so loud it drowned the rush of the tailrace.

"I'm sorry," Edward said.

Fulton just grunted.

"I just… I don't know. I snapped. I didn't want to fight him in the first place."

"Could tell, the way you swiped him even after he dropped his sword."

Edward was shamed once more. "It was fucking Edmund's games. If it hadn't been for that, we'd just have had a little dance, father would have been disappointed in me, but we'd have come back to the table, and…" He trailed off.

Fulton was silent still, and reproach flowed from him like a wave.

"You don't want to be here, do you. I don't blame you." Edward knew he was being selfish. "Go, then." He knew he'd see him again soon, even if neither of them wanted.

Fulton relaxed. "It's all right," he said. "I accept your apology."

"It won't happen again, I promise."

"You have a nasty temper," said Fulton.

"I'll try to control it."

"Bit bloody late, now."

"What can I do to make up for it?"

"Probably nothing."

Edward would find something. A present. A coin, although Fulton would be insulted by that. He didn't do what he did for money. Edward didn't actually know Fulton's motive, and dared not ask in case he stopped. Honour? Duty? No-one forced him, but still Fulton stayed close to Edward in spite of the suffering. "I don't take you for granted, you know."

"Yes you do, you're the fucking Prince."

"No I don't. That's the point. If I didn't suffer too it would just be meaningless cruelty."

"My heart bleeds," Fulton snorted.

Edward roused himself early the next morning, to give himself time to read before Ellin came, before he was called. He'd caught Alfred playing with the hounds yesterday evening, romping happily with them until he noticed Edward watching, when he suddenly remembered the agony of his bruises and weaselled away cradling his arms, first one, then the other, not knowing which was supposed to hurt most.

Edward read from the Book of Esther loud enough that Alfred must wake. Hearing the scripture would do him good. He translated the Latin as he went, skipping the boring bits and the repetitions, because he knew this was the only way Alfred would get to hear much of God's word. He never concentrated in church, that was plain to see.

Edward liked Esther. She was brave, yet circumspect in the way she manipulated King Xerxes. She had learned the lesson of Vashti's demise; she was like his own mother. He liked Mordechai too – loyal to the King, yet uncompromising in his faith in God when Xerxes' satrap Haman turned against Mordechai's people, the Jews. He hated Haman, the vain minister who assumed that when the King wanted to honour a man, it had to be he, Haman, who stood in line for glory, not Mordechai. Haman wanted Mordechai to be the first Jew to die, so Esther bravely revealed to the King how Mordechai had secretly saved the King from a palace plot.

Edward read on, knowing that Alfred's ears were open even

if his eyes were shut. When he read of how Xerxes ordered Haman to be impaled on the very pole that Haman had set up for Mordechai's execution, Alfred grunted his approval into his pillow.

"Then Mordechai was honoured, and was allowed to issue an edict in the King's name, granting Jews in every city the right to destroy and kill any armed men who might attack them." He paused. "Might attack them? That's a bit strong, isn't it? Anyone might attack anyone. Does that mean the Jews could attack a stranger at will, if he was armed? What do you think, Alfi- Alfred?"

Alfred said nothing. Edward would have to take the matter up with Fulton. If Fulton would speak to him after today.

He skipped on quickly, recalling the bones of the story from his reading last year. "So, well, the courtiers went out, and Mordechai dressed up in splendour – befitting the King's first lord, I suppose – and people converted to become Jews out of fear. And there's some stuff about dates. And then in the city of Susa they killed five hundred men, and they killed… Oh my God" – he couldn't help blaspheming – "The Jews killed Haman's ten sons!"

Edward paused to let this cruelty register with his brother, and he knew that it had, because Alfred turned over. "What do you think? Is the Bible saying that it's all right with God for sons to be punished for what their fathers do?" This was troubling. Their father was the most powerful man in the country. Might he and Alfred suffer for Aethelred's misdeeds? Was the St Brice's Day slaughter a misdeed? The Danes would surely say so, and they were mostly Christians now, weren't they? At least the ones settled in England. They hadn't even converted out of fear.

"The rest of the Jews in the provinces came together, and killed seventy-five thousand of their enemies. Seventy-five thousand, Alf! But they did not plunder their possessions."

"That's all right then," Alfred said.

"God is saying that it's right to look after your own people," Edward explained. But his troubles with The Word grew. "I must admit, I'm not sure how this fits with Thou Shalt Not Kill, Love Thy Neighbour and Turn The Other Cheek."

Alfred sat up, and turned to perch on the edge of his bed. "Mordechai turned out to be as much of a bastard as Haman," he said. "The only difference I can see is, he came out on top."

"Is that the lesson you take?"

"Yeah. Don't you?" Alfred rubbed his eyes, bored now and ready to move on to the day's major excitement.

Edward didn't always like Alfred, and knew they were very different to each other. But he couldn't imagine life without him.

They sat in silence in the hall until Frethi came to lead them to the King's chamber. Fulton was already outside, waiting as they entered. The steward closed the door on him.

Aethelred was seated, with Edmund standing just behind his left shoulder. The fat Reeve Wilmaer stood against the side wall next to Bullward, the King's head husceorl, who held the thin switch of birch as if judgement was already given.

"Come stand here, Alfred," Aethelred said, indicating the space to his right. So Bullward was right. Only the punishment was left to be decided.

"Do you have anything to say, Edward?" said Aethelred. No preamble was necessary.

"I'm sorry," said Edward. He turned to Alfred. "I'm sorry. When you hit me… I know you didn't mean to-"

"Did," said Alfred.

"I know you didn't mean to hurt me like you did, but I just saw red."

"Anger is fine," said Edmund. "It's losing control of yourself that gets you killed."

"You hurt your brother, deliberately and unfairly," said Aethelred. "You have to learn."

Edward's head turned downwards, like half a nod.

"Alfred. You were wronged. You can choose the punishment."

"Two dozen!" His unbroken voice couldn't carry his outrage, and cracked the word "dozen" in two.

"No! that's too much," cried Edward.

"You have no say," his father said. He looked at Edmund.

"It was done in anger," said Edmund. "And Edward stopped. Not planned, or wantonly cruel. A dozen, at most."

"Two!" said Alfred again. "Look!" And he rolled up his sleeves to show livid bruises on his arms.

Edward touched his own cut and swollen cheek, but said nothing.

"I say then, eighteen," pronounced Aethelred. He nodded at Bullward.

Bullward opened the door and pulled Fulton in by the arm. Wilmaer placed a heavy rectangular oak stool in the middle of the room, which Bullward pushed Fulton over, letting him grip its far edge as he'd gripped it before. He unknotted Fulton's waistcord and pulled his braies to the floor. He turned up the shirttail, exposing Fulton's ravaged buttocks.

"Eighteen," repeated Aethelred. "Edward, count."

Edward could barely watch, and his vision swam as it had earlier, but he listened and counted carefully lest his friend suffer a nineteenth stroke of the birch.

Bullward was neither weak nor lazy, and the first blow cracked like an axe splitting a log. Fulton's pink flesh was raised with eighteen cruel welts, oozing red. Where strokes overlapped blood flowed freely. Fulton held back his cries for five strokes, but by nine he had lost all control. His screams filled the hall, heard by Emma, by Ecfrida, by Goda, and by all the ceorls and servants and thuws.

Edward's sobs came too, although they were drowned by Fulton's anguish. When it was over Edward went to his best friend, his only friend, and pulled up his braies, knotted the cord, and led him out with his arm protectively around Fulton's shoulders.

Fulton clung to him as he had those times before, and Edward knew himself unworthy of such loyalty.

9. The Dance

(Fleada)

"Giving yourself to a man is no way to win him."

Before Witan, the council. Before council, the feast.

The tables' thick boards, polished from use and spilled fat, proudly supported hams and steaks, roast suckling pigs, ducks and pheasant, cheeses and butter, breads, pickles, pears in honey, and apples. Jug upon jug of ale, mead and wine were brought and poured by the serving boys and girls. At the far end, away from the high table, children played on the floor. Men and women left the hall to piss or shit or vomit, and returned. Some couples capered, dancing and jigging, then left the feast and failed to return. The gleemen played valiantly, but little could be heard above the shouted conversations, the laughter, insults and arguments. The scop sat on his stool sipping ale, awaiting his call to give yarns and poems to those staying for a quieter time before sleep.

Fleada stood behind her mistress, dutiful but idle because Aethelred's servants delivered food and wine to the table. Apart from remaining attentive to any sign from Aelfgifu, she was free to observe. Some names she knew. Nothman got drunk and noisy, while Leofric got drunk and quiet. Reeve Terning was positioned further back among the Mercians, alongside a young cleric Fleada had never seen before. He wore a habit, but wasn't a monk, was he? Monks don't have long hair, or rings on more fingers than not.

Eadric talked seriously with the King and another young man, tall and dark, who could only be the famed Edmund

Ironside. They must have mentioned Aelfgifu, for Edmund's eyes turned to her. Aelfgifu too noticed, and Fleada blushed with her.

Further away, Eadric's wife Eadgyth talked avidly with a younger woman. They held hands and engaged in deep whispers. With their similar faces, this made them sisters. So there were five of the King's offspring at the table. Fleada wondered if Eadric would be slighted at this reminder that he had no heirs. Then she wondered if that was the intention. Then she wondered if she was being stupid – of course the Princes and Princesses were at the King's table. She scolded herself for pretending to understand matters way above her station.

Aelfgifu was almost next to the Queen, with only the younger Princes Edward and Alfred between them. One ate slowly, and even from behind Fleada could tell from the movements of his head that he, like she, was observing and listening. The other Prince ate like a wolf, and didn't look up until his platter was bare. While he waited for someone to put more ham or pie before him, he seemed not to know what to do.

Before the feast had started, the two Princes had been called to meet Eadric. Polite pleasantries done, he had shown them his jewelled dagger, and the matching brooches that fastened his cloak. Gold they were, with garnetstones surrounding a single ruby. Rubies! He said they were brought by Danes who travelled and traded down a river that led all the way to the fabled cities of Constantinople and Byzantium. Were they really traded, Fleada wondered? Or did blood colour those rubies and garnets?

Again she told herself to stop thinking.

The Princes loved the trophies. Alfred gripped the dagger before him, and stabbed at air. Edward turned a brooch over and over in his hands. Eadric smiled at him, and said to

Emma. "Your boy loves fine things."

"He has good taste," Emma agreed.

Aelfgifu too had looked on. Her foot bounced under her seat. She hadn't liked the boys getting attention. She'd seen Eadric's brooch before, of course, but never had he shown it off to her, not that Fleada knew of.

"He'll not defend the kingdom with jewellery!" Aethelred had snapped. "Nor even with daggers. Women's weapons. If it comes to daggers, the enemy's too close, and it's too late."

"You are right, lord." Eadric smiled again. "About the dagger. But it would be unwise not to recognise the part jewels may play in defending the realm."

"Hmp," was all Aethelred said, then he ordered Edward and Alfred to return the treasures to Eadric, and get back to their places.

Fleada was stood next to the boy who attended to Prince Edward as she attended Aelfgifu. Well, perhaps not exactly, but in everyday matters the boy was Edward's servant and companion. He was permitted to eat and drink standing, as was she. She was getting bored, and her legs ached, so to relieve the tedium she asked him his name, quietly, barely moving her head.

"Fulton," he replied.

"I'm Fleada," she said. "Lady Aelfgifu's handmaid." She couldn't keep the pride out of her voice, although she tried, because if Fulton was a Prince's personal servant, his status was higher than hers. "Boring, isn't it."

"I can cope," he replied. He looked tired, as if he'd had a long day.

"Wouldn't you love to sit down though?"

"No thanks," he said, in a tone so sharp and unwarranted that she shut up.

As they ate, Fleada watched, and she divided the company into those who actively made conversation – mostly the men –

and those who watched and listened, like Prince Edward, and his mother the Queen. Fleada knew from the set of Aelfgifu's head that her eyes were on Prince Edmund Ironside. He, definitely a talker not a watcher, was unaware, until he glanced up and saw her.

Queen Emma noticed all, for she smiled at Aelfgifu. "You blush so prettily, my dear. It's a talent you must never lose." She spoke across Edward and Alfred. "Tell me, are you Mercian by birth?"

Her mistress was surprised to be spoken to. "Oh!" she squeaked, then gathered herself. "I am Northumbrian. My father was Elfhelm, Ealdorman of Jorvik."

"But you are known as Aelfgifu of Northamtun, are you not? And Northamtun is Mercia, not Northumbria."

"My mother's family was from Northamtun," Aelfgifu said, as if admitting to a naughty secret. "I have nothing to do with them. My Godfather wanted me to be known that way. To make me more acceptable to Mercians, I suppose."

"Ah yes," Emma said. "That sounds like Lord Eadric. You said your father was Ealdorman of Jorvik. Is he no longer?"

Aelfgifu paused, then said expressionlessly "Both my parents were murdered. No, he is no longer."

"Oh, my dear, that's terrible. Isn't that terrible Edward?"

Edward said with obvious sincerity "That is very sad."

Alfred raised his head.

Aelfgifu was demure, yet graceful. Fleada was proud of her. "I was young. I have only the vaguest memory of them."

"A mercy," said Edward.

"Eadric has been good to you," said Emma. "But he is not a relation, is he? Not family?"

"No," said Aelfgifu. "Yet he has done as much for me as any kin would, and more."

Alfred reached for Aelfgifu's arm to get her attention. "Who killed them?" he said. "How did they do it?"

Fleada watched Emma close her eyes and sigh.

After much food had been consumed and much ale drunk, the trestles and benches below the King's table were shifted aside. Youths came to do cartwheels and tumbles, followed by a dangerous barechested sword dance, executed to the beating of sticks and tambours. Harps and lyres and flutes sounded, and girls arrived to perform a flower dance with the boys. Then the girls danced alone, and their moves became increasingly suggestive, and downright bawdy. Cheers came from all quarters, but were not full-throated until King Aethelred showed his approval by clapping. The girls began to expose more of their legs and much of their bosoms, and were showered with coins and suggestions.

Fleada wanted to dance too, not for the chance to catch someone's eye but for the joy of it, and to join with those girls' fearlessness when they were together. She hoped for their sakes they would not be split up later in the evening. Too many drunk men about. But maybe some of the girls would love that.

The gleemen played popular tunes to which all could sing and dance, and the great men and women of Saxon England wove lines, made arches and circles, in pairs, quartets and eights, coming together with a clap and a whoop, parting with a skip and a jig. In some dances women made a circle around the men; in others the men lifted them by the waist and let them down again.

Fleada watched as dancers eloquently spoke their thoughts through their movements. One girl drew the most attention. She was the most beautiful in the room, and she wasn't Aelfgifu, no matter how much Fleada wished otherwise. She was taller, with hair of flowing gold, huge eyes of purest flaxflower blue, and perfect heart-shaped face.

"Who is she." Fleada asked the boy Fulton, who stayed as she did in post behind his master's empty seat.

"Cynethe. She's Princess Ecfrida's handmaid."

This meant for most men that she had the advantage of not being a noble. She heard the distaste behind Cynethe's giggle as she firmly relocated Eadric's hands away from her bottom.

"Which is Ecfrida?" she asked.

He pointed out the girl she's seen talking with Eadgyth. "Your Lord Eadric's sister-in-law."

Eadric was still fondling Cynethe's behind.

"I see why he's called The Grasper," Fulton said.

Fleada choked. "You must be careful what you say."

He shrugged. "Probably," he said. "Yeah. But sometimes when you think they are all shits, you just have to tell someone. Prince Edward's not a shit."

"Neither is Lady Aelfgifu. Why tell me?"

"I was guessing you know it too."

Fleada was stunned into silence.

She watched Aelfgifu take every opportunity to come together with Edmund. Her smile was as pretty as her blush had been earlier, her movements lithe, her skips hopeful. When Nothman got between her and Edmund, which he boldly contrived to do too often for it to be happenstance, she did not smile at all. Next to the Atheling, Nothman was a provincial donkey.

Fleada asked Fulton if he wished to join the dancing, if he was allowed, but he shook his head and leaned on the chair just vacated by Edward. So she left the morose boy, stepping in to the dance to divert Nothman, at the price of his roving palms.

When Eadric put his hand on her bottom, she let him leave it there far longer than a maiden ought, knowing that Eadric's favourable regard was good for her mistress. It would do no harm to her either, but this thought she pushed away, for she was revolted at where it led. Fulton was wrong. Eadric was not a shit. He was good, and kind.

Prince Alfred seemed to be learning from the Mercians, and when he got the chance, he squeezed Cynethe's behind. She slapped his hand away, but pretended to find him amusing. He pinched Fleada, who had to skip rudely away from him, prince or no. When Nothman did the same she wondered if her posterior had some talismanic life-giving property, like the relics of a saint.

She wriggled away, but he pulled her back. "Don't worry girl, it's not your arse I want. Get me close to your mistress and there'll be reward for you, don't you worry." Another squeeze, this time of her breast, left little doubt what he considered a reward for the likes of a handmaid. She didn't squirm away from him, although she wanted to. She was amazed that he thought this might win assistance, or make her do anything other than keep Aelfgifu as far away from him as possible. He gave her tit a final squeeze and moved on. Fulton was wrong, but not about Nothman.

She searched for Aelfgifu, and was relieved to see Edward nervously approaching to ask her mistress if she might accompany him in a dance. She assented, as she must, and danced with a gusto that made it easier for the poor shy lad to forget his awkwardness and join in the spirit of the jig. He was about Fleada's age, and thus younger than Aelfgifu, but seemed such a boy. Not even a youth, not yet. She wanted to hug him.

Aelfgifu looked over his head at Edmund whenever she could. Now there was no embarrassment to her gaze, even when he nodded to her and smiled. The dance took her away from Edward now and again, and sometimes she would be face to face with Edmund. The energy that she had put into her pairing with Edward was now replaced with a slower and more studied grace. Fleada was as proud as ever for the way she held herself.

Emboldened, Alfred had moved on to Ecfrida. She slapped

his face, though he seemed more stung by the laughter of those around. When he pinched Fleada's rump a second time then a third, she lost her redhead's temper, and slapped the horrid boy's face as Ecfrida had.

King Aethelred roared with laughter at his youngest son's pink cheek, and Fleada slipped shamefully back to her place behind Aelfgifu's empty seat at the table. "Do you know how close you came to a flogging?" Fulton said.

She could no longer see Aelfgifu dancing. There she was, in a corner that candles and torches struggled to illuminate, chatting with Edmund. They both leaned against a tapestry, they both laughed.

Fleada parted from Fulton and placed herself nearby, watching as Edmund moved closer to Aelfgifu, who did not retreat but shaped her body sympathetically to his. Her shoulders were back, but her hips were forward. Fleada tried to shape her body the same way, but knew she was no swan. Aelfgifu saw her and lifted her eyebrows, though what that might mean, Fleada had no idea. Stop standing like a goose, probably.

Edmund lifted the tapestry's hem and backed into the darkness behind it, drawing Aelfgifu gently by the hand. With most of the feasters' eyes either clouded by ale and wine or still on the dancing, their departure went unnoticed.

Before the hanging fell back flat against the wall Aelfgifu looked over her shoulder at her. Fleada knew the meaning of that glance.

She sidled around the edge of the hall, and carefully peered behind the tapestry. There in the shadow was a doorway. She ducked behind, and opened the door. It led onto a corridor. One direction was lit by a single torch in a sconce. The other was completely dark. Voices came from the lit end, the common accents of the servants, and the sound of water splashing. The kitchens, surely. The other way was silent and dim, and there she turned, her eyes working to find their night vision.

At the end of the corridor was another door, stouter than the first. An external door. She lifted the heavy oak latch, and pulled it open. With the moonlight, and distant torches on a wall beside the hall's main entrance, outside was lighter than within. Some steps led to the ground. A few yards down a slope, a wooden extension to the main hall stood on timber posts to lift it to the same level. Two figures, barely discernible, leaned against one of the posts.

She descended the steps and silently approached as close as she dared. Her purpose was not to spy or to peep, but to be nearby in case Aelfgifu needed assistance. Away from the talk, music and laughter of the feast, she could hear their words despite the low tones.

"I will take the fight to Sveyn Forkbeard," Edmund was saying. "He breaks his truces, he harries the coast, and pays no price."

Fleada wondered if he was unwisely revealing battle plans, or merely boasting.

"You should come to live in the south," he continued. "He'll be minded to retaliate, and Eadric's northern lands are most in danger.

"Eadric will not let me come to harm."

"Lunden," he said. "Or Oxenford. Surely you feel safe down here in the south?"

"I do feel safe," said Aelfgifu, and the gentleness of her tone implied that she wasn't talking about marauding Danes.

"You are safe," Edmund said, and he put an arm around her and pulled her close.

Fleada closed her eyes, and when she opened them it was as she knew it would be. Her mistress was being kissed by Prince Edmund Atheling. Aelfgifu's face was upturned, and her body curved to his as it had done back in the hall, but now they were moulded together. Her hand went to his hair, then moved down to grip his shoulder, responding as his hold became firmer.

He eased her backwards, between the posts and under the building where it was dark. Fleada could just make out his movement as he removed his cloak and spread it on the ground. He pressed Aelfgifu down, and lay beside her. They kissed again, there was a rustle of clothing, a small "Oh!" from Aelfgifu, and indeterminate movements.

These were motions of passion not of fight, and Fleada stayed still, wishing she couldn't hear, but listening for sounds of struggle or any sign that her mistress was in peril. She crept closer and into the same dark. Edmund was on top of Aelfgifu, and she was holding him there… until he rolled off.

"I'm sorry, I'm sorry," Aelfgifu whispered. She had pushed him away. She was rising, straightening her dress, and stepping out from under the building.

Fleada went to her, and removed her shawl to wrap around Aelfgifu's shoulders. Behind, Edmund sat on his cloak, looking foolish and un-princely.

She led Aelfgifu back towards the steps, and heard Edmund call "Aelfgifu, my lady…" She looked over her shoulder, to see Edmund risen, standing there, his cloak draped limply over his hands. The sound of the door opening came from above, and there was Eadric at the top of the steps, looking from Aelfgifu to Edmund.

When they returned safely to her chamber, Aelfgifu sat for Fleada to unplait her hair and brush it. She confessed that Edmund was the first man she had kissed. Fleada knew about the boys Aelfgifu teased, knew about the games she played with the sons of thegns around Eadric's homes in Mercia, and even with some of the bolder ceorl youths, those not scared, or too callow to realise the risk of taking liberties with their Ealdorman's ward. Fleada had played such games herself. Boys were one thing, and not to be feared. But a man! A Prince! Edmund Atheling, heir to the English throne!

"Was it scaring?"

"It was exciting. Not scaring."

"He has a beard."

Aelfgifu pulled Fleada in front of her. "Oh Fleada, you must kiss a man with a beard!"

"What did his bristles feel like?"

"Rough. Like Hector and Paris." Hector and Paris were the girls' favourites of Eadric's pack of lurcher dogs. "I wanted to rub my face there. And when he pulled me close, I felt…"

"What did you feel? Tell me! Please…"

"Edmund Ironside... He's also Edmund Iron-front."

Fleada gasped, and they fell on each other's shoulders trying to hold down the guilt-laced laughter swelling inside.

"I meant…" There were tears in Fleada's eyes. "I meant, how did he make you f-"

The door opened, and in strode Eadric. They were instantly silenced. Fleada returned behind Aelfgifu and concentrated on her task.

Eadric pulled the second stool away from the wall and sat astride it, arms folded, staring at Aelfgifu as she picked up her silver mirror to watch her hair being brushed. She turned it so she could see Fleada's eyes. Better than having to face Eadric's.

He spoke firmly. "Giving yourself to a man is no way to win him."

Fleada felt Aelfgifu stiffen. "I did not give-"

"In truth it's the first step to losing him."

"There is nothing to lose."

"What possessed you to go outside with Edmund? It's as

well no-one else saw you leave. I'd have had to spend all night pacifying Nothman and Leofric."

"Why should I care about them?"

"You know perfectly well why. And that's aside from keeping your honour. Because your honour is Mercia's honour, and Mercia's honour is mine."

Aelfgifu was contrite. "I'm sorry if-"

"I asked a question. Why Edmund?"

"I liked him. I think he liked me."

"He liked something about you, for sure. I wonder what it was?"

"I made him laugh."

"Not when you left him standing like a donkey you didn't." But Eadric chuckled, and Fleada felt Aelfgifu relax under her brushing. "Edmund, eh? His fire is fanned, it seems." Eadric nodded to himself, and rose. "I wish you a good night's sleep."

He left, and Aelfgifu stood. Fleada began to help her undress, taking her outer clothes and folding them onto the chair. "Never mind that. Go warm the bed."

Fleada quickly took off her own outer garments, her shoes, her hose. She removed the pan of warmed stones and slipped under the bedclothes on Aelfgifu's side, and rubbed her feet together in the hot circle where the pan had been. She thought the mattress was at last fully aired. She shuffled to the cold side when Aelfgifu got in beside her.

"He has no idea, does he," Aelfgifu said.

"No idea? You mean, that you knew exactly what you were doing?"

"Yes."

"You were always going to push Edmund away?"

"Of course I was."

The boys around Coventre had a name for girls like her mistress, but Fleada did not speak it. "Did you know I was there, just in case…?"

"My darling Fleada, of course I did. That's why I love you." She turned to face Fleada and hugged her. Fleada stayed within the warm embrace until it loosened. "I need to sleep," Aelfgifu said, and Fleada nodded and withdrew. "So help me." Aelfgifu rolled onto her back.

Fleada put her hand onto Aelfgifu's small breast under her linen shift, and nuzzled at her neck. "Now," her mistress ordered, and placed Fleada's hand lower under the warm blankets. Fleada felt her hidden wetness, and stroked.

Aelfgifu pushed her head down, and as she moved to kneel in the dark, Fleada thought, yes, you really did like Edmund, didn't you.

10. The Traitor

(Godwin)

"They deserted the King."

Godwin realised he wasn't breathing. He backed silently away from his father, Ham and Gewis, before allowing himself air. He crept back to his friends, and slid under the blankets next to Eg. He held himself still and silent, but his mind raced.

It never crossed his mind to go without Eg and Sel. It never crossed his mind that either would spurn him. Cudbert? No, it would be wrong to test his loyalties so. He listened to his friends' breathing, and to snores from beyond. He was sure Arni was one of the snorers. For an hour and more Godwin watched The Archer cross the sky out over the sea. He lifted his head slowly to check that his father, the captain and the Headman had finished their grim conversation and settled themselves.

When he thought everyone was as soundly asleep as they ever would be, he slid again from under the blanket. He took his leather bag and sneaked to the remains of the fire, stepping carefully around the bodies sleeping under blankets and moonlight. He slid the knife from his belt and hacked off as much meat from the pig's carcass as he could find. It wasn't much, but it would keep them going for a day. After that, they'd find fruit or roots, trap rabbit, tickle trout, or use his mother's coin to buy a chicken.

He crept back to the bed, and held his hand gently over Eg's mouth. As soon as Eg twisted for better air, he whispered "Shhh". He reached to do the same with Sel. "Pick up your things," he hissed, "Follow me. Say nothing." They looked at each other, but they followed, tiptoeing silently, making their way up the track to the edge of the village. Godwin pulled them aside, and looked back to see that no-one had followed. All was still under the moon. Then the moon was covered by cloud.

"What the fuck are you doing?" Eg hissed.

"Shh. I'll tell you." In urgent whispers, he explained what he'd heard his father and the captain say. "We haven't been chosen by the King, nor by Eadric, nor by anyone. He's sold the men a lie. He sold me lie. What he's planning, it's not for England."

"I don't get it," said Sel. "What are they planning?" Selferth wasn't stupid, but he lacked imagination.

"Piracy," said Eg, reliably sharp. "They're going to rob boats, and keep the loot. Maybe rob villages too."

Sel's mouth was an open hole. Godwin waited for him to understand what he'd been told. "But," Sel said at last "…they'd be no better'n Norsemen."

"You're right," said Godwin. "We could never go back to Comtyn. Anywhere in England, we'd have to hide from the King's true men."

"We don't know that," said Sel. Incapable of deviousness, he could never see it in anyone else.

"We don't know much," said Godwin. "Except it's treasonous. He said it himself: we'll be hanged, or worse. Not to mention being lied to by my own father, tricked into leaving home never to return. How is that different to being taken by Norsemen as a slave? I want no part."

"What do we do?" said Eg.

"One, we stick together. We… We go back to Comtyn and say we were never here." And as he spoke a realisation stopped his breath. He almost lost balance, and had to shake his head to collect his thoughts as the full enormity of his father's plan hit him.

"What?" said Eg.

"Them in charge of this fleet. They'll see our boats are missing, if not in Scorham, for sure in Sanwic. They'll look for my father. And when they find he's stolen twenty boats, they'll take their revenge… That Brihtric, he'll take it out on our kin. It's not just that we can't return home. We shan't have no home to return to."

Eg was silent, absorbing this. Sel was silent, trying to understand.

"Ealdorman Aelfric would not allow it." said Eg. "Not Mercians."

"Could he stop them? What I've heard about Brihtric, he's to be feared. The only way we might save our village is to go to Aelfric and denounce our fathers. Aelfric may be able to make a plea for us with the King, and keep the Mercians away."

"How? He'll be in Wintancaestr."

"He'll be in Lunden," said Godwin. "There's a Witan coming up. Father was invited."

"Where in all England is Lunden?" said Sel.

"It must be north of here." He looked at his two best friends. "You both have your bags?" They did. He started up the track that headed inland, northwards. Eagbert followed.

Selferth did not.

Godwin turned. "Sel, come on!"

Sel stood and shook his head. "I'll not leave my father."

Godwin growled in frustration. "You'll not get him to come with us. He's loyal to mine."

Selferth just stood there.

"Sel! You, me, Eg… we are brothers."

"No we ain't. My brother's buried back in Comtyn."

"If you want to see home again you have to come with us."

"Cain't leave my dad."

"I'm leaving mine."

"Your dad's a traitor, according to you. Mine ain't."

"We got to, and we got to leave now," said Eg. "Someone might see we ain't there, thinking it's a bloody long crap we're all taking."

"You go. I won't say nothin'."

Godwin went to Selferth, held his shoulders, and looked at him. Grey had appeared in the eastern sky, but with the moon now blocked by heavy clouds gathering in the west, it was still too dark to see the details of Sel's expression. But his eyes would be narrow and sad, and his jaw thrust out, his standard look when he knew what he was going to do but was confused as to why. There would be no changing of him. Sel was months older than Godwin, but not as ready to walk his own path.

Godwin sighed. "All right. We'll go back to Cudbert and wake him. We'll bring him back here, explain the truth, and he can make his choice." Cudbert was honourable. Even if he chose not to come, and Sel stayed with him, he'd not wake Wulfnoth, and so Eg and he would have time to get clear of Brimclif. Probably.

Godwin told Eg to stay there, while he and Sel crept back down into the sleeping village to where Cudbert slept. He left it to Sel to wake his father, hush him, and draw him back up to where Eg waited.

"Cudbert, my father has lied," Godwin told him. "The King has not appointed anyone to harry longships. My father… He wants to make pirates of us all. I heard him, with Ham and this Gewis fellow."

Cudbert stared at the three boys. It was still too dark to make out an expression, but then, Cudbert's face was always carved of oak.

"We want no part in it," said Eg.

"We was leaving, but I'll stay with you," said Sel, and stood closer to his father.

"I'm your father's man," said Cudbert to Godwin in a voice deep and low.

"And you swore to him you would protect me," said Godwin, "So you must come with us."

"I'm your father's man," Cudbert repeated, "Not yourn."

Godwin shook his head. "We can't stand here debating. Make your choice. Break your oath to look out for me, never see Comtyn again, and watch Sel quartered as a pirate right next to you if ever Brihtric catches you all, or come with me and try to tell Ealdorman Aelfric that we all were duped."

"By your father."

"Yes."

Cudbert just stood there, with Sel beside him. Godwin knew they were lost to him.

He turned and put his arm around Eagbert's shoulders, and began to walk. "You and me then, Eg."

The unmistakable sound of sword being drawn came from just in front of them, and Arni stepped out onto the track. His steel shone in the faint pre-dawn light, and the tip wagged as Arni shook his head. "Turn around now."

"You followed us," said Eg.

"Too much sneaking about. First I thought you was out to steal something. Didn't want to miss out. Then I hear all this about pirating."

"It's true. Let us pass." Godwin stepped forward, and Arni lifted the sword.

"I know it's bloody true," he said, "That's why I can't let you pass."

"You're not going to kill me," said Godwin, shaking his head.

"Cut a big slice out of you though."

Cudbert drew his sword too. "Do that, and you drop right here."

Arni laughed. "Touch me and you're a dead man. My father will see to that. Wulfnoth needs him more than he needs you."

"Be that as it may. You touch Godwin, and you'll never know."

Godwin stepped forward, closer to the point of Arni's sword. "Two of us, Arni. We're just boys. Let us go. We make no difference."

Arni swiftly drew back the sword. Whether he meant to strike for blood, or turn the blade to hit him with the flat, or not strike at all, or just feint to test whether he'd flinch, Godwin never knew. With a speed that belied his large frame, Cudbert moved and struck Arni's sword arm just below the shoulder. Arni screamed. His bone was splintered. His sleeve was suddenly black with blood.

He fell to his knees, still screaming, and immediately noises rose from the village. Calls turned to shouts.

"Run!" said Godwin.

It was Cudbert who moved first, pushing Sel ahead of him. Eg stepped past Arni. "Told you," he said. "About swords, and trouble." He picked up the weapon in question, and ran.

They fled up the track. Godwin looked back. In the dim first light, he could see men beside Arni. He recognised Arni's father Ham. He recognised his own father. He saw them, and over a distance of two hundred yards, they saw him. They didn't recognise him, Godwin could tell. His father called "Wig! List! Gormond!" and Godwin turned again.

"Run!" he repeated. Wig, List and Gormond were the three fastest runners Godwin knew. They were men, and he couldn't match them. Eg might outlast them over a distance, but they'd be onto him before his slightness and stamina gave him an advantage. Sel was burly, a carthorse not a hound, and Cudbert the same, and older. Godwin sprinted and quickly caught up with the others.

"This way," he called, and ran off the track to his right,

where a field ran up towards thick woodland. Trees were silhouetted against the eastern dawning. He couldn't tell how deep the woods might be, but they were their only chance.

Wig, List and Gormond caught up with Sel and Cudbert. Cudbert turned to fight, and the three circled him. They were fearful, knowing that one on one, he had the beating of each of them. More than this, they had no wish to attack their fellow, this man they'd known all their lives, Wulfnoth's trusted right hand man. But their Thegn had instructed them, and they would do as they were commanded.

He had held them up in their chase, that was good enough. "Cudbert!" Godwin called back. "Lay down your sword."

Cudbert surrendered, and with him, his son.

"Eg! The trees!" Godwin called. He ran up the hill, fighting for breath, fighting against the burning in his thighs. The trees came closer, and he passed the outliers into the black woods where he couldn't easily be seen in broad daylight, let alone now.

He looked back, as Eg crashed through the undergrowth to join him. Down the slope the three chasers had stopped, knowing they could not track their quarry in the trees.

They were listening. A rising wind made the leaves shiver and rush like water, but the three seemed to know that Godwin and Eg had paused.

"Godwin?" Wig called. "I know it's you, I know that voice. You best come out. Your dad'll be mighty mad at you, and putting it off ain't going to make it better."

"Ain't his dad he has to worry about," List said to him. "It's Arni's dad."

"Let's go back," said Wig. "We'll not find them in there. They'll come down, they got nowhere else to go." The three turned and tramped down the hill.

Godwin waited, thinking hard, as Sel and Cudbert were led back to Brimclif.

"What'll happen to them?" Eg asked. "Arni's dad ain't the forgiving type."

"True," said Godwin. "He'll want him killed."

"Your dad wouldn't do that."

"He'll have to do something. Cudbert might lose his sword arm. He won't be able to fight. Won't be any good as a pirate, or a sailor."

"Pretty fucked as a farmer too," Eg said.

It was true. And it was Godwin's fault. "Follow me," he said.

"Again?"

They skirted the edge of the woods where it curved above the village, to a bluff where the villagers hacked away flints for walls and chalk for lime, that marked the eastern edge of the village. They hid behind bushes at the top, and with dawn done and morning upon them, looked down on the men gathered below. Wulfnoth and Ham stood at the centre of the village, facing Sel and Cudbert. Of Arni there was no sign. Godwin couldn't hear what was being said, but clearly Wulfnoth was trying to establish what exactly had happened, while Ham interjected shouts. "He could have murdered him!" "It doesn't bloody matter why!" "I want his head!"

Godwin and Eg scrambled down the slope at the edge of the little quarry, and crouching, made their way to the back end of the canopy they had sheltered under when they took their food. Here, Odylia sat by her semi-conscious brother with various leaves, roots and seaweeds laid out beside her, which she was pulping in a mortar and pestle. Arni's wound was dressed, and no doubt she'd spread a poultice under the dressing. Herbs and seaweed might feed his lifeblood but they can't mend bones, and he'd surely lose the shattered arm.

Closer now, Godwin could hear what was being said, although he couldn't see through the crush of bodies. "You won't have his head," Wulfnoth was telling Ham.

"I shall, even if I have to take it myself," Ham shouted.

"It will be the last thing you do," said Wulfnoth. "This is my man." He was silent for a moment. "But justice must be done." He drew his sword.

"No!" cried Sel, "You can't! He was protecting Godwin."

Wulfnoth was quiet for a moment. Then he spoke loud enough to make sure that all heard. "An eye for an eye, a tooth for a tooth. An arm for an arm. Cudbert is a fool. He was aiding my coward of a son in running away. And he must pay."

Godwin clenched his teeth at this dishonour. Even if his father didn't believe his own words, Godwin knew that Arni was right, there was no turning back for Wulfnoth, and he needed Ham as captain of the boats more than he needed his own husceorl.

Godwin gripped his sword, not because he could use it – brazen bravery would be folly – but because it gave him courage. Then he loosened his grip, and drew his knife from its sheath, knowing what to do, knowing it was a coward's ploy which might not work, and knowing that it shamed him more than being called a coward by his own father.

Arni lay there, protected only by his small sister. Godwin crept up behind her, held her, and put the knife to the girl's throat.

Odylia screamed, and struggled.

All eyes turned.

Eg moved swiftly to withdraw the small seax she'd been trying to free from her waistband.

The men parted as Wulfnoth and Ham barged through.

"Stop!" called Godwin. "Let them go."

The captain put up his arm to restrain Wulfnoth, who laughed. "He won't harm the girl," Wulfnoth said. "I brought him up better than that."

It was true. Godwin remembered his vow not to hurt a woman, not to be wicked like his father, as his own mother said he would be. Yet here he was, threatening this girl's life. He nearly gave up. But if he surrendered he'd have to rejoin the treason, so he'd be like his father anyway, and Cudbert would pay for keeping his own oath. And what would Odylia's fate be? He had his suspicions.

He tightened his grip on her. "And my grandfather brought you up better than to be a traitor to the King, a pirate, and a liar to your men!" he shouted. "I'm glad I dropped closer to his tree than yours."

Wulfnoth's eyes blazed.

Odylia was stiff with terror, but did not struggle against Godwin's firm hold. Behind them, Eg stood over Arni with Arni's own sword, to stop him lunging to save his sister.

Godwin called to the crowd of his father's men. "There is no mission from the King! You will not be harrying Danes, you will be pirating from any boat you find. You will be raiding villages just like this one here, only in Flanders and Normandy. You'll be no better than the Norsemen!"

Wulfnoth gave a small laugh. Godwin knew it was insincere. "You seem to have picked up the wrong end of a very long stick, Godwin boy," he said. "You've convinced your friends, and look what's happened. My comrade's son will lose an arm." He put his own arm around the captain's shoulders "So for justice's sake, my own loyal Cudbert must now lose his."

Godwin didn't so much feel his anger rise as watch it, like he might watch a boiling pan of milk. He could decide whether to let his anger foam over and fall spitting onto the fire, or whether to remove it from the heat. Spitting was for children.

He lowered his voice. "I know when you're lying, father. I've heard you lie so many times to mother. You are betraying the King. That's why we've come to this godforsaken hamlet on the edge of nowhere. You men of Comtyn and Bosham," he called. "Listen to me! If you go with my father, you will never be able to return to your homes."

Wulfnoth turned and shouted to his men. "He's a young fool! An idiot who thinks a rook is a sparrow and a fox is a mouse! You will be able to go back home, I promise. But I promise this too: you will not want to stay there. With me, you will be rich men, richer than ten lifetimes in Soussex. We'll be able to go anywhere! And those who wish, you can fetch your kin to be with us."

Now he was sincere, Godwin knew. And so did the men, who cheered their leader, greedy fools that they were.

Godwin tightened his hold on Odylia. "Let them. I don't care. Just spare Cudbert, and let us leave."

Wulfnoth looked at Godwin. "Your problem is, boy, that you think you have coin because you have a knife to that girl's throat. But it is coin you won't spend. I know you, you'll not harm her, so hand her over, take your beating, and let us set sail."

"Spare Cudbert." He tightened his grip on Odylia.

"I can't do that," Wulfnoth said, and he spoke with sadness. "Now put down the knife and let us be done." He stepped forward, and Godwin pressed the knife more firmly to Odylia's throat. He knew he would press no harder. Cudbert would not even want him to.

Ham pulled Wulfnoth back. "No! Don't play with my daughter's blood. He has his coin, it's bigger than mine. Your husceorl for my daughter? Aye, but your man shall not set foot on my boats. Not him, not his son, not your son, nor that scrawny ferret with him."

Godwin watched his father's face. Not a flicker. Just a hardening to granite, and he knew himself disowned.

"Untie them," Godwin said. "I'll take Odylia into the woods, then I'll release her to come back down to you."

Ham turned to Wulfnoth. Wulfnoth nodded. "Gormond," he said. "Do it." Gormond unknotted the ropes around

Cudbert and Sel's wrists. The pair joined Godwin as he backed away saying loud to Odylia so all could hear. "Don't struggle. You'll be back with your father in less time than it takes to milk a cow."

They walked up towards the woods as swiftly as they could. Godwin kept a grip on Odylia's wrist, and Eg kept a look over his shoulder to check they weren't being followed. If they carried on up through the woods and turned towards the sea, they'd come to the clifftop. They could get their bearings from there. And then he'd let Odylia go. No sooner, just to be sure.

It was not as far as he thought it would be. The trees grew more stunted on the thin chalk soil, and they came out to grass, shrubs, and the cliff edge. He relaxed his grip on Odylia's wrist. "You can go now." She took a few steps away, but no more.

Eg called out "Godwin! Something's happened."

Godwin turned. The cliff was a good vantage point over the Brimclif cove. They couldn't see the village itself, but they could see boats putting out to sea. From the little antsnests of activity on each deck, with oarsmen not in place, and sails flapping in what had become a stiff breeze, they were departing in a grievous rush.

"Best run," Godwin said to Odylia, "Or you'll be left behind."

She didn't move.

Godwin walked up to Eg, Sel, and Cudbert "We'll sit here till we're sure they've all gone, then we'll have to go back down to take the lane inland." From his bag he pulled out the meat he'd sliced from the pig carcass. "May as well eat this now. We'll need to hunt for more."

The others ignored him. They were looking past him towards the sea. He turned.

Just come into view around the chalk cliffs to the west were the massed red sails of the longboats of Dertemuthe, glowing in the light of the rising sun against dark clouds beyond.

"That's why the rush," said Eg.

No-one moved as they watched Wulfnoth's fleet beat through the waves away from the shore, now using oars as well as sail. They all knew they must wait and see whatever unfolded on the sea below them. Even Odylia seemed to have resigned herself to losing her father and brother.

Godwin numbered two dozen red sails before he stopped counting, and that was less than half of them.

"Dertemuthe boats are faster 'n ours," said Sel.

"We're bad outnumbered," said Eg.

"We should be with our people still," said Cudbert.

"We are," Godwin told him.

Fifty and more fast boats filled with Brihtric's angry men, against Wulfnoth's twenty. None of them wanted to see the inevitable battle, to see men from families they'd known all their lives drowned, impaled, captured. Godwin hoped Wulfnoth's fleet was swift enough to be over the horizon of their sight before the Dertemuthe fleet caught them. It seemed unlikely.

The clouds in the west had spread and now covered most of the sky. The wind had stiffened, and lifted whitecaps off the waves. Godwin wondered if it was weather that any boats should be putting out into. But there they were, and the wind added to the redsails's advantage.

"Wulfnoth's heading south, straight out to sea," Sel observed. "He's making it easy for them. Why ain't he fleeing along the coast?"

"It's only a matter of time afore they catch up," said Eg. "Looks like your father's plan is doomed before it started."

It was a plan Godwin wanted no part in, but the prospect of it being so lamely thwarted added disillusion to his shame for his father. Then he remembered. "They're not armed, them Dertemuthe boats, or only lightly. They were all to arm at Sanwic. Our men have weapons chosen for fighting at sea."

The clouds massed higher, slate grey, and the wind grew stronger still. It had swung round and was now in their faces.

"They're turning," said Odylia.

Godwin had forgotten she was still there.

"Ours are reefing their sails."

He'd forgotten too that she was a seafarer's daughter. She was right. The Dertemuth fleet had to tack into the wind to keep away from the cliffs. Their speed advantage was lost. Wulfnoth's boats' sails were being hauled up.

"Wind so strong as this," Odylia said, "sails are worse'n useless. Sails can turn a boat over. It's oars you need." The Dertemuthe boats were dropping the spars, sails and all. Men gathered the folds on the decks. "They're inshore, so they got no sea-room."

All the boats were struggling, but it seemed to Godwin that under oar, the Dertemuthe boats were less stable, and rocked more wildly as the waves grew higher in the ever-rising wind.

"They're coming in," Eagbert said.

The Bosham boats were blown closer, and no oars tried to pull them away. Godwin saw a glint of red on one of them. And another, and another. "They lit the braziers," he said.

"Dangerous," said Odylia.

"For who?"

The Dertemuthe boats were numerous, but they were now trapped between the cliffs and the Bosham fleet, only a few hundred yards offshore. Men drew swords, but few had bows. The boats were directionless, facing all ways, as if they had no overall commander, or if they did he could not communicate with his captains. They were all too close. Boats collided. Oars broke. Two boats became locked together beam-on to the waves, listed, and were swamped.

"Fishermen," Odylia said. "Ain't never sailed so close together before."

Wulfnoth's fleet closed in. Smoke trails arced across the sky as the first fire arrows flew far on the wind. Most sputtered into the waves, but many found their mark, landing in the lowered sails still spread on the decks. Sails were woven of hemp, linen or wool, but all were rubbed with animal fat, as the Sea Wolf's had been. The fire arrows were hungry for the fat, and soon a dozen boats were ablaze, and sailcloth, wood, tar and rope were eaten greedily by orange flames. Oarsmen abandoned their benches and jumped overboard. Unsteered boats clashed with others, unrowed boats were blown remorselessly in towards the cliffs.

The Bosham sailors shot plain arrows as their oarsmen held them steady, away from the defenceless redsails.

One boat after another was abandoned. Many could not swim, but they chose water and hope over fire. Some held onto oars and planks, but all were being blown in towards the cliffs.

Godwin couldn't see where the waves whipped up by the squall pounded the rocks below them, but he could hear, and the roar made him fear for any man who would soon be dashed there.

Wulfnoth's men lowered their bows. They were cheering, and although no sound reached the clifftop over the noise of wind and waves, their celebration was plain to see by the fists hitting air, by the claps and the hugs. His father stood, braced at the stern of Ham's boat, leading the cheer. Hemming was next to him. He waved his flags, and boat by boat the crews settled at their benches and pulled oar, pulled them out to sea, towards Flandre.

Godwin was sure he'd never see his father again.

Godwin, Eagbert, Selferth, Cudbert and Odylia returned to

Brimclif village for what Godwin prayed would be the last time in his life.

Ash stood tethered under the shelter. "Eg," Godwin said, "See if you can find the saddle and reins."

"They were taken in there," Cudbert said, nodding at the largest home in the village of tiny hovels.

"That's the Thegn's hut," Odylia pointed out. So he was a thegn.

"Thegn of Shittington," said Cudbert. He drew his sword and entered.

Godwin turned to the others. "There's no point trying to find Ealdorman Aelfric now," he said. "I need to ride and warn Comtyn and Bosham, because when Brihtric and Eadric hear about this, they will have no mercy in their anger."

"What if Brihtric's already sent a troop?" said Eagbert, as an outraged yell, quickly silenced, came from within Gewis's hut.

"Brihtric can't know what my father was up to, and won't work it out until he hears of this disaster."

Thegn Gewis's protests rose once more, until Cudbert's growl silenced him.

"I'll have at least a day," Godwin continued. "He won't be able to muster a troop and march it there as quick as I can ride."

Cudbert emerged from the hut with saddle and bridle, followed by Brimclif's leader himself, hopping as he pulled on a boot. Cudbert started saddling the horse, talking as he did so. Ash stood calm and patient.

"How far to Comtyn?" Godwin asked.

"Took me three long days to get here," Cudbert said. "Could be done quicker, maybe, but push him and he'll lame up. He's tired. He'll need food and rest along the way."

"Hey," said Gewis, realising what was going on. "That horse is mine."

"Petition the King," Godwin said. "See how far that gets you." He turned to Eg and Sel. "You follow with Cudbert, make your own way as best you can."

Eg and Sel weren't looking at him. He turned.

Stumbling into the village from the direction of the beach were three bedraggled men, wet, and unarmed. Four more followed. Godwin wondered how many of the Dertemuthe men would get their feet back to land and make their way here, and whether they'd worked out the part Brimclif played in the Bosham desertion. Not that this lot appeared to have any fight left. Was there a leader among them?

"Come," he said to Cudbert. The pair marched towards the ratlike survivors, and Gewis made as if to follow. Godwin turned to him. "These are Brihtric's men. You're the last person who wants to stand before them."

Gewis shrank back, and went into his hut, probably to collect his valuables and make ready to run.

They walked towards the shipwrecked sailors, who halted at the sight of Cudbert's sword.

"We was…" one started to say.

"We know," Godwin interrupted. "We saw from the clifftop. Where are you from?"

"Defenas," said the man. "I am Caum, of Totness. And you?"

"I am-" began Godwin, "Arni, of Brimclif. This is Bert."

Caum of Totness looked at them suspiciously. "And this place is Brimclif?"

Godwin nodded.

"That was the Bosham boats that put in here," said Caum. "They deserted the King."

This man was not just a soldier and oarsman. Godwin guessed he was a boat captain, or a husceorl. The men were half-drowned and cold, with their weapons abandoned, but if more washed up, they could turn angry. He had to be careful.

"Yes. They came here, they stole food. Like Norsemen." He spat onto the white ground on which they stood. "Some of us ran and hid in the woods. They were too many." He didn't care about Gewis's fate, but there was no reason for the few crones and greybeards still here to perish for their leader's greed. "Does Brihtric know what has happened today?"

"He will. Two boats got away, and they'll head back to Scorham."

"Not easy. The wind's against them."

Caum inspected Godwin suspiciously, and took a step forward. Cudbert drew himself taller and took a fresh grip on his sword, and Caum halted. "You name Brihtric. You know a lot for a pisspoor village boy."

"I heard talking."

Caum seemed satisfied, but he was a man used to taking charge. "Have you got shelter here, and food for the King's men, those of us as get out undrowned? It might help Brihtric think favourably if he has to decide whether your people aided the traitors…"

"Brimclif is loyal," said Godwin.

"Aye," said Cudbert. Eg and Sel added firm nods and hard faces.

"You should go down to the beach and help your comrades," Godwin said. "I will get a big pot of stew made. And I will ride to Scorham. The boats that have gone back, they may not know there are survivors here."

Caum paused, and narrowed his eyes. "No, boy. I will ride to Scorham. You stay in your village and help our men."

The man had an air of authority and could use it well. He wore a bawdrick over his shoulder, but he'd let the sword it held sink. Godwin could not back down. "And watch you steal our only horse, never to be seen again? No. And you'll not call me a pisspoor village boy again, Caum of Totness, not while you're armed with no more than wet rags."

Caum snorted, and turned, and led the dozen men who had gathered behind him back towards the beach.

Godwin returned to Sel and Eg, calling "Now let's get out of this pisspoor village."

"What about me?" said Odylia.

"She's mine," said Gewis. "I did my part."

Godwin recalled the overheard fireside conversation between Gewis, his father, and Ham. "Is that so?" he asked Odylia.

She spat. "A horse and a wife he was to get, for his help and his silence. I've lost my father and brother."

"You've still got family around Bosham?"

She nodded.

"Cudbert?"

"I'm supposed to look after you. And my boy, of course. Eagbert, if I must. The girl is nothing. She'll slow us."

Odylia glared at Cudbert. "If it wasn't for me, you'd be dead, or as good as." She spoke as if she'd volunteered to have her throat slit. Godwin had to smile.

Cudbert turned and looked at her. "Forever in your debt, I'm sure."

"She's promised to me!" Gewis pleaded.

Cudbert looked him up and down contemptuously, and turned to Godwin, his decision made. "Aye, I'll look after her."

"And you," said Godwin to Gewis. "Those sailors have gone down to help their comrades who survive the sea. You will feed them. I told Caum that Brimclif was stolen from. Godwin and all were never here. I am Arni, a village boy, who after he's gone to Scorham to report the survivors here, will disappear to make his own fortune. Stick to the lie, you may live out the day. You may even be rewarded for your help, though you won't deserve it."

He opened the purse that his mother had presented him, and gave eight of the twelve silver sceats to Cudbert, then whispered to Ash, stroked his nose, and swung himself up into his own saddle. Ah, so much more comfortable than a rowing bench. Eg handed him a flatbread which he put into his bag. "Good thinking. You have some for yourselves?"

"Don't be stupid, 'course I do."

"Then follow as quick as you can. Get a dozen miles stepped out before you rest."

He steered Ash onto the track up the valley, and dug his heels into his horse's flanks.

11. Father Stigand

(Edward)

"The most handsome priest."

"Because," said his mother patiently, "because you are the elder. Because Alfred will fidget and shuffle and not pay attention. And because… Edward, in this world, we always need friends. People who don't just owe us, or fear us, but who like and respect us. Bishop Hugo, you may never see him again. But, you just might. And you can be sure he will report to the Duke what he thinks of you. He will note that Alfred wasn't there, and you were."

Edward sighed. It had been sunny, and Fulton, who knew when weather was set or changeable, had promised it would be the same tomorrow. It was good that Fulton was his friend again; they'd planned to go fishing, and Edward would let Fulton take all their catch home to his family. Now it seemed he must spend all morning attending the Norman emissary's audience with King Aethelred; then all afternoon with his mother in her private meeting with this Bishop. He really wasn't interested in the health and travails of her family across the southern sea, and he was certain there would be no chance to discuss matters scriptural.

After fishing, he'd planned to seek out that priest who'd arrived with Eadric Streona, Father Stigand. Edward had tried to discuss the story of Esther with Father Benjamin, who held service for them when they were not obliged to join the Bishop Elfhun's congregation in the Cathedral. But Benjamin had said nothing that lit any flame in the gloomy cave of

Edward's vexation regarding The Lord's word. Perhaps Stigand, much younger but seemingly better travelled, had more insight.

"Yes Mother, I'll be there when the Bishop is called. Should I ask after the Duke?"

Emma smiled. "No, dear. It's for the King to undertake such formalities. I will of course ask after my other brothers and sisters. You should ask after your cousins. They are closer in age to you. Not Richard, but yes, enquire about the others. It will go down well. And you should know your relationships."

His relationships to these cousins and second cousins whom he'd never met? Whom he never wanted to meet? He wondered which of them would ask about him on Hugo's return.

"Duke Richard, he is the second Duke of that name. His first son, who is your cousin and my nephew, will be the third Duke Richard."

"Yes, Mother."

"And your other cousins are..?"

"Robert, Adeliza, Eleanore and Mathilde the baby."

"Good. Well done."

Edward could have recited their birthdays had he cared. He wondered at the gap between Adeliza, just a few months older than he, and Eleanore, eight years younger. But he thought it impolite to ask, and devious to pretend that he was interested.

Edward was surprised to be suddenly drawn into Emma's embrace. Formal kisses were her usual display of affection, delivered for onlookers' benefit, not his. Being hugged, feeling his mother's arm around his shoulder, feeling the warmth of her body, was strange, and discomforting. The talk of her family meant little to him, but it must have moved her. He pulled himself away, then regretted it. Now he could not return.

"Go. This evening is your own. Perhaps you could spend some time with Alfred. You have some making up yet to do."

He had no making up to do. Not with Alfred. His brother could practice his swordsmanship, his archery and his riding on his own.

Edward left. First he asked Arsindis if she'd seen Alfred or Fulton. She was a strong-featured Frankish woman who rarely smiled or frowned, or blinked for that matter, and who seemed at times to be more a strict aunt than a servant to Emma. He was sure she guessed that he'd only asked for Alfred for the sake of appearance. "Alfred is with Wilf somewhere. As for Fulton, have you tried the kitchens?" Perhaps she had a heart after all.

He wandered around the halls towards the kitchens. If he happened upon Stigand first, he'd ask for a time when they might discuss the Book of Esther together. And the prophecies of Archbishop Wulfstan. Surely a priest could not dismiss these as lightly as Edmund had?

The kitchens were a-bustle with women preparing food for Eadric's men, complaining about the work and who was going to carry that many turnips. Boys scurried, or slacked if they could get away with it, but none knew Fulton's whereabouts. Fulton sometimes lingered with the husceorls – he wanted to join their number in a few years, an ambition Edward approved of. The idea of Fulton one day being his head husceorl appealed greatly, because who do you need to trust more than the chief of your own personal guards? But Fulton was not there, nor was he in the woodyard, nor at the butts, nor even by the brook with the washerwomen who were always rude but never dismissive.

Nor did Edward see Father Stigand.

He realised that he was putting off returning to his room to start on the Book of Job, because that Book offered questions about the nature of God's will and benevolence more troubling even than Esther's. He shook his head at himself, and wandered down to the lake on which he would no longer be fishing tomorrow. On the bank, propped up on its side making a shallow cave, was the small boat that had hidden Fulton and himself on many an afternoon. It was a place few people wandered to, and the boat's hull screened them from any who might approach until they came all the way around the stern. It was a good place to be alone.

As Edward came closer, he heard a voice, a man's voice, deep and accented. He couldn't make out the words, and anyway the tone was too low to be conversational. No reply came. Curious now, Edward stepped quietly through the meadow grass. Who was there in his private hideaway, talking to himself? Perhaps Stigand, with his uncommon East Anglian accent, had found this spot as a place for solitary prayer? Churches, chapels, they were often crowded, rushed and busy, and for a cleric rarely a place of peaceful solitude. Prayer was indeed a private matter, especially between a priest and God, so Edward was reluctant to progress. But the voice dropped to silent contemplation, and Edward felt entitled to move on. If Stigand resumed praying out loud, he could retreat, or cough. He could wait for him to finish, and then perhaps have the conversation he wanted.

He skirted to his right and sidled down to the lakebank. There were reeds in the water, and if he stepped into the shallows and crouched, he could get much closer without being seen.

The prayer resumed. "Sweet she was, like a ripe pear" the voice intoned as from a reverie. It was not a line from any prayer Edward knew.

"Too young for him, but too old to be childless still. And she wanted to be filled, there was no doubt of that. I'd even say he needed her filled too. Rich in wealth and power, but poor in seed. Such was her complaint, before she lost her bridle and soaked my seed up like parched soil. I only hope the moon was with her. Doubtless we shall hear in a couple of months. And if not, I'm as certain as sunrise that she will welcome me back."

Edward knew enough of life to realise that the topic was not horse breeding. He had felt sure it was Stigand who spoke, however unpriestly his words. Was it not a prayer, but a confession to having broken the Sixth Commandment? Who was the wicked wife being spoken of, who the betrayed man?

Guilt at his own sneakiness was confronted by curiosity, but curiosity had excitement by its side, and guilt slinked away without a fight.

"I think he knew. I think he wore his horns willingly. He could have watched, if he'd asked nicely! I'd happily have aided him if he wanted to service his own wife. I'd have done to him what you are doing now-"

Aha! thought Edward. You're not alone. But in whom do you confide? He pushed through the reeds, carefully and slowly, so the mud made no squelch. He saw sandaled feet, and legs stretched out, long and lean, so at first he wondered if they belonged to a woman. Was she the listener? But no, the calves were toned muscle, and sprouted golden hairs. The plain dun-coloured cloth of a habit spread beneath them on the grass. Father Stigand it surely was.

"-and in all honesty, I'd have done it better. But you're new to this. Well, be grateful. This skill that will serve you well if you use it wisely. You'll need every device at hand to stay in with your little friend as he grows older, trust me. Something tells me he will relish you too."

Edward cowered down behind the curtain of reeds until he was kneeling in the shallows as if in prayer. He knew he should rise and creep away, but he couldn't. Someone else was there, kneeling beside Stigand, praying. Stigand had his hand benevolently on the other's head, and the other knelt with his right arm across Stigand's knees and his left hand out of sight in front of him. His head and body moved rhythmically as if he was chanting, but no sound issued. Stigand's eyes were shut, and his face wore the beatific expression of spiritual enlightenment.

He allowed himself the sickening realisation that the smaller of the two was Fulton, that he had found both those he sought at once. Tears stung his eyes. Why would Fulton pray with Stigand, alone? What device did Stigand mean? His curiosity and excitement were turning bilious. Guilt hadn't fled after all, and he felt shame at his eavesdropping. His sickness grew with the knowledge that this was neither prayer nor confession, it was a bragging, and he himself was surely the little friend.

He breathed "Fulton," hardly aware he had formed the name.

Fulton's head jerked up and turned, his mouth open and dribbling. Stigand's pizzle stood tall and shiny, transfixing in its size.

Edward's stomach turned inside-out like kneaded bread, as blood filled his face until it felt near to bursting. Stigand's pintle was huge, like a pillar of some Roman temple, like the trunk of a fir, like the thigh of Hercules, or so it seemed to him. He'd seen teorses before, but never one so stout, never one that pointed heavenward of its own levitation. His own became a bone in the mornings, and somehow it was hard now, but it was a pup compared to Stigand's mastiff.

Had Fulton had the impure thing in his mouth?

He had.

How could he? Why would he?

Edward's strength gave way. He slid sideways with a splash into the shallow water. Fulton closed his mouth and Stigand covered himself, but it was Edward who felt naked as he rose and tottered dripping from the reeds. He ran up the slope and away, to his room, hoping Alfred would not be there. He dashed past wenches and ceorls before they perceived his mortification, though he did not fully understand what he had witnessed. Fulton and Stigand had not lain together, not exactly, but surely that awful act was a mortal sin that the whole world would suffer for.

Why did he too feel sinful?

Why would Fulton open his mouth for Stigand? Was he forced?

Edward suddenly felt a great anger madding within, in a rush like water over the millwheel. Anger at Fulton for his betrayal. It was surely betrayal. Anger at Stigand for taking his friend, whether willingly or no. And anger at himself for the image of that treetrunk pizzle seared into his head.

He barely knew what happened from one minute to the next as his father met with Bishop Hugo the following morning, alongside The Queen and Prince Edmund.

The Bishop was from Bayeux. He dressed in great finery, with fine woven wool, furs, and jewelled rings. He brought greetings from Duke Richard, from the Frankish King, Robert of the House of Capet, and even from the Pope, for Hugo had been to Rome. King Robert was to go also, and he was being called The Pious. Edward wondered what piety truly meant.

Hugo brought gifts: a silver box jewelled with garnet for the King; another box, smaller but gold, for the Queen; and barrels of cidre, already stored somewhere. He brought news, too, that Edward's grandmother had been ill, but was improving. "My mother is past seventy," Emma said. "She has no right to improve. It's unnatural. I hope I don't live so long."

Edward wondered what such an old person would look like.

Richard's youngest daughter, Mathilde the baby, niece to Queen Emma, and Edward's fourth Norman cousin, had also survived a serious illness. The child had made it into her second year, so the leeches were offering assurances that she would live a long and healthy life, and Hugo prayed to God to make them right. On Duke Richard's behalf he said how pleased he was that Goda had recovered, although he had not known she was ill.

No-one had mentioned his other cousins, and Edward knew this was the time to ask after their health, but he could not concentrate. All he saw was Stigand and the shiny thing which seemed not part of his body but somehow a separate beast of its own rampage, and Fulton's open mouth, dripping. Edward kept his own mouth tight shut even when he felt Emma's nudge.

He was saved by his father launching a tirade about Danish and Norse ships still provisioning at Fécamp and Huniflet and Deppa. "Don't think I don't know!"

Hugo wheedled no, they must be getting their supplies in Flandra or Brittany, and Aethelred must take that issue up with Count Baldwin or Duke Alan; and the King said don't worry, he would, but he didn't trust any of the three conniving bastards who were all marrying each others' daughters. What was the use of having a Norman wife anyway?

Edward was brought back at this, for he felt the heat of his mother's ire at being so ill-valued as Queen and Consort. He recalled the lack of respect shown to Queen Vashti, and forced himself to concentrate, to see if there was something he could do or say to portray Saxon royalty in better light. He couldn't track back to the subject of his cousins now.

"Boats," he said.

All eyes turned to him.

He himself didn't know where the notion arose, or how it

floated above the churn of his mind.

"Did you say something Edward?" asked his father, as if not believing he'd heard a cogent word.

"I was, I was, I was..."

"Don't stutter, boy. Speak."

"I was just thinking," Edward said, forcing himself to coherence. "We now have a royal fleet. I'm sure your Grace and the Duke know this already. We haven't been able to keep our boatbuilding secret."

"We know nothing of that," Hugo said.

Edmund snorted at such a blatant lie, and Edward was glad that he did, because for one small moment he feared he had revealed the King's biggest military secret.

He spoke slowly and carefully now, lest he give away more details, like the fleet's size and its destination. "The boats are for trading around the coast under royal charter," he said. "I was thinking, perhaps the Duke is open to more trade across the sea. Our boats can provision in Normandy under the Duke's protection. We can provide the same for Norman boats on our southern coast. Your havens get trade, to replace what will be lost... I mean, trade that was lost when the Danes and Norse were turned away."

"Now that is a telling idea," said Edmund.

Hugo nodded thoughtfully. He knew, the whole room knew, that this was a reciprocation that the Duke could not refuse.

Emma picked up the mantle. "We should have as many Norman boats as possible here, for trade, and for pilgrimage, and exchanges of scholars."

"And for swift passage to Normandy should Sveyn Forkbeard get close to Lunden," said Hugo sourly, his suave demeanour dropped at the implications of Edward's suggestion.

"Hah!" cried Aethelred, seeing the obvious and speaking

what he saw. "We shall have boats regularly in Normandy. Then let the Vikingr provision there! We'll burn their ships, and cut the throats of any traders who sell to them. Hah! In the Duke's name, of course."

When Bishop Hugo departed, Edward basked in the rare warmth of approval from Aethelred, father and King, from Edmund, brother and Prince, and best of all, from Emma, mother and Queen, who hugged him again.

They took their midday repast separately, the King and Prince in one hall and the Bishop and his Norman entourage in another; leaving Edward, Alfred and Goda with their mother. Alfred had been instructed to join them to hear about the morning's proceedings. He had brought a wicker basket with a strapped lid, inside which were half a dozen mice that he'd freed from the cages of rodents bred to feed the falcons. He'd put ears of corn into the basket, and seemed to want to make pets of them. Edward gave it a day before Alfred forgot to feed the mice, and they finished the corn and gnawed their way to freedom.

Alfred was plainly more interested in them than in what had passed that morning. When Edward saw him glance from the mice to Goda, he decided he'd have to intervene at some point.

After they had eaten, Edward said "Mother, I need to tell you something."

"Today Edward, you deserve the ear of anyone you name."

Alfred looked on expectantly, for though Edward rarely did anything to be noticed, and Alfred was used to being sole recipient of elders' approbation, he recognised when his brother was in their mother's favour, and was curious.

"It is something not for Alfred or Goda."

Emma looked hard at him through narrowed eyes, before turning to his brother. "Alfred, leave us for a few minutes will you please. Take your sister."

"But-"

"Alfred, listen to your brother. This is not for you."

Alfred knew his mother was not to be argued with, and left. Goda followed obediently.

Emma turned to Edward, waiting.

"It is something I'm not sure of, Mother. I heard a conversation but I cannot say who it was between, save that one half was Father Stigand."

"Go on."

"He is from Elmham, in Norfolk, yes? But he has been the last few weeks with Eadric and Eadgyth in Mercia."

"In Coventre, yes."

"I- I- I-"

"Edward, don't stutter."

It wasn't a stutter, it was care in choosing the right word. "I believe that he has…" What was the way to say this? "I think that Stigand has lain with Eadgyth."

Emma's head lifted and her eyes widened. But she did not doubt him. "Eadgyth? Perhaps you should tell me exactly what you heard."

Yes, that was easiest. "He was boastful. He said she was a pear, a ripe pear. He said she wanted to be filled. That means she wanted a baby inside her, doesn't it?"

Emma paused before replying, and suppressed a chuckle. "It might do."

"He said he was poor in seed."

"Who was?"

"Eadric. He didn't name him, but he said he was rich and powerful, and Ead means wealth, and Ric is ruler. I don't believe Stigand said those words by accident."

"That would explain Eadric's lack of progeny. And perhaps his lack of interest in his wife."

"He said he thought he knew. I mean, Eadric knew Stigand was with his wife."

"Stigand is surely the most handsome priest I have ever set eyes on. Well well well."

He was hugged again by his mother. Three embraces in two days, warm ones, spontaneous ones, not formal or for show. He hugged her back, lost in the rare love he felt from her, that he wanted only to return.

She held him even as she mused out loud. "Stigand is Eadric's breeding bull. Perhaps. If not, he is Eadgyth's pleasure bull. Either way, it presents us with an opportunity." She held her son at arm's length. "Edward, you have excelled yourself today. You have good instincts. It makes me proud, and hopeful for you."

He smiled. Why would she not be hopeful?

"Now, two things. One, who was Stigand speaking to?"

"I- I don't know. I hid myself and didn't see. I think it was one of the kitchen girls." Edward's good instincts told him not to mention Fulton. Instincts, and a deep mysterious hurt.

"Do you think he was going to bed her?"

"I don't know. How would I tell?" What exactly did "bed her" mean? "Perhaps."

"He was boasting. He is venal. Of course he aimed to bed her."

She was satisfied. Fulton was safe, at least from Emma.

"What was the second thing?" She had forgotten, he thought, distracted by thoughts of the vileness of the venal priest.

"Oh yes," she said. "Tell no-one. Not even your father. He would not know how to use the secret."

Edward knew this was so. He wished it wasn't.

"Do not tell Edmund. It's possible he might have been told by Eadgyth herself, or by Ecfrida, if I know sisters. But if so, let him think he alone is privy to it. And – Edward, I don't know what you confide in Fulton, but you must learn – some things are not for him to know. For his own sake."

"Yes Mother," he said, suddenly wishing he could go back to yesterday, when he and Fulton were both more innocent.

Emma was warm to Bishop Hugo when she met him again that afternoon. They conversed in French, which Edward could follow more easily than he could join. At first, Hugo would not look at him, but with mugs of his own Normandy cidre to drink, he began to relax. Edward partook of a small mug, and liked the sweet tang on his tongue and the balm inside his head. Emma denied him a second measure.

Hugo talked of Normandy, and Emma's family, which amounted to the same topic. The peace in the west between Normandy and Brittany was strong, built as it was on two reciprocal marriages. Duke Richard had married Judith, sister to Goffroy Count of Brittany, while Richard and Emma's sister Hawise was recently wedded to the Count. This peace allowed Richard to use all his strength to bring barons who opposed him to heel, and they were bowing one by one to his overlordship. He had endowed monasteries in Caen and Rouen, where another of Edward's uncles was Archbishop. Cousin Adeliza was betrothed already to the Burgundy heir.

Surely Emma had plans for his and Alfred's marriages, but Edward couldn't guess who or where. For the most obvious English or Norman alliances, only cousins were available. Aelfgifu was the exception, but surely she'd go to Prince Edmund. He couldn't imagine himself with her. He couldn't imagine himself with any wife.

"Your nephew Richard is studious," Hugo reported, "As befits the next Duke. He is intelligent, he learns well from his father, and is equally pious."

The second son, Robert, was in Hugo's estimation equally clever, if not more so, but was far from studious. "He prefers to ride, and often goes too far alone, with no thought for safety. He doesn't know he is followed at a distance by his father's stewards."

"Ransom would be expensive," Emma said.

The thought that a Duke's son might be kidnapped and held for gold was startling to Edward. That had never happened here in England, even though England was caught in this endless conflict with the Danes. Normandy seemed at greater peace with its surrounding provinces, whether through marriage or might, but in some ways appeared more dangerous.

"And my other cousins? Adeliza and Eleanore? You haven't spoken of them."

Hugo was startled at the question, and stuttered that they were in good health, as far as he knew. Edward suspected that girls, once safely past infancy like Mathilde, were of no further interest until husbands were sought.

"It is the Duke's wish to talk of Rameslege," Hugo said.

Emma nodded, appearing unsurprised. "I thought you'd raise the matter with the King this morning," she replied.

Hugo looked at Edward. "Perhaps this notion of Prince Edward's makes it timely for the King to honour his promise."

The marriage between Emma and Aethelred was the first outcome of the failed invasion of Cotentin. The second brought the prohibition on the Danes using Normandy ports, allowing Aethelred to claim that although defeated in battle, he got what he went for. The third arm of the treaty was the estate of Rameslege to be granted to the Abbey of Fécamp, in addition to land at Steyning already given. Edward knew that as yet only the first had been honoured.

Emma spoke firmly. "If it were proven that the Danes have indeed been denied access to Normandy's shores, I am sure the King would consider the grant of land at Rameslege to be a very small price."

Hugo didn't bother to repeat the morning's denial. "If we prohibit them, the Danes will raid Normandy – your homeland – as they raid England!"

"Which shows that both sides of my family have the same enemy, dos it not?"

Hugo laughed sourly. "You pay the gafol to keep the Dane happy. We look away when he uses our ports. We each have our method."

"They buy their provisions, they don't steal them. They enrich you, with money that England gave them. Richard should know how this rankles with the King. England and Normandy have a natural alliance, and a mutual enemy. Richard should reflect on that."

"Your new fleet," Hugo said, "that your son almost convinced me was for trade alone… If that changes the balance, if it repels the Danes, then we will lose their visits anyway."

Edward had thought the afternoon's meeting would be purely about family. He realised that his mother had let him in on the true business of Hugo's visit. He suddenly felt five years older.

"Yes, the fleet is vital," said Emma.

"Is it large enough to stop the Danes at sea? Are the sailors skilled enough? Are the fighters fierce enough?"

"I don't know its size," Emma said, and Edward wondered if she was telling the truth. He recognised her split loyalties, one half to England, one half to Normandy.

If she had to make a decision, with whom would she make her primary alliance?

"I do know that it is not battle hardened," she continued. "That much is obvious to all. And as you and Richard also know, when it becomes a strong fighting force, the fleet can be turned south as easily as Danes can sail past Calais. More easily, for Normandy is closer. If Aethelred wishes to revisit

Cotentin, it is with the same aim as it ever was: not to make war on Normandy, but to defeat the Danes. You must tell Richard that in the long term, his interest is to be closer to Aethelred, not to Sveyn."

Hugo nodded. "I will convey your view."

"And convey this. I want more of his ships trading with England. I want a Norman boat always at Suthamton. Do you understand? Always. And I will raise the matter of Rameslege with the King."

When Hugo left, Emma asked Edward if he had questions about the discussion.

"You want a ship ready to take us to Normandy, if Danes threaten the south," he said.

She nodded.

"Do you think war will come?"

"The noise of battle grows louder in my ears," she said. "Don't worry, Edward. I will always keep you, Alfred and Goda safe. Do you have other questions?"

Edward had many, but they didn't concern Hugo and diplomacy with Normandy.

"If you think of any, come to me at any time. I will try to answer my best, little Prince." And she hugged him again. Four in two days. The last time he had received such blessed affection was in his infancy, before memory. Or so he supposed.

As he left and crossed Emma's ante-chamber, he saw a stack of four pins of Hugo's cidre, separated from the gift to Aethelred, destined for Emma's private store. A taste of home for her, Edward thought. He was half-Norman, was he not? And therefore entitled to a share.

Arsindis was not to be seen, so he turned one onto its side, and heavy as it was, rolled it across the courtyard and returned unchallenged to his room. Alfred was elsewhere and the basket of mice was gone, so Edward expected to hear a scream from Goda at any time. Edward unstopped the pin, and tilted it to pour cidre into his cup. He lay on his bed and drank, and felt that giddiness return. He drank more, until he suddenly wanted to cry.

It wasn't from guilt at stealing the cidre, nor this time of having spied on Stigand and Fulton. Eavesdropping was not wrong if it revealed sin, surely? So was it at the confusing and shameful nature of what he'd witnessed? Was it his fascination? Was it that Stigand had stolen Fulton from him?

He let tears fall, and when they stopped, he prayed for his sins, whatever they were, to be forgiven. He must now read of Job, whose sufferings at the hand of God were so much worse than his own, in spite of Job's intransigent Godfearing uprightness.

Was God testing him, too?

Was he prideful in thinking that God would even notice him?

But God noticed everything. God saw men's hearts.

The Book of Job gave Edward consolation. His sufferings were not those of Job, who lost his wealth and his family at God's hand, whose body was tortured with crippling pain and ugly sores. And yet Job remained steadfast in his praise for the greatness of God. "He giveth and he taketh away," Job said. His undeserved suffering was God's lesson for men: respect My infinite power, glory and knowledge; do not assume to question it. "Where were you when I laid the foundations of the earth?"

Well, Edward could be steadfast too. His sufferings were not destitution and boils, but only confusion; and his questions were not of God, His thoughts, His actions, His purpose. They were of men, their thoughts, their actions, their purpose.

It was darkening, and rather than light candles to read by, he left the bible. The bible was eternal, it could wait another day. He drank more of the cidre. If he had questions, he could return to his mother; she had said so. She might have meant questions about the Danes, about Normandy, about the arts of diplomacy, but surely she would try to answer questions about men too. He could ask about Stigand without mentioning Fulton; he could say that it wasn't a kitchen girl he was talking to, but a stable-boy or a ceorl. He could say he saw… But could he say that? Could he ask, without describing details, whether Stigand might share the same embraces with boys and other men that he shared with Eadgyth?

His mother would guess some of what he'd seen, and would extract from him the rest, and Stigand would be banished.

Yes, Edward decided, he would not withhold anything, save Fulton's involvement. He felt that Stigand now stood between himself and Fulton like a huge pillar that may not be mentioned. He wanted Stigand gone, and Fulton back.

He made his way out from his room, and towards his mother's hall. Again he staggered across the yard, only this time he rolled no barrel. He was the barrel.

Arsindis sat in the ante-chamber, but he paid her no mind until she stood and said "You are not to go in. She sleeps."

"She said I could. She invited me."

"Not now, Edward," Arsindis snapped. "Your mother is tired."

"Oh, right. So she's not asleep now, just tired." He was being rude. His head floated uncaring on a pool of cidre, and it pleased him. He pushed past her.

She reached for his shoulder. Her fingers dug hard as she pulled him back.

Arsindis normally scared him, with her glowering face and harsh words. But normally he was neither cushioned nor angered by cidre.

How dare she?

He shook her off, and marched to Emma's door. When Arsindis grabbed him again, he turned and slapped her. The shock on her face was from such an uncharacteristic show of temper, not from pain. You should have seen me with Alfred, he thought. Count yourself lucky that I hold no birch sword. She reeled backwards, and in that moment Edward reached the door, opened it, and stepped into the room.

His mother was kneeling on her bed, leaning forward, facing away from him. Her hair hung like a waterfall over her naked back, and her arsehole puckered and swelled as she moved like a poplar tree in the wind. He recognised Stigand's muscled legs, and the hairs golden in the candlelight as he lay on his back beneath her with that pizzle shiny again, disappearing then reappearing. Stigand, with his head and shoulders raised on pillows, saw him, and his surprise turned to ill-suppressed laughter.

Emma was slower to react, but her moans stopped and she turned. Her breasts swung like waterbags. Edward would remember the pendulous motion forever, the anus, the thick stem that was gripped, the things no son may see. Her expression slid swiftly from outrage to horror to an animal snarl.

Edward wanted only to kill Stigand. His hand went to his dagger but before he could take a step forward Arsindis threw her arms around him. She held him fast, hauled him back outside, and shut the door.

12. The Candlers

(Walt)

"Somewhere to sleep means under a roof."

Walt was accustomed to solitude. Nights and days he'd spent on that hillside, sleeping in his shelter and foraging alone in the woods and valleys around the village with only Jack and sheep and rabbits for company. He could even be lonely at home with his mother and Djorka. They never sought to exclude him, but sometimes the bond between them did so, as if the loss of his father that had wounded all of them was easier for a son to bear than a wife and daughter.

Go find your ma's family, Baker had said. All Walt knew was that his mother had brought them from somewhere called Northumbera, which lay in the far far north. If they hadn't had to come south he'd still have a family and a home. He didn't know how big Northumbera was, but surely if he could get there, someone would know his family. The thegn, or the priest, or the scire reeve even. Was Northumbera as big as Norwic?

There was a path called The Erming Way he'd heard of, old and straight, that lay beyond the fens. Travellers knew it, or so it was said, by the avenue of cherry trees along its verges. He knew of some vast and empty fenlands too, and that they were impassable save by coracle or punt, so he'd need to veer south to find this Way. He might miss the trees and cross over it without knowing, or take some other track by mistake. But surely he'd meet people he could ask. South, west, north, and even if he went in circles, he felt that somehow he could close in on Northumbera. The most meandering of rivers inevitably reaches the sea. He just hoped to do so before the river froze over.

And there was the place he'd heard of called Jorvik. That was north too. Was Northumbera in Jorvik?

Walt had essentials in his bag, which when it wasn't over one shoulder was always to hand, ready to be grabbed. It held his flint, strong cord for guys and light string for snares, hooks and the small net, his knife, and Portheof's seax; and the last of the food he'd taken from Croming, which he'd eked out for two days. A waxed cloth and a blanket were rolled and tied together with a loop to be slung crosswise over his other shoulder. Wrapped inside was Benna's doll, whose sticking out arms made a cross, almost. When he had time he'd strip some willow bark to weave a proper cross for Jesus, and a web against the nixies. Meanwhile the sprig of rowan he'd cut would have to keep him safe at night. He had two sceatts, his mother's buried hoard that the Vikingr had not found, in a small leather pouch tied around his waist, out of sight.

He spent a day looking for food to sustain him for a further day's walk. If he saw a cave or a tree hollow, or an abandoned hut or any other kind of shelter, he would stop there. Such places were rare, but to be caught in the rain at night was the first step towards the coughing sickness, weakness, and a lonely collapse in an empty forest. Always damp, never warm, barely eating… he would give himself a few days at most. Shelter was vital.

The soils grew cresses, fat hen, nettles and chickweed, but these were thin sustenance even when boiled with grains stolen from fields. There were wild carrots and parsnips to chew and spit the fibres out. Turnips helped, but turnips were grown close to villages, and were dangerous to filch.

He searched low for the last pignuts hiding in the undergrowth if he could spot their tiny leaves, and high for the first small sweet chestnuts that a stick might bring down. And – a happy day – a wild apple or pear tree in fruit. He soon craved fish or meat.

Mushrooms abounded, and some that were similar enough to those he knew he added to a leaf stew he brewed one evening. They brought him a nightmare of horned warriors rising out of the ground to stab at him with axes of fire that hacked his limbs off and send them skywards in different directions so he could look up and see himself spread across the dark like spinning constellations, and there were his mother and sister too, smiling, until boars appeared and started eating their hands and feet.

He woke up sweating, and retched the food up with two fingers down his throat. He stayed awake until dawn, then found some chamomile to suck, which settled him.

He followed a slope down to a shallow river where he could drink and catch fish. He deposited shit on the riverbank downstream, then looked for a nice springy sapling beside a rabbit-run, and cut sticks to fashion a snare across their little path. He threaded his cord through the circumference of the net and tied a slipknot.

By the time these tasks were done, his shit had attracted a dozen flies, which he trapped in his kerchief. The flies went onto his hooks, as did worms he dug up, because different foods lured different fish. He set the baited hooks up the river a few yards, hanging off a cord spanning the flow.

He cast the net where the stream was wide and still, allowed it to settle, and then sprinkled crushed flies onto the water. He waited like a rock until ripples gave away a fish's interest in the flies, then he waited longer because more fish would gather, until the time felt right to haul the cord to lift the net and close it in one. The minnows fled through the net – he needed a finer mesh for them – and bigger fish were swift in sensing the new current and fleeing on it. He was not good at river fishing, he was too used to the catch from the sea. So he repeated the process, going back to his shit for more flies. By the afternoon all he had were three crayfish and a small dace. He hoped for a rabbit in his snare or a perch on a hook. The trap was sprung but empty, and the hooks bare.

Three more nights passed, and he was weakened, dispirited, and ever hungrier. The more he needed good snares, the less he could be bothered to make and set them. The more he needed patience as he fished, the less he was able to sit without fidgeting until the fish were lulled.

He realised exactly how mean the foraging was when making do without a trowel, how unhappy the fishing without a good net, how true the saying "twenty snare for decent fare".

He could walk on, or he could spend a day foraging, fishing and rabbiting, but not both.

He approached a village. Croming had always dealt cautiously with strangers, but they were not sent running by youths with stones. They were shown steel and made to understand that any crime would meet summary justice. Then, if Elferic deemed the stranger trustworthy, he or she would be given food and shelter in return for labour in field or forest for the common good. There had been no thefts that he knew of, no rapes, no murders.

Some villages, he discovered, were less hospitable.

He was dirty and clearly no craftsman, no cobbler travelling with rolls of leather; no travelling potter with a wheel on a cart; no healer with bags of herbs and potions jangling on a leather necklace; no jeweller with a big companion to protect him from theft. He entered the hamlet and drew suspicious looks and slow answers when he asked for the Headman's house.

The Headman was not there. A boy went to find him, and Walt stood by the cottage door as the sun moved past its zenith, wondering at what point he should simply walk away to leave himself time to find shelter. If he was to be spurned, he didn't want it to be at dusk.

Eventually a man strode towards him, his once fair hair and beard now greying at the sides, his arms tattooed, his eyes glowering from under heavy brows. He was followed by four youths, his sons perhaps, or his husceorls for the day.

Walt had to turn his head slightly so his good ear could pick up the Headman's words. "You going to fuck off straight 'way, or you first going to waste my time telling me how useless you are?"

Walt took this as an offer to hear what he might contribute. "I can dig, I can cut. I can mend roofs before winter. I know sheep, I-"

"We ain't interested in your shaggin'," the man said to make his gang laugh.

Being the butt of jokes was a fair price for a hot meal. "I can fish and mend nets…"

"Ah, you're from the coast. Where?"

"Croming."

"Croming had a visit from the Norsemen, maybe?"

Walt was silent.

"What's your name, orphan-boy?"

"Walt. Walt was my father too."

"And the Norse chopped his balls off. Look at you, runt, they should have done it twelve years ago."

Walt didn't say thirteen. "No, my father was killed eight year ago."

"He was killed, eh? Who killed him?"

"Elfhelm, Ealdorman of Jorvik." Walt was unversed in the

ways of deceit, of saying what a man wished to hear and avoiding what he didn't.

"Killed by an Ealdorman! What, in a fight? And you're far from Jorvik because your father made an enemy of an Ealdorman."

"He was hanged for stealing a goat." His father stole no goat, nor did anyone accuse him. The story was the family's protective coat of mail. "But he didn't do it."

The Headman laughed. "Of course he didn't. No-one never stole a goat, and yet, goats get stolen. What's to stop you not stealing a goat from us?"

The young men behind him chortled as Walt tried to make sense of the Headman's sentence. All he could find to say was "I'm no thief."

"Ah, so not being a thief runs in the family!" The Headman leaned close and grinned. His teeth were as brown as his eyes. "Bring me a letter from Ealdorman Elfhelm vouching for your honesty, and you can be goatherd for a week. Can you do that?"

Elfhelm's injustice still pursued him. Learning quickly, Walt refrained from voicing his certainty that the man could not read. He shook his head.

"Then you'd better fuck off then, before one of our goats catches your eye. Or one of our sheep."

The young men cackled, and Walt turned. He had four hours to find shelter somewhere in the woods beyond the village. Three, because he'd need to walk an hour to be clear of the Headman's domain and the village's livestock.

"Why are you walking boy? Run!"

He held his head firm and kept walking until he realised the young men were running after him, then he fled as fast as he could as sticks and stones hailed around him. They could have caught him, but they didn't want to, they just kept him running for near a mile, until they got bored or reached some boundary, when they stopped and turned back. Walt collapsed face down, panting, feeling the ache in his legs and a sharper pain at the back of his head. He touched it there, and found a swelling and dried blood matting his hair. He hadn't even felt the stone strike.

Once, he'd been a dreamer, playing tales of adventure in his mind. What a fool he'd been. Adventure was misery heaped upon woe. But for all his gloom, he knew it could have been worse. They could have stolen his bag, and searched him for the sceatts. They could have beaten him.

It could have rained that night.

Next morning he walked the ache and the dewdamp out of his bones. He thought about his father, wishing he remembered his face, wishing he knew more about him, wishing he could understand what had happened. He had been one of Elfhelm's husceorls. Walt knew, because his mother told him, that his father stayed loyal, yet was hung with a dozen others. Why would an Ealdorman of honour do such a thing? Why had his mother needed to flee Jorvik with her children, and told them to tell the story of a stolen goat because she feared a bounty still on them? What turned Elfhelm against his men?

When he came to another village he resolved that unless he saw a positive sign of welcome he should walk straight through, as if determinedly about his own business and nearly home. He watched for expressions of friendliness or enmity on the faces that regarded him, and jumped when he heard a sharp call "Hey!"

It was from a scrawny elder with a thin grey beard that hung like a billygoat's from his rodent face, who beckoned Walt to where he sat on a stool outside his hovel.

Old and in poor repair, the hut leaned as if pressed by a gale. Planks were askew, their fixing pegs sprung or nails rusted, with gaps a palm wide between them. Frayed timber at the base were signs of rot. Walt was no carpenter's apprentice, but even he knew that wood must be kept clear of the ground. Yet the man's shirt with its fine linen weave, and the glint of gold chain about his neck, showed he was no pauper.

He was cutting hemp string from a reel to equal lengths, and laying them across his lap. "Looks like you've travelled far, boy."

"A ways," Walt replied.

"Far to go, boy?"

More miles, more days than he knew. "Just a few more hours."

"Needs be back home before dark, do you?"

He was leaving home. "Aim to be."

"You don't want to be walking at night. Where you headed?"

"North- Northam."

"North Northam? No North Northam in a day's walk of here, nor a South, East or West Northam." The man turned and called over his shoulder into the hut. "Gro, you know a North Northam?"

Gro? A Danish name. Bodil's mother was a Gro.

A cracked female voice from inside. "'Bout a half day walk, cross the river and down Thetford way." The accent was strange to Walt's ears, and sharper than he was used to. The further he got from Croming, the more words changed their sound.

"That's Northwold, fool." The man turned back to Walt. "Means you Northwold?"

"Yeah, North Northwold. That's what I said."

"Well you walked in from Northwold side, so I reckons you gone marched straight past it."

"Oh," said Walt, now not knowing what to do. To keep up his lie, he'd have to retrace his path. He remembered wading the ford. Was Northwold the village he'd had to flee?

“’Salright,” the old man said “Not my business where you be going. It’s a wise traveller keeps his story to hisself. But you look a hungry dog. Is you a hungry dog?”

Walt was starving. He had to find a stream to net in, or a rabbit run, or some wild roots or chestnuts before the day was out. Or to work for a meal, but he wasn’t going to ask. “I’m not a hungry dog,” he said.

“You’s not a dog, granted,” the old man said.

Why do the old always need to sound cleverer than the young?

“Gro,” he called, “Come you out here.”

A woman, equally stoatish and only a bit less bearded, emerged from the hut. Her wrist was bound and her arm slung under her bosoms.

“In’t a dog, he say. Prob’ly tell us he be honest, too. You honest boy?”

“Yes I am.”

He turned to his wife. “Told you. You think he look…?”

She scrutinised Walt. “I’d say he honest. Still wouldn’t…”

“Me neither.”

Walt wanted to walk away. Of course he was honest, his mother had always taught him to be so. When he spoke a truth, he expected to be believed, so if someone didn’t trust him, why should he trust them? But the man was leading to something, and it might be to his advantage to at least discover what. He could walk away at any point.

“Is you thinking…?” she said.

“I is. What do you…?”

“Do it matter if he in’t? What’s he to…?”

“That’s what I…”

“Settled then. Why not…?”

“A try. Why not. Say.”

Husband and wife seemed to know what the other was talking about, but Walt had no idea. After a moment’s silence, he realised the old man's last word had been addressed to him. "Say?"

"Yes. What do you…?"

"Say?" Gro finished the sentence.

"What do I say to what?"

They looked at him as if he was an idiot. "To workin' a day," the man said, "In change for…"

"Food," Gro finished again.

He wasn't going to leap, dog-like. "Then I'd need to walk at night."

"Don't you worry 'bout that," the man said.

"Food. And somewheres to sleep," Gro said.

"Come yer," the man said, rising, and led Walt around the hut with Gro following. Against the back wall stood an open-sided lean-to lodge with a roof of sloping thatch, which sheltered a thigh-high furnace lit with gently glowing charcoal. The raised hearth was topped with a large iron grille on which sat a wide cauldron holding a bath of steaming water. Inside the tank, set in the water, was a smaller, deeper tank with a glazed interior, filled with hot oil. Walt recognised the smell of beef dripping hanging in the air. He saw how the furnace kept the water hot, and the water melted the fat without burning it.

The man told Walt his name was Petwin, and he and Gro were candlers. The strings across his lap were wicks to be dipped. Efreda made candles in Croming, but they were simply bound reeds set into small bowls of tallow, fit for a ceorl but not for a church. Churches had dipped candles. There was a monastery nearby, Petwin told him, whose monks made candles for themselves and for the local churches. But the monastery couldn't get tallow enough because he would pay farmsteaders more for their beef and mutton fat, and yet he sold candles to the churches for less than the greedy monastery. Petwin was plainly delighted at getting one over the monks.

"Now boy, dipping candles be a four hand job, but…"

"Injured my wrist," said Gro, lifting her arm from the sling.

"Fitting the wheel."

"That cart," she said, nodding to a two-wheeled donkeycart resting on its shafts, with a log under one axle. A wheel was detached, and its new iron rim told its story.

"So we only got three hands," Petwin said.

Walt wondered why there wasn't some other person in the village who could help them. Probably there was, but they'd want more than a meal, and already had a bed for sleeping.

He showed Walt how to tie each end of the strings to a small waxed finger-shaped pebble, and drape them over a wooden batten so the strings hung down on each side, held in notches cut into the batten that stopped them slipping. Each batten held a dozen strings, allowing twenty-four candles to be dipped at a time. With Petwin at one end of a batten and Walt at the other, they dipped the row of weighted strings into the tallow and hung them on a larger rack, "So's the wick can soak up the tallow," Petwin explained. The rack held twelve battens, meaning they could make two gross candles in a session.

Next to the bowl of melted tallow was a half barrel of cold water. They dipped the two dozen primed wicks once more, lifted them out, and this time sank them into the water to cool. They repeated with a second batten of soaked wicks, and took the first set from the water, back into the tallow, then back to the water, rotating the pair. With each dip the candles came out thicker and more tapered as the tallow flowed down before hitting the water.

When Petwin judged the candles thick enough, they started on another two-dozen pair. It was indeed a job for two, one at each end of the batten, either side of the furnace and the cooling basin. It was not heavy work, but needed four sound arms.

It was hot next to the heater, which Petwin kept stoked by

adding small amounts of charcoal on a shovel. Soon Walt's clothes were bone dry, then they dampened again as he started to sweat. He was glad to drink the water brought by Gro, and later, as the afternoon wore on, the beers which slightly eased his ever-growing hunger.

They worked in silence, and Walt's mind drifted. He wondered how much the churches paid for the candles, and how much Petwin and Gro paid for the fat that they rendered down for tallow. He began to understand their jewellery and clothes. Candlemaking was easier than shepherding out on the hills. Were there sheep in the north? What would he do there, to get food and lodging? If all went badly, could he look for a place with a lot of livestock and a lot of churches, and ideally no monastery, and be a candler?

By late afternoon they had two gross candles hanging on the rack. Petwin cut the weights off the base with fleecing shears, and offered a ladle of tallow to the candles' bases to seal them off. The final task was to shave surplus wax off the pebbles. Petwin put them into a bag, ready for the next dip.

They finished the job just as a light drizzle began to fall, which looked set for the evening. Walt was grateful when Petwin told him to carry the glowing charcoal embers on a shovel to place under the pot inside the hut. Gro told him to chop carrots and meat that had been kept cool in another earthenware bowl of water. He was so hungry that he wanted to eat the meat raw, but after she rapped his hand for stealing a slice of carrot to chew he didn't dare ask even for a rip of bread. He only had an hour to wait until the pot boiled and the meat was sufficiently cooked, an hour partly filled by bringing all the candles into the hut lest they be pilfered from the rack if left there overnight. Petwin showed him how to place them in rows so the fat and thin ends alternated like interlocked fingers, and the stack built up tightly.

The couple seemed to have exhausted their conversation

for the day. Walt didn't mind. He just wanted to eat, and to sleep, so when he'd spooned the last of his bowl of stew into his mouth, he asked if he could lie down in a corner now. He began to untie the rolled-up blanket and cloth. "I'll cover myself with my blanket, and face the wall." Gaps in the wall would make it draughty, but at least he'd be on the plank floor, lifted above the ground-damp.

They looked at each other. "Can't sleep in," Petwin said. "Didn't…"

"…say nothing 'bout sleeping," Gro continued.

"Not in here."

They wanted to cheat him. Walt's weariness made him snap quickly. "You said food, and somewhere to sleep."

Petwin raised himself from his seat and stood over Walt. He thrust Walt's bag into his arms. "Sleep where you like."

"But not in here." With her good hand, Gro picked up the knife she'd used to slice the carrots. Walt's own knife was at his belt, but by the time he'd dropped his bag and pulled it free, she could have stuck his guts five times.

"Somewhere to sleep means under a roof," he said.

"Not in here." Petwin pushed him towards the door, his fingers on Walt's thin shoulders.

"Not our roof." Gro followed, with the knife.

"It's raining." Walt could hear it beating down even through the thick thatch roof.

"Can't stop rain..."

"Can we."

"Try under the…"

"Shelter."

Petwin shoved him outside into the rain, threw out the waxed cloth, and shut the door on him. Water dripped from the eaves into his eyes and onto his cheeks. He turned and slunk round to the tallow shelter. The hearth had a vestige of warmth, so he huddled in its lee, the cloth around his shoulders. His blanket was still inside the hut, rolled up around Benna's doll.

The wind blew the rain in sideways, so if he lay down his feet and head were exposed. There was small chance of sleep, all he could do was curl himself up like a river rat and brood. Was this how they had achieved their comfort – by underpaying? What did they have to lose by denying him floor space? Privacy? Did they fear he'd sneak off with their valuables? As it was, they had his blanket. Would they cheat him of that too when he went to reclaim it in the morning? He didn't want to reclaim it in the morning. He didn't want to see them again, or hear their disjointed talk.

The wind changed direction so he had to move around the cooker to keep out of the rain. The ground on the other side was soaked and muddy. If he could move the water cauldron and the bowl of tallow to sleep upon the hearth he might find some warmth and be clear of the rain, but they were too heavy to shift.

He lay shivering, unable to recall a time when he'd been more miserable. He should have run out from that holly bush in Croming and begged to be taken with Djorka. Even if they'd been parted, life couldn't be worse than this. He should have tried to look after her.

He told himself he stayed for Benna's sake, not knowing then that she and Portheof were dead. Then he felt disgust with himself, for the truth of it was that he'd been frozen by fear.

The rain let up, the clouds cleared, but still the wind scythed through his wet clothes. It howled around the hut, and made the nearby trees roar like a cataract.

Moonlight let him see a gap in the wall, wide enough to take an arm. He crawled from under the shelter, squelching through the mud like a lame goose. He lowered his bag and knelt, putting his ear to gap. The wind did not not quite drown the snores from inside, Petwin's heavier, then Gro's lighter, conversing in sleep as they conversed awake.

He put his fist into the gap, and pulled at the rot-softened timber, working it free inch by inch until he could angle it aside. The little noise he made was covered by the wind. At each widening of the gap he paused, and listened to the snores. If they changed rhythm, if they stuttered or became a snuffle, he stopped motionless until they settled back.

The gap needed to be less than a foot wide for Walt to slither through, slowly, carefully, like he had once reached inside a ewe to find the lamb that she could not expel. He shouldn't even be sneaking like this, he should be standing up to walk in, grab the blanket they had stolen from him, lift the door-bar, depart before they woke. But wake they would, and they'd cry "Thief", and the village would wake too, and he'd be stoned with no chance to explain. So he crawled on, around the pile of two gross candles they'd stacked earlier.

The blanket would be on the floor where he'd left it when he'd stood to face Petwin. He reached out, found the rough familiar wool, and gathered it to him. His feet were still outside, and he crawled backwards and out, wriggling past the stack of candles. He was almost clear when he decided that he had earned more than just a bowl of stew for his labour. If not a dry place to sleep, then surely a pair of candles that he could sell somewhere, or trade for shelter, or even eat. He felt the contours of the stack, and his hand and found two loops of wick, and pulled the two attached pairs. When they didn't lift free smoothly, Walt thought they were simply stuck to their waxy neighbours, so he tugged, and the four candles suddenly came loose along with the dozen or so that had been resting on them. They rolled down the pile with clatter, and if there was one thing bound to wake Petwin it was the sound of his candles complaining at being moved, like sheep do when herded in the morning.

"Hey," he called, and Walt pulled the four candles and his bundled blanket with him as he wriggled backwards as fast as he could. He ignored the one length of sound timber that scraped skin off his back. He grabbed his bag and cloth, and ran towards the setting three-quarter moon.

"Thief!" came Petwin's cry from behind him. "Stole our…"

"Candles," Gro finished.

People emerged from other huts. Walt knew well how to steal from one was to rob the whole village, how they'd never thieve from a neighbour, and how they'd watch out for one another. He knew too that he'd given the village's youths an opportunity to prove themselves men, just as he'd want to prove himself if a thief robbed Croming. His only chance was to disappear into the dark woods.

He nearly made it, but he was young, and hampered by his baggage. Four older boys caught him up and, like hounds, pulled him to the ground. Two knelt on his hands while a third took his knife, and a fourth held up the candles. "These?" someone said.

"Ours." It was Petwin's voice, panting.

"Candles," said Gro, panting harder.

"Who else's would they be?" said a youthful voice.

"Mine," Walt cried. "Payment, because they-"

A heavy hand crashed into his cheek and when his head stopped reeling he was swallowing blood.

"What shall we do with him?" said the youth.

"Hang him." Gro this time.

"From a tree." Her echo.

An older, sterner voice came. "He was helping you with the dipping."

"Paid," said Petwin.

"Food," said Gro.

"They promised me a bed," Walt got out, struggling against the three boys who held him down. One of them cuffed him again, and his face was pushed sideways into the soil.

"You always were a mean pair of fuckers," the older voice said. Was he the Headman? "Here, take your candles and fuck off home."

Walt heard their muttered words fade away. "Paid him," "Fed him," "Ungrateful…" "Little…" "Bugger…"

The youth repeated his question. "What shall we do with him?"

"Do what the fuck you like," said the older voice. "Just don't kill him. And give him back his stuff. We ain't murderers and we ain't thieves." His footsteps disappeared through the mud.

Not murderers, not thieves. But they took the words to mean all else was permitted, and they proved themselves men in ways he never knew existed. They turned him over and lowered his braies, and he struggled, and more blows to the head made everything a whirlpool of pain, disgust and shame. They left him leaking blood and mucus and spunk and tears.

They took his knife, and his bag with all its contents, so it turned out they were thieves after all. Lying there near naked, Benna's doll somehow in his hand, Walt wished they were murderers too.

13. Witangemot

(Eadric)

"To pay? To fight? Make up your bloody minds!"

The Great Hall was guarded by ten husceorls. One stepped forward as they approached, but Eadric ignored him, and called over the guard's head "Bullward! Mercia's greetings to you!"

The King's chief husceorl was watching arrivals from a raised rostrum beside the door. He said lazily "Welcome, Lord Eadric."

"How many are yet inside?"

"Most of 'em. Well more'n half full." Bullward had checked Eadric's arrival at several Witans, and knew by now that he liked to be neither among the first to arrive, nor among the last.

So they entered, and joined some ten dozen pairs of feet standing on the hay spread over the packed dirt floor. The feet of ealdormen, and ealdor sons, of thegns, of bishops, reeves, and other favoured men, gathered at the Great Witangemot to advise King Aethelred of his people's prayers. Eadric let Nothman and Leofric lead him through the throng, barging rudely past lesser men who turned in anger, then backed off when they saw who was coming through. They paused to greet Ealdor Smerdon respectfully, as instructed.

The greatest nobles were favoured with stools and benches at the front of the crowd. Here, they greeted Aelfric and Athelmar, the Ealdormen of eastern and western Wessex, with embraces and kisses. If he'd been Aelfric and Athelmar he would have waited outside to ensure their entrance followed Mercia's, or at least accompanied it. Or failing that, been the very first, and stood indoors to welcome everyone as if it was their Witan, as if they were again in Wintancaestr. Perhaps they needed to sit down, for – unlike himself, today at least – their hands and necks were heavy with gold and jewels. Do rich men add to their ostentatious loading as they get older and weaker to divert attention from their shorter steps and rounder shoulders? Which of the two, under their layers of fine linen and wool and unnecessary furs, was the fatter, the flabbier? Was he looking at himself a score of years hence? He'd be happily fat, but he'd not wish to be on these front benches. He wanted higher.

He likewise greeted Ulfcytel, just arrived from East Anglia. Ulfcytel asked if Father Stigand was well, and if he was to come to the Witan. Eadric told him he hadn't seen Stigand for days, and was surprised not to find the priest standing there beside his employer, patron of his abbey. "And your wife is in good health?" he asked. The two men's wives were sisters, daughters of the King.

"She was when I left." Ulfcytel usually chose to speak too little rather than too much; Eadric doubted he would say a great deal today. Yet he wasn't taciturn, and he looked upon the world with a benign and inscrutable smile. Under that trimmed beard was a strong chin, and Eadric knew not to underestimate him. East Anglians had followed Ulfcytel to victory in battle, though he was not warlike by disposition.

Both Ealdormen had the same interests here, and he'd get Leofric to nudge Ulfcytel when he needed a display of East Anglia's support. "Ah, but you should have brought her," Eadric said. "Did she not wish to see her family?"

"Her sisters, perhaps."

Then not her father, Eadric surmised. "The King laid on a fine feast."

"We eat well enough in Norwic."

"And long may your bellies be full."

He moved on to greet Archbishop Aelfheah, who was with Hlothar, High Reeve of Cantware. No conversation was required or desired.

He sat down with his charges and, as they waited, he whispered to them how to arrive first at a meeting, how to arrive last if you want to impose, and how to appear modest and friendly, one of the crowd, as they had. Such ploys mattered.

Behind the high dais dark tapestries hung. To the side the fire was stoked with logs, but was yet to be kindled. Doors left open did little to remove the smells of so many men. Two small round windows in the gable end allowed some daylight, but it was as if the masons who built it had feared to insert more than the tiniest of holes into the stonework. Thuws came to light torches in sconces set into the stone at each end, clear of the timbers and the thatch, but the hall remained gloomier than a church.

Prince Edmund entered from the back of the hall, where the doorway gave access directly from the royal compound. He seated himself on a chair at the dais, carefully shifting that damned sword so it rested on the floor behind him. No-one noticed Eadric's snarl at the sight.

The sword Edmund carried marked his status as Atheling, but it was not his sword. It did not belong to the King, nor to England, still less to Wessex or any Wessex-born Atheling.

It belonged to Mercia, for it was no less a sword than King Offa's own, bane of the Waelas, subduer of the Anglians, and indeed terror of Wessex. Offa, the great Mercian who built the walled dyke to say to the Waelas "no further", and ruled from there all across to Lindesege, East Anglia and the eastern sea, and from the Humber to Soussex, Cantware and the southern sea. Not until Offa was dead did Ecgberht push back

Mercian overlordship of Wessex at Ellandun. Ecgberht claimed Offa's sword as a trophy.

Then came the heathens from the east, turned from raiders to invaders, and Mercia had been trapped between Wessex and the Danes ever since. Alfred forcing his daughter Aethelflaed onto the weak Mercian ruler, and then having the scribes name her Lady of the Mercians, that was a joke. Bequeathing Offa's sword to his grandson Athelstan Atheling, was an insult.

Edmund had an empty chair to his right, and the empty high throne to his left. Queen Emma came with her sons, and seated herself on the other side of the throne to Edmund, with the boys beside her.

So Aethelred was blooding them to the Witan. Or Emma was.

Aethelred's Reeve Wilmaer entered through the back door, and stood in the vacant space at Edmund's right. He raised his hands, and let a hush settle over the room. "Aethelred, son of Edgar called the Peaceable, heir to Aethelstan, heir to Alfred the Great, King of England, King over Strathclyde, Northumbria, the Five Berhs, over Mercia, Hwicce, Anglia, Cantware, and all the Saxons East, South and West, and the Defenas."

Strathclyde? Northumbria? The Five Berhs? Sveyn will laugh when he hears, Eadric thought as he stood and bowed at the entrance of his King.

Aethelred wore a crown, a thin ring of gold with a simple cross at the front, but was dressed more plainly than he had been at the recent feast. Eadric smiled at not being alone in having reason to display modesty.

"Welcome, Ealdors, Thegns, Bishops, Reeves and all," Aethelred said, and sat. Those few before him who had chairs and benches, they seated themselves too.

Aethelred announced some minor victories against Danish

and Norse raiders. The successes were few, and Eadric knew there were many more raids, many towns looted and sacked, whose residents fled at the first warning of a Viking approach. Woe to those caught by surprise. The biggest of the small victories was an incursion towards Coelmaersford, as Edmund with a force of East Saxons had managed to capture and take prisoner over one hundred Danes. Edmund bowed his head without rising, as cheers from the assembly threated to lift the thatch clear of the rafters.

The prisoners were now penned and guarded in a field, slowly dying of their wounds. They appealed to the King for mercy, with a promise to go north never to return. "I am minded to slaughter them," Aethelred said, "as they sought to cut down any who stood in their way. But the noble Archbishop makes plea on their behalf. Aelfheah, speak."

The old Archbishop stood. He stooped somewhat, but held his head as only a man who answered first to God and second to the King could do when face to face with the latter. Eadric noticed young Prince Edward sit up, and his brother too. He wondered what their views on the issue were. He would watch them.

"They do not just plead for mercy, your Majesty," said Aelfheah in his gentle tone that many had to strain to hear. "They also plead to be shown the path to salvation. They wish to know the word of Christ. I have gone into their midst, and already-" Aelfheah needed to pause as a ripple of mutterings flowed across the hall.

He went into that crowd of imprisoned Danes? They were disarmed, but could so easily have held him for ransom, or more likely torn his limbs off. The Archbishop is a fool, Eadric thought, or he'd had a visit from a winged angel bringing clear and loud assurances from God himself. He considered the first the most likely.

"-already, a number have been baptised."

Archbishop Aelfheah was famous as the priest who had baptised Olaf Tryggvason, the Norse King, some twenty years before. And it was true that after his conversion, Olaf's ships never raided England again, and Olaf turned his warriors east to create a Christian Scandinavia and thus ensured Sveyn was forever his enemy. When Olaf was killed, the old gods returned to his people. They probably never went away.

The Archbishop was still speaking. "I believe that if we show them Christian mercy, they will honour all the promises they make. They will go north, and plough the land."

"So we should love our enemies?" Aethelred said. "Is that the view of all?"

Voices rose. Eadric recognised Smerdon's. "Kill our enemies! That's what they're farr."

"We will look weak, we will look feeble. Sveyn will think us lacking in stomach."

"Save them for Saint Brice's Day!"

"One hundred fewer Danes!"

"One hundred fewer Danes makes no difference, even if they break their oath. But a demonstration of our mercy, this might, might…" the speaker clearly wasn't sure what such mollification might achieve. But perhaps he had a point. Would that more Vikings were peaceable farmers, Eadric thought. Mercia would be safer.

"Kill all bar one," Nothman shouted. "Take that one to Sanwic and let him see the great fleet assembling there, and let him report to Sveyn Forkbeard, to show what will befall any of his ships that sail south!"

Eadric stood and raised both hands, and others quietened to let him speak. "Forkbeard knows of the fleet already," he said. "If you stand on the cliff at Dofras, you can be sure that one of the boats you will see between there and Flandra will be his."

Nothman sat down, embarrassed at being contradicted. The

fool was told what to say, and yet he says different, Eadric thought, and gave him not so much as a glance.

The hubbub rose again, then fell, for the other Archbishop, second only in rank to Aelfheah of Cantenberh, was standing. Eadric settled back to hear what Wulfstan had to say, and how he'd say it. It wasn't often one got the chance to see two Archbishops lock antlers.

"Your Majesty," Wulfstan began. His words addressed the King, but his eyes were on Aelfheah. "His Grace speaks from his merciful heart, and he humbles us all. But remember, these men are born heathens. They are chosen by Satan himself. They serve the Antichrist. Their pleas for baptism cannot be genuine. A man will promise anything to save his life."

Cheers rose from the vengeful.

But Wulfstan held up his hand to hush them. "And yet," he said. "And yet, baptism gives their souls to God whether they will it or no. If it were otherwise, baptism would have no meaning, and all our souls would be in peril. Those who are baptised must be granted all that we would grant ourselves. That is, a fair trial for crimes they committed, and justice no less and no more than any Englishman might expect. Those that have not killed or maimed or stolen should be freed. Those that have, must be executed in accordance with law. That shall be their mercy. Then let us see how many genuinely wish to come to the Lord."

"And those that do not?" asked Aethelred.

"They will suffer eternal torment in hell, and there is no reason to postpone it."

Eadric decided that religious debate merely diverted the Witan from considering the advantages or hindrances to the cause. Besides, he was bored.

So he stood once more. "I support the noble Archbishop." He let people scratch their heads for now as to which idiot he favoured. "Know your enemy's weaknesses…" He turned to

Leofric. "Were we not talking of this? The pagans' distance from God is one weakness – on this all can agree. But it is not so great a weakness as the division between Danes who worship their false gods – their Wotan, their Thor, their Freya – and the numbers woken to the true God and his blessed son Jesus Christ. I say to you, Archbishop Lupus, to baptise a man only to behead him is a fool's way of appeasing the pagan hordes we face-"

Wulfstan stood, angered, gesturing and pointing "It is not the pagan you need to appease, Eadric, but God himself! The day is coming when you will realise who the fool is!"

Eadric did what he considered best with angry men who pretend to know more than they do. Ignore them. "And to Archbishop Aelfheah I say: Go, baptise them. Tell them not to return north simply to farm, but also to spread the word of Christ. Tell them the joys of heaven, tell them the place they call Valhalla is no hall of dead warriors, but a place of torment and torture. I say this: love our enemy, and he will be our enemy no longer."

He sat down, and the hall was quiet.

Eadric looked down modestly, but his eyes were not so low that he couldn't see the dais. Little Prince Edward seemed about to clap his hands, but refrained, and contented himself with nodding. His brother looked disappointed – Alfred seemingly wanted a massacre. Edmund was impassive, probably accepting that his one hundred prisoners made little difference either way. The Queen was stone-faced.

And Aethelred, King of England, looked around, trying to read the assembly.

Reeve Hlothar stood. "The Danes raided Eassex. The Danes were captured by East Saxons. Let them decide their fate." Hlothar was Aelfheah's man.

"They were captured by Edmund!" Aethelred said, and turned to his son. "Let Edmund decide."

Edmund merely said "This is neither an axe I wish to grind, nor a cross I wish to polish."

Ulfcytel stood. "Aye," he said. "The Reeve speaks right." He sat down. Eadric wondered if he'd sensibly chosen to direct his support to Hlothar rather than to Mercia, or if he'd just been slow to rise.

There were murmurs of approval from around the room, and those wanting blood were hushed. Eadric doubted they were shamed. They were won, or at least silenced, by the Reeve's point, based as it was on a principle of local determination. Just as Eadric had advised Aelfheah they would be.

"Then Lady Leofflaed," Aethelred said. "Let us hear your mind."

A stout woman with grey hair plaited in a long ropey tail stepped forward between benches. Leofflaed was daughter of Byrtnoth, the hero who lost so bravely at Maldon. Then her husband Oswig had been killed by Danes just a few years ago at Ringmere. Their son Elfwin would be Ealdorman of Eassex had he not preferred a monastic life in the fens at Ely. Leofflaed had as much reason to want vengeance against the Danes as anyone in that hall. "Kill them, and God loses their souls," she announced. "Baptise them, and we do God's work."

Eadric wondered if perhaps she had been listening to the Wolf's sermons and taken the wrong message. Or if she'd been influenced by her monk of a son. If so, perhaps the two hundred silver coins Eadric had promised her may not have been needed to sway her thinking. Still, take your cape, even if you wear a cloak.

Thus was Aethelred's decision made. "So be it," he said. "Archbishop Aelfheah, I applaud your bravery. The strength of the Lord is in you. Do your best to convert them-"

"And those you don't convert, cut their bloody throats,"

someone shouted from the back.

Aethelred held up his hand. "No! Speak words of mercy and salvation, and act as you speak. Even pagans talk."

He can't make a decision, Eadric thought. But once he's sure which way the wind blows, he follows it with all sails raised and full.

Aelfheah sat down, saying "Thank you, Majesty. They will carry the Holy Spirit north, whether they know it or not."

The mutterings resumed, as the Witan's attendees discussed the decision among themselves. No-one else shouted, and those who disagreed spoke the quietest.

Aethelred stood, and slowly the room hushed, for all knew the main purpose of the gathering. The decision to be made by the King – or perhaps announced, if by faint chance he had already made it – would affect their lives, their people, their lands, and their purses.

Gafol. The taxes that the people were now calling Danegeld.

"As you all know," Aethelred said in tones so sombre he might have been speaking at a burial, "Sveyn Forkbeard lives in expectation of continued gold and silver. And we therefore have another stark choice. You all know the option: we raise taxes, we convey our wealth north. Or we refuse to bow any longer to his extortion, in the certain knowledge that the Forkbeard will muster, and march overland, and sail around the coast. No city, town, berh or ham will be safe, not from Lyccidfeld to Dofras, not from Yernemuth to Escancaestr."

He paused, and looked across the room. "You are asking: How safe are we anyway? Have I not just reported incursions into Cantware, into East Anglia, and along the coast? I know too well how Sweyn Forkbeard milks us dry, how he bleeds us with his treaty, and then these animals, they come to bleed us again!"

"Not all are Sveyn's," came a shout from the back.

"They're his brothers, his cousins," came another.

"Who we give mercy to," came a third.

"The Norse rovers follow no overlord."

"Aye, Sveyn himself wars on them from Denmark," rejoined the first caller.

"He says he does! In truth all he does is direct their dragonships to Saxon villages to keep the Danish ones safe!"

"They have sailed to Swanawic," came another voice. "They sailed from Cotentin."

"Aye, and to Suthamtun – next they will be in Wintancaestr again, then maybe you will listen!"

Those disgruntled by Aelfheah's success were having their say another way, thought Eadric. He must be careful here; belligerence did not serve Mercia.

The King raised his hands higher. "I do listen, I do hear. Last year I paid the Beard twenty-four thousand silver coins! Until last month he kept his promise not to attack us from his strongholds in the north."

"But not his promise to stop the Norsemen!" came the call.

"How long does it take us to raise twenty-four thousand coins?" Aethelred asked of his Reede.

Wilmaer replied "Two years."

Aethelred shouted to the far reaches of the hall "And this year he doubtless expects the same again!"

Aelfric of Wessex stood, cleared his throat, and began to speak. He was old, but his voice was loud and clear, and it hushed the hubbub that pervaded the hall. "We paid Forkbeard to stay north of the Trehynt, but his people moved into the Five Berhs. Step by step the Danes come closer, and open a free path for him. Soon they will cross Watling Street, not as an army but as farmers, and I tell you, that is more dangerous to we Saxons, we English."

"You speak as if England is Wessex alone!" yelled Nothman. "When already they encroach on old Mercia."

Eadric had no wish to rise and draw further attention to Mercia, so he gave Nothman has fiercest stare which said "Speak no more." Leofric whispered something to his older brother. Leofric understood.

A shout came from behind. "What do you expect when you fear to oppose them?" Smerdon again, cheered by many Wessex thegns.

"I say this," Aelfric resumed. "We must march north, and take back what we have given, aye, and more! We should be demanding tributes from Sveyn!"

The problem that Aelfric would not see, and had no need to see, was that when Danes stole at will from the south, they stole from Englishmen, not from their own kin. If the south took to raiding the north, they would pillage other English more than the recently settled Danes. How Sveyn would love that, especially when he named himself protector of the North. Aelfric's old eyes saw no further north than the Ciltern Hills.

"Give the Forkbeard more tribute, and we may as well give him all England," some other Wessex thegn shouted.

A rumble rose, and the word "treason" was heard. Aethelred took the ring of gold from his head and held it high. "The English crown is a Saxon crown. A Christian crown!" He showed them all the cross, and stabbed at it with his finger in case they missed the point. He re-crowned himself. "The English crown will never sit on a Danish head!"

A voice shouted "But English crowns may sit in a Danish purse!" and Eadric had to hide his smile.

Then Athelmar, Ealdorman of Western Wessex stood, as if he and Aelfric had planned their argument in advance. "We paid gafol. We paid heregeld, to build the fleet. Is this new strength to be used as a shield, or as a sword? Shall we defend our coasts, or shall we take men up the Humber and to Jorvik, and attack Sveyn where he sits?" Most of his point was lost amidst the rising volume of shouts and argument breaking out across the hall.

It was as Eadric knew it would be. The south, further from Danish warriors and with full grain stores, resisted paying taxes which primarily protected Mercia and East Anglia, whose villages slept and woke in fear of invasion from the north. Aelfric and Athelmar didn't object to collecting the taxes from their people, just to passing it on.

Eadric stood.

Nothman stood too, and turned to the assembly crying "Hush! Hush for Lord Eadric." He was trying to ingratiate himself. Eadric wished he wouldn't. Fortunately few heard over the rising disordered arguments.

"Bishop Hugo was here, an emissary from Duke Richard," Eadric began. It rankled that he'd not been allowed to meet the Bishop. "May we humbly ask what was discussed, apart from marriages and maladies?" Some laughter came from those who heard, and this hushed others. "May we ask in particular if the possibility of a loan from the Duke was discussed?"

Aethelred heard, and spoke none too loudly to Eadric, as if they were having a private conversation. "Duke Richard has battles of his own to fight."

Eadric knew the King's pride was stung by the idea of borrowing from Normandy, but still, a seed planted long ago had to be nursed as a sapling.

Before Aethelred had time to frame a further response, Edmund stood. The Ironside.

Victor of numerous skirmishes not only against the Danes but also against the Waelas clans who raided Glocaestr and Somorsaet he may be, but Eadric thought "Ironside" was as undeserved a sobriquet as his own. He saw a young man spoiling for a fight but unable to locate his true enemy, so reduced to bullying.

The room hushed, eager to hear what the next King would say.

"The Norsemen live by plunder. They are still the Vikingr of old. But the Danes? They want land."

"Our land!" someone shouted.

"Yes. And land cannot be plundered, it can only be ruled. So war must come. Not raid and counter-raid, but battles. Battles in which one fyrd will fight another, and the victors will rule the land, for none will be left to oppose. We have a clear choice. Who do we want the victor to be? Who do we want our ruler to be? Our King, heir to Alfred the Great? Or a man from far away who wishes to subjugate all the peoples around the Eastern Sea to his command? There is no decision to make, for we are English."

Eadric had never heard Edmund speak before, not to an assembly. He had judged Edmund a warrior only, but his simple and forceful words told another story. A worrying one.

"Then, if war must come, we must do two things. Our fyrd must be more battle-hardened. And we must choose the days and the fields on which to fight."

The Wessex Ealdors led the men behind them into clapping, sparking renewed clamour and argument.

A voice called "Byrtnoth fought at Maldon! Which of us wants to end up like Byrtnoth and all his fyrd?"

Brave but foolhardy, Byrtnoth was killed and his men massacred at Maldon. Many here had known him, and he had been well-liked. It was a narrow defeat to the Norse King Olaf Trygvasson, before he converted. Olaf had taken no heed of his own losses, and his victory seemed not worth the price of his men's lives. They butchered the vanquished through the night, and only darkness allowed a few at the edge of the field to crawl away to recount the brutality. And that was the point, because Olaf's Norse dead had bought him

England's first gafol payment. Ten thousand silver pounds kept them away for three years, until Olaf joined Sveyn Forkbeard to fall on Lunden, a siege which cost another ten thousand to lift.

"None of us," shouted Edmund. "Which is why we must do these two things!"

Most were not listening, but had turned to dispute with their neighbours.

Aethelred raise himself to shout over the noise. "This doesn't answer the question of gafol!"

He was right, thought Eadric, but it veered the waggon of opinion in a certain direction, the wrong direction. He didn't like it. Sveyn wouldn't like it either. He wondered how to pull the horses back towards a settlement that kept fyrds and battleaxes out of Mercia.

Voices yelled "Raise more silver!" and "Gafol! Buy us time."

Others called "To battle!" and "Now we have a fleet!"

A chant of "Ironside, Ironside" rose from some corner.

Edmund shouted "Who will draw sword with me?" and the chants turned to a cheer before resuming.

Faces spat words into opposing faces, shouts became pushes, open palms became fists. The young Prince Alfred stood and raised his little seax blade. Next to him, Edward's mouth hung open. By all accounts the boy was more used to civilised theological debate with priests, and had never imagined such chaos.

Aethelred waved his hands as if flapping flies from a horse's back. "To pay? To fight? Make up your bloody minds!" Few heard, none heeded.

Eadric rose again, not sure what he would say, but seeing the need to bring the debate onto a manageable path. The buying time argument might keep both sides happy for now. But before he could raise his arms and attempt to quell the storm of argument, a face appeared before him. A face he was surprised to see: Brihtric's second husceorl, Pol.

Pol spoke in his ear. His message took half a minute to convey.

Eadric had one question, "My brother?"

Pol said "He was not there."

Eadric looked up at Aethelred, who had seen Pol's arrival. Eadric went to the dais.

Such an approach, unbidden, was unheard of. Those who saw were hushed. The truce spread, and all eyes turned to Eadric. Aethelred and Edmund leaned forward to hear his words.

Good. Eadric wanted both to hear this. "The fleet. Terrible news. News beyond belief. A squadron of boats was led away from the main group, it seems. Brihtric sent his fastest after them, but the deserters turned. A storm rose, and our boats were trapped between fire arrows and the cliffs. In all we have lost some sixty boats, and countless men."

Aethelred slumped back into his wooden throne. Edmund beckoned Aelfric and Athelmar forward, and Eadric repeated the news to them.

"Do we know who commanded these traitors?" asked Edmund.

"I'm told they were from a place called Bosham."

"It is near Cicaestre, by Seolsey," said Aelfric. "The commander would have been the Thegn of Comtyn, Wulfnoth Cild."

Wulfnoth! Eadric remembered him. The man spurned by the King in favour of Brihtric as the fleet's commander. Well well. He furrowed his brow in an expression of regret. "Betrayed! By a Wessex man."

"Capture them! Kill them!" said Aethelred. "Kill them all, and hang his kin."

Such decisiveness! "I'll send word to my brother." Not that Brihtric would wait for permission to exact his reprisal.

"No," said Aelfric. "This is a Wessex matter."

Eadric spoke as much to Edmund and the Wessex Ealdormen as to the King. "I think," he said, "I think this shows that Wessex, which most wants war, is least ready for it. I think we must buy time."

He returned to Nothman and Leofric knowing that more gafol payments were secured. This was worth the loss of a few boats, especially Wessex boats, and the slight to Brihtric's pride. He silently thanked the treacherous Wulfnoth Cild.

14. Pebbles

(Emma)

"Rich as an emperor. Mean as a bastard."

Queen Emma was seated at her table by the window, peering at itinerary maps of Cantware in the sunlight. The maps were lists of villages and landmarks along each routeway, far more useful than God's view maps like she'd seen in Cantenberh and Wintancaestre. Here was the river crossing at Meddestane, and thence the road to Cantenberh, Sanwic, and Dofras. And here was another list by way of Seven Oaks and over the Weald to Rameslege and the minor haven at Rye.

She read the placenames, but when she turned her head to look out of the window, the itineraries fled her mind. The yard outside was empty, lacking its normal bustle. With the Mercian retinue returned home, and Bishop Hugo Normandy-bound, the King's halls were quiet.

After the Witan, Lunden was quiet.

All was much the same as it had been a week ago, Emma reflected. There was still a fleet, albeit a few score boats lighter. The loss could be made up in a couple of months. The rift with Normandy was yet to be closed. Viking raiders still roved the coasts. Thuws ground the corn of England still, thegns ate the bread, and reeves collected gafol and skimmed a share like cream before passing on the coins. Their ealdors and the King took their dues, leaving the bulk to make a pay to Sveyn via the trusted Eadric, who doubtless skimmed again.

And yet somehow all felt different, as if the first movements of a landslide had begun. The pebbles were small:

Wulfnoth Cild's desertion, Aethelred's feeble grip on the Witan, Eadric's feeble grip on his wife. Edmund's minor victory at Coelmaersford.

The King himself was busy with envoys to Scorham and Sanwic, trying to discover the exact number of vessels stolen and destroyed by that man Wulfnoth. Emma thought it made little difference – they were bound to lose scores of boats the first day they confronted any substantial Danish fleet. That was the price of strengthening those who survived, of tempering them, like a smith hammers hot steel at his forge.

She got Aethelred to order six of his boats to accompany Bishop Hugo. Each captain carried the woolcloth and the silver- and pewter-work at which England excelled, to trade for provisions. Provisions they didn't need, admittedly, provisions that could be haggled over and bought more cheaply in England. But the one-sided deals would please some Norman merchants and encourage further trade, and word would get to Duke Richard. Hugo carried a message that Norman boats would be offered safe harbour and free provisioning if they came to Exencaestre, Suthamton, Scorham and Haestings to buy more of what England offered. He carried too her private letter to Uncle Richard, demanding that there always be a Norman boat moored at Suthampton.

Alfred spent his time practicing the archery, riding, falconry, and other little man skills that so engaged him. The master of arms, the stablemaster and the falconer all seemed to like the boy, and Emma knew how important it was for him to learn confidence among such men. Alfred would return to supper tired and full of himself. Little Goda had wanted to join the falconry, which showed how much better she was, but Emma judged her not yet strong enough, and the leech agreed, so she was somewhere inside the royal halls with Hendi.

Edward was avoiding her. He had spent days in his room reading those thick bible tomes. Something had passed between him and Fulton, perhaps the last currents after the flogging the boy received. Whatever, it had taken a while to heal, but now they were walking and fishing together.

Had Edward told Fulton what he'd seen? Emma doubted it. He would know full well that her warning not to speak of Stigand and Eadgyth, for Fulton's own good, would apply even more to Stigand and herself. Edward was nothing if not discreet.

It must have been a shock to the poor child. But there were things a boy has to learn, and like a battle survivor, he would now be stronger for it. If it distanced him from his mother, wasn't that what becoming a man entailed? Emma took no action.

The event soured her memories of the angelically handsome Father Stigand. When at the feast Eadric had introduced him as Ulfcytel's emissary from East Anglia, her first thought had been that he was young for an ordained priest, which meant he was either precociously clever or had influential parents, or both. Her second was that he stood tall, with the bearing of a soldier more than that of a cleric. Her third notion was to stare into those deep blue eyes and let him read her. The rest was easy.

He'd had to leave, of course. It was a shame, for the yieldsome parts between her legs tingled at the memory of him, his hair soft like a girl's, and the smoothest unblemished, skin of his broad chest. She could have used his muscled vigour for several more nights. But much more of that and a visit to the herb-witch would be inevitable. Pain and illness would follow, but anything was preferable to contriving Aethelred's bulk on top of her, the insanity of pregnancy, and the torture of birthing. She quailed at the thoughts.

Arsindis should have been flogged and dismissed for allowing Edward past the door that night. But her servant was utterly discreet, and loyal. Loyalty is not a river: it must flow two ways. What might she tell the world if Emma was not loyal to her in return? The reality was that she couldn't be punished, but only retained or killed. Emma had none of her Norman family around her, and her old friends were lost, so here Arsindis stayed.

She was annoyed when Arsindis entered the room to announce Prince Edmund Ironside, and positively angered when Edmund pushed past with no ceremony or formality. "Do you know what he's done? My father, your husband?"

"Get out!" She flicked her fingernails at Arsindis, who retreated. The woman was failing Emma badly. Two of the King's husceorls were obviously needed to guard the door.

Emma redirected her frown at Edmund before turning back to her maps. She traced her finger down the Cantenberh route to where waves marked the coast. "Sanwic." she said, "Where Caesar landed. Wippidsfleet and Thanet, that Hengist and Horsa took. The sea is a moat, but England does not treat Cantware like a castle." Somewhat composed, she looked up at Edmund. "I know what he's done, my husband, your father. He wants to bring the boats, those that remain, up the Tamys. Do sit down, Edmund."

Edmund stayed on his feet and paced between the door and the chair, barely glancing at her.

"But that makes mock of the fleet's purpose," she said. "Does it not? The thegns along the south coast would not have been so helpful if they knew their boats were to protect Lunden." Relocating the fleet made Lunden safer, so she had not tried to dissuade the King. But the Danes could sail past Dofras to attack the south coast with the same impunity as ever. She asked Edmund if he considered Rye now vulnerable.

He answered curtly. "Rye is a sprat. Rameslege is an oyster with no pearl. No-one wants it. That's why my father gave it away."

"He hasn't given a single reed."

It was barely fifteen years earlier that King Aethelred and her brother Duke Richard had been embattled, when Aethelred tried to take Cotentin to stop Danish boats using the peninsula as their base for ravaging Wessex. Aethelred was stalled by the Normans, then forced to retreat, but when he brought more men across the sea, a settlement was reached. Emma's marriage to the King of England was the first part of the agreement. At seventeen, she couldn't help being excited at the adventure ahead, the panoply of marriage at Cantenberh, and enthronement as Queen, no less. She'd never be Queen in France. How proud was her mother – normally such a sourgoat – who was from common stock! Aethelred had been more than twice her age, but he seemed jovial, and had agreed that their first son would supersede Edmund, Aethelred's eldest by his first wife, as the next king.

A dozen years on, who was called Atheling? Edmund, not her Edward. Who held Offas's sword? Edmund wasn't displaying it today. He carried one he'd do battle with, tarnished along the flat but honed to a sheen along the edge.

The third leg of the settlement was the gift of lands to her own endowed Abbey of Fécamp. The hundreds at Steyning enriched Fécamp, but as yet the land and waters of Rameslege did not. It was something she had long wanted to address.

Edmund did not. "I didn't come to discuss Rameslege, or Sveyn's next attack, or where father wants the fleet." His irritation was carved into the set of his jaw.

Emma judged Edmund arrogant and not half as clever as he thought he was, but this conversation would have to be endured. She pushed aside the maps and turned to him. "What then. What else has he done?"

Edmund at last seated himself on the sheepskin-covered chair. "Ten thousand. Ten thousand pounds of silver, for Eadric to transport to Sveyn Forkbeard."

Emma shrugged. "What precisely is your problem? Is it too much? Or too little?"

"My problem is, it's both. The last payment was twenty-four thousand pounds. If pacify him we must, until we're ready to stab him in the guts, the payment has to be at least that. What we don't do is flick his ear."

"A low payment leaves the King more money to build more boats, and to arm and feed a strong fyrd. Isn't that exactly what you want?" Emma felt the urge to add the word "idiot," but refrained.

Riled, Edmund sprang to his feet again. "Cutting the gafol screams that we are preparing for war! So Sveyn can prepare too, and meanwhile deliver us a bloody reprimand. We don't know where, and we don't have a hardened force to oppose him even if we did."

What is a warrior to do when going to war is forbidden? She was not inclined to take Edmund seriously. "We should reprieve that Wulfnoth Cild, and bring him back. Not for his boats, but to summon up a timely storm."

For a second she feared her flippancy would spark a tantrum, or better, that he'd leave. But after a glare that would cut leather, he damped his anger and sat once more. "That's the other thing that vexes me."

It was not obvious to Emma why this might be. "There's little point being vexed, Edmund. Wulfnoth is gone, there's nothing we can do."

"It's not the man. The King has told Eadric that Brihtric may burn Wulfnoth's village of Comtyn and take his hides. And a place called Bosham, where the boats were built and probably most of the sailors came from. Wulfnoth was thegn of both. Brihtric has permission to kill anyone who stands in his way, which means anyone he can find. And he must especially seek out Wulfnoth's family."

This was no surprise, and less concern. She said so.

"But Brihtric!" Edmund cried. "He'll take a force of Mercians from Scorham, raze the vills, and slaughter anyone who can't or won't run. Wessex men. No, Wessex women and children, since most of the menfolk are gone. Then how will Ealdorman Aelfric react? He'll be insulted. Worse, he'll fear rebellion when word spreads. If their Ealdorman can't protect them, why should Wessex folk pay those taxes? Why should they come when levies are called?"

She could understand an Ealdorman's pride, and she knew that Wessex and Mercia had been rivals, if not enemies, for longer than they had been allies. "And so…?"

"So Aelfric will muster a force, and he'll attack Brihtric's men in Scorham. If he captures Brihtric, Mercia will have to pay a ransom. He'll hate that, Eadric will. Rich as an emperor. Mean as a bastard."

It was true. There was no such thing as a gift from Eadric, only a purchase.

"So once he has his brother back, he'll send a force down to attack Oxenford or somewhere in Wessex. Then Aelfric will retaliate. Our two strongest lords fighting between themselves!"

"Cloud in the south means sun in the north," Emma said. "Sveyn Forkbeard might die laughing. But these places, Comtyn and Bosham, they must burn. The King is right in that."

"Yes, they must burn. And Wulfnoth, he signed his own kin's death warrants."

She realised why Edmund was heavy of heart. "You have to go there, don't you. You have to get there before Brihtric. You have to give the order. Aelfric will not raise men against you."

Edmund nodded. "You have the King's ear, and you know his moods better than anyone. I don't wish to confront him, but I do want to know how he's likely to react."

She considered his uncertainty. "This is a small matter to him. As long as people know the price of treason, the King will not care who lights the flame or wields the sword."

Edmund nodded. "And the gafol?"

He meant, could she change the King's mind about the ten thousand pounds. "He'll not be told he's wrong."

Edmund sighed, as one who had long ago given up arguing with his father. "One path would be to match the ten thousand pounds of silver with a separate payment," he said. "I could perhaps raise a thousand, or two. But never ten."

He fell silent, waiting for her to speak. She realised why. "No," she said. "Stop there. I cannot get silver from Normandy, and I will not. Even if Duke Richard has it, even if he'd make a loan without the King's seal on the charter, it could not be done in any time that might appease Sveyn."

Edmund remained stone-faced.

"You don't like that path in any case."

"You're right," Edmund said. "So if we do not want to flick Sveyn's ear… might it be better if the payment didn't get to Sveyn at all? The roads teem with robbers."

What on earth was Edmund thinking? "Even if that could be done, a failed payment could bring Sveyn's ire even more swiftly than a derisory one." And if that ire was directed at Lunden… "There's nothing to be done," she said.

"There is one thing…" Edmund's head was frozen. So were his eyes.

Ah. Now she would learn the real reason for his visit. "Which is….?"

"The Five Berhs. A treaty with Sveyn reinstating the old agreement with Guthrum. It only sets down what we know to be true. It could buy us time."

The Five Berhs. England's eastern heartland, stretching from Mercia to the Eastern Sea. So Edmund was prepared to let it become Danelaw once more, in word as in deed. To sacrifice it like a scachis piece. The earth she felt trembling under her feet was the soil of England.

She had viewed Edmund as a belligerent, who saw only the way of steel, not that of silver; and the sooner the clash of hard metals drowned the clink of soft ones, the better. Now she saw that Edmund was capable of playing a longer game. How unexpected. How refreshing. "And you want… what?"

"I want you to do what I cannot. Fathom his mind, and plant a seed."

"You cannot do that?"

"I'm not a woman. I'm not a wife."

Emma's inward smile did not flicker onto her face. She was one of those, certainly. The other was in some doubt, in the eyes of God and one of His servants. She nodded at Edmund. "It will not be quick."

"Do your best."

"You had better go and do your worst, to those people of… wherever it was," she said. "Before Brihtric gets there. Aelfric and Eadric at each other's throats won't encourage Aethelred to renounce any of the realm."

As he left, Emma wondered if perhaps she had found an ally. Edmund Ironside. Who'd have thought?

She returned to the itinerary maps. Perhaps Meddestane, not Seven Oaks, was the better route to Rameslege and Rye.

Aethelred demanded that his family here in Lunden, be they few, should gather for repast. Having issued the order, he immediately relented, allowing Goda to eat in her own room with Hendi, who had come down with the same pox.

It was the first time since the great feast that the others had all been together. Having just finished eating honeyed breads with cheese, washed down with ale, the King was ladling stew from his bowl, and was in a jovial mood. He asked Ecfrida how she had enjoyed the dancing, if Nothman had caught her eye, or Leofric perhaps? Ecfrida was predictably shy in the face of her father's twinkling teases, and sipped wine to cover her blushes.

"Nothman is a man to set a girl's heart a-flutter," Aethelred said. "Don't you think? But Leofric, he got the serious blood, from his mother most likely. Did I see him smile all evening? I did not. Did you, Emma?"

She shook her head, wondering if Alfred would be as handsome as Nothman, if Leofric was as clever as Edward, if people would come to talk about her boys in the same way Aethelred characterised Ledwyn's. She chewed her bread, having declined the stew. "He does have a dour demeanour," she said, before realising that she had stepped into the same place as Leofric's mother. That was not her plan for the evening, so she drank more wine. "Leofric has the most powerful frown in the land. The Waelas are fearful lest they be turned to stone by a single glower."

"Ha! Yes. Stay away from the male Medusa of Mercia, 'Frida my girl." He obviously liked the music of that, because he repeated "The male Medusa of Mercia."

"I only wished to talk with Eadgyth," Ecfrida said.

"Quite right!" said Aethelred. "And did she tell you of any marriage plans between the girl Aelfgifu and one of the brothers?"

That was a likely match, Emma knew. It would help Mercia become one again, extending Eadric's influence. He had a dilemma: which brother to put Aelfgifu with: the elder, or the cleverer? With Eadgyth already aligned with Eadric, she could see how Ecfrida marrying into the other half of Mercia was an idea that appealed to Aethelred. Emma wondered if

Ecfrida might be found a match in Normandy, or if that privilege awaited little Goda alone, in a few years.

Ecfrida shook her head at Aethelred's question.

"Well, you were talking like six-year-olds discussing… well, whatever little secrets six-year-olds discuss. Come on, tell us."

Ecfrida blushed again, more deeply this time. "Nothing. She said nothing. It was just… girl's stuff."

She knew! Eadgyth had told her. Emma glanced at Edward. He was looking into his bowl of stew, hovering his spoon over a dark island meat – beef, perhaps – then a lighter one – chicken? – as if either were more interesting than his father's jollying.

"Nothing interesting or important then," Aethelred said to Ecfrida, bored already. "Unless she's with child, of course."

"She's not." Ecfrida blushed again, which was as much confirmation as Emma needed.

Edward raised his eyes to stare at Ecfrida. He had only looked idle, but he'd been listening hard enough. Emma was sure that he had made the same deduction: Eadgyth had told her sister about her indiscretions with Stigand.

For once, she was annoyed at her son's attentiveness and insight. "And how were the falcons, Alfred?" she asked of her other son.

Alfred's eyes lit up at her unexpected interest. "We caught two young rabbits, and an adult. A mallard, two teals, and some voles and moorhens."

"The lazy bastards will always go for the little things," Aethelred told him. "Bullies, that's all falcons are. High speed bullies. And good luck to 'em."

Alfred didn't know if this was to demean his new falconry skills, of which he was proud. "The mallard, and the big rabbit, we gave them to cook. They're in the stew!"

Not beef and chicken, then.

"That's my boy. Keep us well fed, Alfie, keep us well fed."

He raised a spoonful of stew to his son. Gravy dripped into his lap. "There's a lesson for you. Speed and power. You don't see a hungry falcon, not as long as there are little creatures still crawling, flying and swimming."

Alfred nodded vigorously. Aethelred the falconer, Emma thought, training his bird. She fixed Alfred with a stare. "And did the falcons get all the baby creatures?"

He could not hold her eye.

"If Goda comes crying to me because she's found a dead rodent in her soup, there will be consequences!"

"Yes mother."

"Think about Wilf, Alfred."

"Yes mother."

Aethelred diverted attention away from his more favoured son. "And Edward. What's new with you?"

Edward just shrugged.

"You know what? Given more time, I'd send both of you to join Brihtric. You're old enough to see how things are done."

"What things?" said Edward.

"How to deal with traitors, that's what things."

Emma winced at her boys having to witness the justice to be meted out on those villagers. But it was true, they had to grow up. Aethelred was right about the little creatures.

When Ecfrida and the boys departed, Emma stayed at the table with her husband. "Bishop Hugo," she began, "He asked me about the promised hides at Rameslege."

"Thought he might," he said. "And you told him that once we get reports from our boats now taking the fat friar back home-"

"He's a bishop."

"The bloated bishop, then. Once we know there's no Danish boats in Duke Richard's havens, then we can talk about Rameslege."

"It would do no harm to show we haven't forgotten the treaty."

"It's him who's forgotten the treaty."

"A positive step would help."

"I'm not giving up land for nothing, even worthless shitswamps on the edge of nowhere."

"I was thinking about a survey. Describe the area in question. Its bounds, how many hides, who lives there now, the livestock and crops it supports."

"Livestock! You mean eels!"

"It's not all marsh. There's freshwater streams, and building stone nearby, I believe, and salterns. It is a good haven, if underused. If we show the place has value, he's more likely to act on the Danish boats. I was thinking of going there to see for myself."

Aethelred sighed at such a trivial matter. "If you want to be cold and damp, that's your concern. Why not send one of Wilmaer's monks?"

"I'll take one. But I'd like to supervise. I thought it would be good for Edward and Alfred to come. As you say, they need to see how things are done, and that goes for boring matters, not just the falconry."

"Edward will take to it," Aethelred laughed, "like a usurer to an abacus. Alfred…"

"There's game down there. He can shoot arrows at geese. He might even hit one."

And so it was decided. She would go to Rameslege, taking Edward and Alfred, but not Goda. With Hendi ill, Emma said, she'd be lonely and she'd fret. Aethelred promised twelve of Edmund's men as escort. "Lunden can't spare any," he explained.

She asked whether he thought Cantware safe, if the fleet moves to the Tamys. "It's only weeks since Edmund caught the last force Sveyn sent. Might he retaliate?"

"Not if he wants our silver," Aethelred said. "And if he does, he'll target Eassex, or Anglia, and a berh that prospers. Not a stinking bog like Rameslege."

Rameslege was a minor concern to both Aethelred and Edmund, but vital to her. She was pleased that on this at least, father and son were in agreement.

Twelve men, plus Theo, Wendel and the waggoners, that made sixteen. Four times that number had set out north with Aethelred's silver on its way to Sveyn, and that force would be added to by Eadric, and then again by Sigeferth and Morkere for the final leg. If that many men protected ten thousand pounds of silver, Emma estimated that the guard of sixteen set the value to Aethelred of his wife, his youngest sons and an unmarried daughter at a few hundred pounds each.

No matter. It had been easy to get him to agree to this trip. On another day, he might have forbidden her to even talk about this land long promised to Fécamp.

She took a breath. She needed to approach her next target stealthily. "Edward was asking me about the seven old kingdoms."

"It's not you he should be asking. What on earth do you know about them?"

"Only very little. But he mentioned the Five Berhs. They were never one of the old kingdoms, were they?"

"That's why they're called the Five Berhs. They were scires in Mercia of old."

"But now they seem to be as one, under… who is it? He wasn't at the Witan, was he."

"Not he. They. Ealdorman Sigeferth of Deoreby, Ledecaestr and Snotengeham, and Ealdorman Morkere of Stamsford. The only two brothers I know who actually like each other. Apart from our boys, obviously. But those two are like twins. Sigeferth is jolly enough. Reminds me of Ledwyn. Morkere, he's a sly one, like Eadric himself."

"Why were they not at the Witan?"

She braced herself for angry shouts, but Aethelred was in a mellow mood. "Pah. Sigeferth writes that he's loyal, but do I see gafol from him? No, he delivers directly to Sveyn. He's about as loyal as Uhtred."

Even the King had accepted the loss of Northumbria, and that Uhtred was Sveyn's vassal.

"I made Sigeferth Ealdorman. But for me, he'd still be thegn of Poxberh."

There was a bitterness in his voice, so for now she'd be wiser to talk about the place, not its leaders. "You named four scires. What's the fifth?"

"Lindesege."

"Where exactly does it lie?"

"By the East Sea, with Northumbria to its north and the stinking fenland south. It was once a kingdom in itself, and proud. But over the years it's become more Danish than Denmark. The Danes sailed west and found a place just like home. Flat, misty, boggy, and full of cowards. You'd think they'd look for somewhere different, but the cowards made it too easy to pluck."

That explained why Aethelred hadn't mentioned an Ealdorman of Lindesege.

"Shittiest of the five shitholes."

"Weren't they once under Danelaw? I do wonder, if they are shitholes, how much would it matter if they were again entreated to the Danes?"

"They won't be entreated to anyone! They are part of the realm! And I don't care who lives there, Danish, English or Babylonian, I am their King!"

Aethelred's voice had suddenly grown to a bellow, and Emma knew there was no more to be said about the Five Berhs for now. "And I am their Queen," she said. "Now, do you mind if I talk to Wilmaer?"

"What about? Oh, yes, your survey. If you must. What difference do a few more words on parchment make?"

Emma sighed. That would have been her next point about the Five Berhs. Mon dieu, she thought. She was the best ally and advisor Aethelred had. He didn't know it, and couldn't be told.

15. Comtyn

(Godwin)

"WHY DO YOU NOT LOVE YOUR CHILDREN?"

It wasn't like being blown about on an endless sea, but still, Godwin had to admit that he had only the vaguest idea where he was.

He'd been travelling three days. He was sore all over, and tired as night, while Ash was approaching exhaustion. The horse had willingly cantered over grass, taken the shock of downslopes to his hooves and forelegs, strained on upslopes, and navigated boggy tracks with buried rocks that could so easily sprain a fetlock.

Yesterday he'd been in sight of the sea. Distant boats racked with the westerly wind. None had red sails. Were the surviving Defenas ahead, or behind? They surely would not risk coming inshore at night. But what did he know? He was no mariner.

What would Brihtric do? What sort of man was he? Was he proud and quick to anger? If so, Comtyn and Bosham could face a swift and terrible reprisal as soon as men could be mustered and marched. If cautious, might not Brihtric await word from Ealdorman Eadric? Would Eadric consult with the King? Two days for a messenger to ride to Lunden and back, commandeering fresh mounts along the way. But the messenger was not the crux, for Brihtric would surely still bring his men, if not to attack the villages at once, then to surround them and let no-one flee.

Either way, Godwin must be home by nightfall.

This morning he'd come up behind a troop of marching fyrdsmen. Sixteen ranks, three abreast. Trained men to march so, not a rabble of poor ceorls or thuws hired from their masters. Two more rode horses. Might one of them have been Brihtric himself? Their march was steady, but paced by two lumbering mulecarts, probably packed with weapons to lighten the men's load, food so they might eat marching, and maybe tents.

He had badly wanted to pass them, to hear their conversation and maybe glean where they were headed, and get a sense of how they were armed. But to try would be to ask for a kicking, so he fell back and followed at a hundred yards. At Arun Dell they pushed ahead of travellers standing in line waiting for the ferry. Wherever they were headed, Godwin would be an hour behind before he got across.

He had cut north, to ford the Arun miles upstream where it narrowed and the faster flow made for a hard and gravelly riverbed. He'd coaxed Ash across a current that would make many a horse panic, swimming himself until he found his footing again. Together they struggled up the bank, and all he knew was to keep going west.

At a hamlet a woman helpfully told him to ride into the sun if he wanted west. "Ain't nothing there but hills and trees, mind. High road and low road."

"Which is best?"

"Both shite. Where you looking for?"

Godwin was cautious. "The Hartings," he said. The Hartings were three villages north of Comtyn.

"Don't know the Hartings. I know the Deans, and Sengelton, they's that way."

East Dean and West Dean! They were but six miles from Comtyn. From there, he'd be on paths he knew. He thanked her, and followed Ash's nose west. Maybe the horse could find the way home from here. They were still short of Wulfnoth's hundreds, but his father used to visit the other headmen and thegns all around. He didn't always take Whitebeam.

Ash would not gallop now, and his canters lasted just a few minutes before he slowed, panting and sweating. Foam rimmed his lips, and Godwin knew he needed water, oats, and a few days' pasture. He dismounted and went to Ash's head, stroking his nose. He quartered two of the apples he'd bought at Arun Dell, and fed seven pieces to the horse, talking with his mouth full of the eighth. "Near home now. I know you're tired, but we can't stop. Mother's there, and Saewin, and Sel's aunt, and Eg's sisters. Do you understand? We got to be back before the sun goes down. Then you rest."

Ash sensed something, and walked on as soon as Godwin mounted, before even being heeled.

They came to beech woods, where roots hid under leaves so only walking was wise. They waded a small river. He hoped it was the Lavant, which wound down to Cicaestr, but here in the valley the trees were dense and Godwin had no idea whether the Deans were north our south. He could only continue west.

At the top of a low hill, a clearing provided a view. He could see a village, and by its stone church he knew it to be Marden. He was on Bow Hill, a mere two miles east of Comtyn! He'd walked up here with Gret for wild berries this early summer, and that copse to his right had witnessed their fuck. His home was just beyond the next ridge, Bevis Hill, named for the giant who slept in the barrow under the hill. Bevis was Comtyn's ancient protector in time of need.

Ash must have sensed home too, or smelled a familiar field, for he started lightly forward.

Where were the men from Scorham now? Would they rouse Bevis?

Fear made him put Ash to a final canter, and the willing horse spent his last energies pounding turf and ripping through dogwood and bullace, and blackthorn fat with sloes. They passed grazing sheep and cattle, and came to fields of ripe barley and oats, golden in the sun and awaiting harvest. Up the far slope, onto the top and the stand of whitebeam for which Ash's sire was named, and he saw at last the houses and huts of Comtyn.

His own house, the village's largest. And the twelve smallest: the wicker skeps in which Comtyn's bees made honey, squatting on their platforms. Cudbert and Sel's cottage, Eg's family's, Gret's, Aiden's, Nothelm and Nin's, Garwig's, Heja's who had nursed him, the house of Toglos, called The Bull, who before he lost his mind had with Cudbert taught Godwin all he knew of swords and daggers and archery. In the chapel of Saint Mary, Brother Snell had taught him to read from a Latin bible and from English deeds of title, for one day he would be Thegn and judge of his people here, and witness to warrants and charters and wills.

His father tried to trick him away from all this. Garwig with his half-head of hair, Nothelm, Aiden and his chin, and all the other ceorls and thuws were sailing God knew where with Wulfnoth, while Brihtric marched on their villages with dire intent.

Ostryth who was Balderstan's wife carried water from the well in two buckets hanging from a yoke, and waved a free hand as she greeted him with a carefree smile. "Not a sailor no more?" Her two young ones Lin and Pothweld ran behind him shouting "Godwin, Godwin," and immediately other children joined the gaggle chasing him to his house. A bee flew by, buzzing her welcome.

He shouted "Mother!" even before he dismounted. The noise brought her to the door, and if she was pleased to see him she gave no sign. Tall, strong, and sharp of face and tongue, Saehild could be as excessive in her anger as she was in her joy; but she could also be stone cold, and withdrawn into herself. Today, Godwin thought, was a day she would rather have been left alone in a shuttered house, when even the return of a son she expected not to see for months was an intrusion.

Saewin the Rabbit had no such reserve, and threw her eight year old body onto Godwin's chest, knocking him backwards onto poor Ash's foam-flecked flank. He caught her, squeezed her breathless until her giggles became gasps, and put her down. "Rabbit, I need to talk to mother. I want you to get water for Ash, please. Then get Ferley." Ferley had taught them both to ride, and no-one was better with horses. "And then as soon as you've found him, I need you to go all through the village and call everyone to gather here, outside our house."

Her reddened face looked at him as if he'd slapped her instead of carrying her indoors, and he winced as if she'd slapped him back. But he had no time for love, and no knowledge of how to use it. "You need to do as I say," he ordered. Rabbit blinked back tears, and complied.

On a good day for his mother, she would have cuddled Saewin herself and chided him. On a bad day she would have screamed at him, ignoring the further tears her ire brought to her daughter's cheeks. But this was a dark day for his mother. She just glared from her shadowed eyes and went into the house again. Godwin followed. "Mother, listen."

"You are not supposed to be here," she said.

"So let me say why I am." And before she could object he told her his father's crimes, the diversion to Brimclif, his lies to the men of Comtyn and Bosham. She listened flint-faced as he recounted the conversation he'd overheard by that fire, and she nodded as if Wulfnoth's action had been as inevitable as his greying beard. Godwin skipped the capture of Cudbert and his own threat to Odylia, in case Sae returned, and because he could hear impatient voices outside as folk gathered to hear his news. But he had to tell her about the sea battle, and the losses to the King's fleet. He needed his mother's support now, and he'd not get it unless she understood why they were all in danger.

"Mother, I rushed here because Brihtric will want revenge against us. He will punish us for father's treason. Bosham too, and all of father's thegnship, the Mardens, Walterton, the Ashlings. I saw fifty armed men on the road! They could be here at any moment."

Saehild closed her eyes. Who knew her thoughts? Was he only confirming what she already knew about her treacherous conniving bullying selfish thug of a husband? Was she contemplating life without him? Was she thinking of her childhood in Wintancaestr, which she sometimes told him about? Or her frequent desire to be dead, which came up too?

But some part of her was with him. "Were they Mercians?" she asked.

"I don't know! Probably."

"Ealdorman Aelfric will not allow it." Aelfric was kin.

"Aelfric is not here!" His father had gone. Did that make him, Godwin, Thegn now? He wished he could be so, and command the people to flee. But a thegn must be warranted by Ealdorman Aelfric, or by the King. That will never happen. His stock was utterly discredited. A village might appoint a headman by acclaim, but for this he was still too young. His mother's voice was needed.

On a good day or a bad one she would already be stood outside their door giving orders to the puzzled folk assembling. But this was a dark day, and she was still within herself.

Saewin entered. "Everyone's outside."

There was no time. He must act like their Thegn. He went to the door with no idea what to say, so he stood on the small stoop and held his hands high, as he'd seen his father do two nights ago.

"Where is Wulfnoth?" Nin called.

"Where's Eagbert?" Eg's mother shouted. She knew that where Godwin was, there too was Eg. It had been so all their lives. Yet today, he was not. She held Cwen and Vikka's hands, and Eg's two sisters waited anxiously.

He gazed at the women of Comtyn who would never see their menfolk again, the elders who would not see their sons, who had lost their thuws. There was Bebbe with her ruddy cheeks, Canoc, lined and grey, Whitstege, tired because she laboured while pregnant, Cawlin Droop with his lazy eye. He couldn't tell them their loss now, not if they were to be safe. He looked over their heads at their limewashed huts and houses, the pens and coops and carts, and all the thatched roofs fated to be burned. No-one must be inside when they were.

"There is no time to explain. All I can say is that my father has betrayed Brihtric and the King, and armed men are coming to take their revenge on us. Cudbert and Selferth and Eg, they followed me on foot. Your menfolk have… they have stayed loyal to Wulfnoth and they sail with him still."

His father had fed them lies at Brimclif, but the chasing Dertemuth boats and the order to turn and give battle must have immediately branded the deceit onto Wulfnoth's brow for all his men to see. By then it was too late. They had to turn and fight or they'd surely die. For Godwin, Wulfnoth's betrayal of the King was less evil than his betrayal of those who trusted him.

Comtyn would know the whole truth all too soon, but for now, he must evacuate the village. "You must leave here. We all must. We must go to friends and family, in the Hartings, or Cicaestr, or even hide in the forest. But we cannot stay here. We will be killed. And we cannot go south. Bosham and all along the Ems, the villages will be razed too. Cenwig, I want you to take Linden, and ride down the valley." Linden was a young cob mare, peat-coloured, full of energy, not as fast as Ash but fresher. He could have called for Whitebeam, but Ash had earned time with his sire. And Whitebeam still felt like his father's horse, and not for Godwin to loan. "Give the same warning to all the people. Give it as if it came from Wulfnoth himself, as if it came from the King. They must run, on pain of their lives."

Cenwig, a lanky lad two years Godwin's senior, did not move. He was not stupid, but demons curdled his mind. Wulfnoth had not wanted him.

"But why, Godwin?" Ferley said.

"Where is my husband?" That was Ostryth.

"Safe last I saw. But you are not."

The faces were confused, not frightened.

"You have to believe me!" he cried, but even as he did so he knew he was not his father. He looked down the village street, expecting to see four dozen armed men and Brihtric on his horse. "Mercians are coming, as wild as Vikings, with swords and torches… You have to run, for your lives, for your children."

"But it's near on dusk." That was Brother Snell. "Where can anyone get by nightfall?"

"The woods. The Hartings. Anywhere but here!"

But his words were not strong enough to make Comtyn save itself. What was it he'd read with Brother Snell, about the prophet without honour in his own land? The faces looking up at him were friendly, but lacking faith.

"WHYYYY?" It was a word like a wail, and it came not from an angry questioning villager, but from his mother. She emerged behind him wearing a coat of chainmail, holding high a seax, glaring at the people with the same fearsome black eyes that had terrified him all his life, on the bad days. "WHYYY has my son ridden two days without pause for you, if there is no danger? Why do you not listen to the son of your Thegn? Why do you disobey, when your own lives are at stake? WHY DO YOU NOT LOVE YOUR CHILDREN?"

Thirty adults and more of their offspring quailed at the roar of the dragon.

16. The Forkbeard

(Eadric)

"I wish to see my wife again."

For the third time in as many years, Eadric wondered what he'd do with a King's ransom. Streona, The Grasper, they called him. If he really was such a clawhand, why did he not divert the fifteen carts in his care and hide them in a stronghold somewhere in Salop, say? Why not build a fortress atop the Wrikin?

Because I'll be besieged by Sveyn and Aethelred both, he thought. His whole being was devoted to the cause of keeping Danes out of Mercia. Hard enough to keep Sveyn diverted without drawing down the wrath of Aelthelred too. Let that happen, and he'd need a plan to become King of all England himself, including Northumbria, over English and Danes alike, beheading both Kings and all their heirs. Nothing less than a reach exceeding even Offa's would do; and if he failed, he'd die.

No. Not yet. Sveyn and Aethelred were aging. Their sons were young and hot-blooded. Nature and battle would take their courses. Eadric had a different plan: to ensure Mercia stood like an island rock while torrents raged around it, to be left safe and high after the floods subsided. Then where will the nobles assembled at the Witangemot look for their King?

Still, ten thousand pounds of silver was a healthy fortune even for Eadric so-called Streona.

He rode with Nothman and Leofric at the head of three dozen of his own men, and three dozen more from King

Aethelred under Bullward. Too small a fyrd for battle, so Sveyn need not fear that this was a ploy of Odysseyan cunning. But plenty strong enough to guard the treasure. Only the King and three other lords were able to match it without a muster that could not be kept secret. Ulfcytel was far away in East Anglia, and Uhtred was even more distant in Northumbria. As for Edmund, he was building his fyrd in Wintancaestr, and would no more go to war over this gafol payment than would Eadric himself. Not this year.

They carried their cargo on barges from Tamwerth down the Tam and the Trehynt to Snotengeham, where they met the brothers Sigeferth and Morkere, Ealdormen of the five Berhs. It was transferred to Sigeferth's waggons, and the Five Berhs' own silver was added. The only person Eadric trusted to oversee this, and to count every ounce, was Thyra. Accounting complete and slate marked, she was sent back to Tamwerth. He'd do without her company in whatever bed he was given, for she was a halfdan, with a Danish mother. She might be seen as a traitor to the Danes, and a target for some ambitious freshbeard seeking Sveyn's attention.

A score of Sigeferth and Morkere's men marched with them on the long trek north to Caestrfeld. Not to protect their silver from robber gangs, Eadric reflected, but from himself. It was an unnecessary precaution based on the perception that the treasure was still theirs. It wasn't even halfdan, it was already Sveyn's, and they should have understood that coveting it was far too perilous. Today he was Eadric un-Streona.

The most dangerous part of the journey was the transfer of the chests from the barges onto carts. The bargees knew their trade, tying the gangplanks with their lower ends resting on the boats' gunwale, free to move with the boat as it rocked in the water. Eadric watched as the bargees, screaming and cursing, ordered his men to lift the heavy chests off the barges in just the right sequence to keep the vessels balanced and level. Eadric let them shout their orders, and made sure his men obeyed. He didn't want a chest falling into the river. It would sink deep into the silt, and take hours to retrieve, with a man diving into the muddy water holding a rope. Quicker to bring it up coin by silver coin.

Sigeferth and Morkere may not have been trusting, but the Ealdormen of the Five Berhs put on a fine feast, and found roofs and fresh straw for the men to sleep on between their guard duties. The horses were given oats, and the mules hay.

The five noblemen sat with Sigeferth's wife Aelswyth, and Morkere's concubine of the month Utta. They gorged on ox and ham, mashed beets with butter, trout, sweetmeats, plums, pears and apples, cheeses blue and white, cakes, conserves, honey and pickles. They drank the pride of the Trehynt valley, its ales, and many flagons were emptied. "I love the north for its beer," Nothman declaimed. "Down south we have to drink their pissy wine. If ever I see grapes growing in Mercia, I shall take my sword to them!"

"Grapes in Mercia?" Leofric muttered. "As like to find tigers."

"Tigers… if you do see any, I'll give you good coin for them." This was Morkere.

"Stick with hounds," said Sigeferth. "A tiger might bring down a deer better, but you'd never get it off him for its meat, so what's the point?"

"And can you teach a tiger the difference between a deer and a horse?" asked Aelswyth. "Or a between a horse and its rider?"

The men laughed, eager to draw a smile from a lady of famous beauty. Aelswyth was chestnut haired, and her hazel eyes shone like conkers freshly fallen in autumn. She was of average size, in truth, but her grace when she walked, the angle of her shoulders, the way she bore her head, made her seem tall. At nineteen years of age, she was much younger than her husband, whose second wife she was, the first having died of the slow fever. A distant cousin to Aelfgifu, she was an exquisite blossom on a poor branch of the family tree. If a girl can't be born noble or rich, God may still grant her beauty, and in this, Aelswyth was blessed.

Nothman moved closer, and looked into her eyes like the gallant swain he was born to play. "And if you could have any animal as a pet, my lady, which would you choose? A tiger? A lion, perhaps? An ostrich?"

A Moorish circus had been travelling the land, drawing crowds to see its exotic animals, the lion, mangy by all accounts, but still a lion, the striped donkey, a buffalo with huge arm-length horns that some called an aurochs. It was the ostrich that most fascinated, and those who saw it had to describe the bird over and over to those who didn't, and explain how it could be a bird but not fly. One artist who drew it on parchment would never need to buy a drink again. Folk thought he invented its strange bundle of feathers, its outlandish neck, and those stilted legs which he claimed outran a horse. They said he imagined its frightening leonine roar. But they looked at the image, and they listened, and they bought him beer.

"I would keep my ostrich with my unicorn and my wyvern," Aelswyth said. She considered the matter. "I think I'd choose a stag, so I'd always have a place to hang my cloak."

"I will bring you a stag trophy for your wall," said Nothman, then he leaned closer still so that Sigeferth could not hear his whisper. But Eadric caught it. "I will always have a peg for you to hang your cloak."

Sigeferth was a hard man to offend, but was too important an ally to take any risk with. And Nothman was not wary of Morkere, who might well take offence on his brother's behalf. Eadric sought a way of pulling Nothman away from the girl.

But Aelswyth spoke first. "Or perhaps I'd choose an elephant," she mused.

"For its ivory?" said Nothman.

"No, for a long and useful life sitting on people who fail to please me. Would my elephant be your friend, Nothman? Or would you be his cushion?"

"I will make him my own cushion, my lady, and I will be yours."

"I have cushions a-plenty. Except – I do have need of a pin-cushion. I hope you get my point."

Beauty, yes, Eadric thought, and wit too. But God had been less generous in granting her happiness. The way she flirted with Nothman and turned her back on her husband told him that her affections for Sigeferth were polite but tepid. Still, if a girl must be wed to man many years her senior, she could do worse than to be matched with the burly, affable, and even tempered Sigeferth.

Morkere, for example. He was as different from Sigeferth as it was possible for two brothers to be. Where Sigeferth was running to fat, Morkere was short, and lean. While Sigeferth was fair and bearded, Morkere was dark, and kept a thin band of hair on his lip, over a shaved chin. While Sigeferth's smiling eyes were open and expressive, Morkere's were black, narrow, and hidden under thick eyebrows like thatch slipped over a cottage's windows. His treatment of criminals notoriously went beyond ruthlessness into the realm of wanton cruelty. Morkere might have got to Aelswyth first, and if he'd done so she'd have had to put up with all the Uttas who came and went. He might not have been as patient as Sigeferth as the poor girl failed to produce heirs.

Still, she was a prize, and Eadric harboured a seed of suspicion that should Sigeferth befall an untimely death, Morkere would not be loth to take up his brother's Ealdorship and his young wife together.

Nothman and Aelswyth continued their prattle and banter. From her raised eyebrows and the tilt of her head, Eadric saw that this was merely amusement to her; but Nothman was serious in his effort to charm their host's wife. Morkere had noticed, and soon Sigeferth must do so too.

"A Waelasman was being chased by a lion," Eadric said loudly. "He saw that the lion was catching him, so he stopped and knelt, and he prayed to the Lord to make the lion a Christian. He turned, and lo, there was the lion, stopped, and settled on its knees. So the Waelasman walked back to the lion to pray with it. When he got next to the lion, he heard the beast's prayer. 'Thank you Lord,' the lion was saying, 'For the food you bring to me today.'"

Even Morkere laughed.

They set out early the next day, leaving Aelswyth in Snotengeham. They comprised sixteen waggons with eight men marching beside each, ten in the vanguard, and a score more bringing up the rear. The road to Caestrfeld was rutted from traffic, and many times they had to halt while an oncoming cart pulled off the track with a grumble from its driver, silenced by a scowl from Morkere. These were traders coming south from lands openly accepting Sveyn Forkbeard as their King, into those notionally loyal to Aethelred.

One cart's wheel collapsed near Blideward, so they transferred its load to the other waggons and abandoned it. "There'll be no sign of that when we return," Morkere told them. "Not even with my mark on it. Robbers hereabouts will have it. They'll come out of the forest on one side, or they'll come down from the hills on the other. With luck they'll meet and kill each other."

Eadric looked at the land they travelled. He'd been through Caestrfeld several times, on his way to Donnecaestr and once to Jorvik, but he'd not navigated this road before. The Pen highlands rose to the west, with his own lands in Stafford beyond. Up there, rough hill tribes still lived their meagre lives on dwarf barley and stunted sheep, and sometimes raided his or Sigeferth's villages. He would send men to punish the Penlanders every year or so, while Sigeferth took the view that punishments just made them poorer and more desperate. The result was that Sigeferth's lands were robbed more than Eadric's, so Eadric refrained from calling him a fool.

The road followed the edge of a forest that stretched away, old and dark, for miles and miles to Lincylene, Torksey and Gegnesberh. The forest was home to packs of giant barghests whose slaver was poison. The mere sight of one could freeze a man's heart. A whole fyrd could disappear into that forest, to be eaten and never seen again. It was a place only the most desperate robbers and outlaws would risk.

He rode next to Sigeferth. "Does the King know you planned to travel with us?" he asked.

"Which King?" said Sigeferth.

"The one in Lunden."

Sigeferth rode in silence for several paces. "Will you tell him?"

"I see no reason to," Eadric said. "We have the same first duty, you and I."

"To our King."

"Indeed, and so we tell him. But really it's to our people. And because we have a good King…" He paused, to ensure Sigeferth absorbed the irony. "…there is no conflict. It is the other King in Jorvik who threatens the people, so we do whatever we must to keep him distant, do we not? We give him silver, of course, but we do more. We befriend him, as best we can. Which is why you, with Morkere, are taking this chance to see him."

"Eadric of Mercia, I am a simple man. Say what you want from this meet, and I will tell you if we can assist."

Eadric smiled. There was no deviousness to Sigeferth, and maybe this likeability served him best. "You do know, don't you, that Sveyn will not be well pleased at the size of this payment."

"I hope he won't be too ill-pleased. I wish to see my… my wife again."

Eadric noticed his pause. Two of his sons and two of Morkere's were guests of Sveyn in Gegnesberh. The youths were honoured, they lived well, and would continue to do so for as long as their fathers were friendly to Sveyn. It was his boys that Sigeferth wished to see again, Aelswyth's charms notwithstanding.

"And I mine," Eadric assured him. "First, I have a gift for him. I want the approval of both you and your brother."

"It will need to be a generous gift to allay the loss, as Sveyn will see it, of some fourteen thousand pounds in silver. What is this mighty prize?"

"I cannot tell you before I tell him."

"But you want our nod anyway? Well, Eadric, as long as this treasure is yours to give, I will applaud anything that keeps Sveyn content."

"It is mine, there is no doubt of that."

"You said 'First'," said Sigeferth. "What is second?"

"I want you not to fall off your horse, Sigeferth my friend."

"Unless your proposal is so surprising that it makes my horse rear, I am safely saddled."

"And is she an even-tempered horse?"

Sigeferth leaned forward to pat the mare's glossy chestnut neck. "Normally," he said.

"In that case… I plan to put something to Sveyn. I will

suggest that we represent to King Aethelred for a treaty be drawn, to formally charter Sveyn as overlord of the Five Berhs."

Sigeferth's hands rested on his saddle, and gripped it hard. He let out a long breath into the autumn air. "I am glad Beech does not speak English," he said.

"This I can't do without your knowledge and consent," Eadric continued. "He'll be angry at Aethelred for this paltry payment, but this notion may temper his anger. And to shoot into the target's eye, it will certainly deflect it away from you and me."

Sigeferth settled into his saddle once more. "I'll have to talk to Morkere."

"Of course. Be sure to point out that this only puts onto parchment what is already true on the land."

Sigeferth pursed his lips, and nodded. "Tell me. If it was Mercia to be passed out of Saxon England and forever into Danish hands, would you consent?"

It was a fair question. To query the word "forever", and to point out Sveyn's age, was not the answer Eadric wanted to give. "How does it help our people, if we swim like salmon doomed to struggle eternally against the torrent of history?"

"Our people. How noble you are, Eadric."

Eadric failed to check his annoyance at Sigeferth's sarcasm. "Stand Aethelred next to Sveyn. Who is the stronger? We fucking English are in retreat. And look at what the Danes do – they invade a land, they settle, then they dissolve among its people like salt into boiling water. The water is forever changed, and cannot be unsalted. They made the north their own, they made Normandy their own, they have all but made Lindesege their own. The rest of the Five Berhs will follow, you know this. East Anglia too. What kind of fool doesn't see the inevitable? Yes, for my people. And for yours. Are we not both men of our people?"

"You're a cunning bastard of your people, Eadric, I'll grant you that."

They rumbled into Caestrfeld at dusk. Sigeferth had sent a rider ahead, and Eadric spotted him standing at the town gate next to a huge bearded man with muscles like boulders. The giant leaned on a battleaxe whose handle came to his armpit, in front of a cohort of a dozen men near as big as he. Sveyn Forkbeard's personal guards were an intimidating group, and this was only a portion of them. Eadric had been greeted by Sveyn's guards before, but recognised none of these faces.

"I am Ulf Egilsson. Welcome to Caestrfeld."

Sigeferth dismounted and hugged Ulf Egilsson. They were like two bears, for what Sigeferth lacked in height compared to Ulf, he made up for in girth. He was followed by Morkere, although the younger brother was dwarfed, and stiffer in the embrace.

"Ulf," said Sigeferth, "You have not met Eadric, Ealdorman of Mercia, and Nothman and Leofric, sons of Ledwyn of Hwicce."

"Eadric of Mercia." said Ulf. "I have heard tales of you from King Sveyn himself." He took Eadric's, Nothman's and Leofric's forearms in turn. "You have brought so many ceorls for us to feed. A man might think you feared being robbed." He looked at the carts, and at the chests his men were already unloading and passing down a chain to a solitary building walled of stout planks. A thin priest stood beside the door making marks on a slate. Eadric knew Father Raegnald, King Sveyn's advisor and accountor. Eadric motioned Reede Terning and Criba, his retainer, to go there too, to watch over the honest weighing of the silver.

Ulf was counting already, nodding his finger at the row of

fifteen carts. He went closer to one of them and counted the sixteen chests it held. Whether or not he had the skills of a steward or a reeve Eadric didn't know, but the frown on his face was like a man expecting venison being served a barm. It revealed his reckoning that the cargo was lighter than anticipated.

He led them into a high-roofed hall that was neither lit nor laid for feasting. Sconces and tables were empty, the fire was small, and only a small trestle held any food at all. Cold beef and pigmeat, pickled cabbages, bread, and ale, all hearty enough, but not calculated to make a man feel honoured. Still, the five of them sat with Ulf, and talked of how the harvests looked promising after last year's failures, of trade up and down the north roads, of Ulfcytel and Uhtred though neither had anything to reveal, and of the Scots who never ceased to cross the old stone wall, or such of it that remained. "The southern Scots have the most solidly built hovels in Britain," Morkere said. "You'd think they'd be content."

They would only talk of important English matters once Sveyn joined them, after the weighing, when he'd know how far short of expectations King Aethelred's offering fell. They talked in English for Nothman's sake. Leofric spoke passable Danish, and Sigeferth and Morkere were fluent. Eadric understood more than he spoke, and preferred to keep this skill to himself.

Eadric looked at Ulf's men guarding the door, knowing another eight were without. Murder and hostage-taking would serve Sveyn no purpose, but still there was the risk, should he feel cheated, angered and insulted by the ten thousand pounds, that one, two or all five of the Englishmen might never see the sky again. Aethelred owed him for this.

Sveyn came in with Father Raegnald. Eadric was relieved to see him more sad than irate, for buoying up a downcast King was altogether easier then damping down an angry one. And less dangerous.

Sveyn Forkbeard had once been built like Ulf, but age and appetite had turned his muscle to fat. His hair was long and plaited, but grew only from the back part of his head. His beard, so thick last time they met, was now trimmed, and not even forked. So much hung on the byname. Eric Bloodaxe, Ole the Strong, William Longsword, and Hrolfr the Walker who was too big for any horse. Would England be at Sveyn's feet if he'd been given the title Sveyn Smallbeard, Eadric mused? Eadric would never be rid of his own byname, but he didn't mind, for it inspired a kind of respect. Better Streona than Unraed.

Sveyn left Raegnald standing, and seated himself alone on the far side of the table. He pulled the beef towards himself. A girl who followed him cut his bread and poured beer into a silver cup doubtless fashioned from some of Aethelred's earlier contributions. Sveyn, King of the Danes, ate slowly, and drank. No-one spoke.

He banged the cup down, and beer splashed his hand. He licked it, looking at the five Englishmen in turn. He spoke quietly in his perfect but strongly accented English. "Eadric. What were you thinking, stealing fourteen thousand pounds of my silver?"

Eadric gave a chuckle that exuded a confidence he didn't feel. "You know I did not, my lord."

"Then what was your King thinking?"

Eadric could only turn out his hands and raise his eyebrows.

"Don't imagine you'll have your one-tenth of this paltry offer."

Eadric had given up on that as soon as he knew Aethelred's decision.

"What he's saying," Sveyn continued, "Is this. Please come

into my lands, Sveyn Forkbeard. Choose your province. I have built a fleet with the silver withheld from you, so you will dare not attack the south. I calculate that you will not attack Lindesege or East Anglia because of the Danes living there." Sveyn looked from one to the other, challenging them to disagree. He chuckled. "On Lindesege he is right. I have no need, I can walk wherever I wish. On East Anglia, I haven't made up my mind. Oh yes, I forgot to say." He addressed Sigeferth and Morkere. "Your sons are growing well. They are healthy. They speak Danish as if born to it."

The anxiety now felt by the Ealdormen was palpable. "Did you weigh the extra tribute from the Five Berhs?" asked Sigeferth. "Four thousand pounds of silver, although we have to buy it from the west."

"That four thousand matches the portion of Aethelred's gafol that comes to you from Mercia," Eadric hurried to add. It was a lie, but Aethelred was not here. Even Nothman and Leofric didn't know that Mercia had contributed about one-fifth share of the ten thousand pounds, or that Eadric held much more in reserve. He would be able to exceed the Five Berhs' extra tribute, if things came to that.

"Attacking the Five Berhs will not hurt Aethelred," Morkere said.

"Nor will an incursion into Mercia," Nothman added.

Sigeferth and Leofric seemed happy that it was their brothers who had stated the obvious.

"Perhaps he calculates that I will pass through the Berhs, and march straight to Lunden," Sveyn said. "Perhaps he has his fyrd hidden in the forest, and will waylay me by Waltham. Perhaps he has fast horsemen to tell them if I go to Oxenford, so they must march there, or to Eassex, or that another Great Heathen Army will fall on Readingam, or Alban's Abbey."

Eadric realised Sveyn wanted the message to go back to

Aethelred that Sveyn could send his army wherever the hell he liked, and thus force Aethelred to thin any planned resistance.

"How can we know Aethelred's mind? He doesn't know it himself," Morkere said with rancid distaste.

Eadric felt like clapping him on the back. Sometimes words needed saying, but he didn't want always to be the one speaking them. Then when he did speak, his words would have more weight. "Perhaps, as you consider, there is one new ingredient to throw into the cake…"

"If you came up with a notion I have never thought of, I shall give you one of your chests of silver back."

"Then I'm confident I shall go home slightly less poor. As we rode up here, Sigeferth and I discussed something."

Sveyn looked at Sigeferth and Morkere. The older brother sat forward, his posture saying that he knew what Eadric was about to say, and agreed with it. Morkere leaned back, but did not look away. Eadric hoped that the brothers had taken the chance to talk together as they rode.

"To speak plainly," he said, "the old treaties between Alfred and Guthrum are eaten by time. The Five Berhs are part of the Danelaw, but then, so once were East Anglia and Eassex who now look upon Aethelred as their King. He would not brook that they are other than his lands. But the Five Berhs? One day Aethelred might want to reclaim them properly, too."

"We do not want war in our lands, or over them," said Sigeferth.

"But then," Eadric continued, "since he does not know his own mind, I judge – we judge – that King Aethelred might easily go the other way. He might formally and openly recognise the current reality, and therefore issue a charter, granting you overlordship of the Five Berhs, all the way beyond Lyccidfeld and Stafford-"

"A line from Watling Street to the Nene River, to be precise," said Sigeferth, "Restoring to legality Alfred's old charter with Guthrum."

"Eadric, Sigeferth, hold your mouths shut," Sveyn snapped. He seemed more angered at the possibility of being given land than he'd been at the niggardly gafol payment.

Eadric recognised that Sveyn might dismiss the idea, but why anger?

"How does such a forfeiture benefit either him or me? What King can command his people if he relinquishes, what, a sixth of his realm without even a fight?"

"Its value would be taken into account in any future gafol."

"It already is," growled Sveyn. "And as for me, you did speak plainly. With apologies to you Sigeferth, and you Morkere, I am already overlord of the Five Berhs. What do I care for charters?"

So Sveyn thought he was being sold a pup. Eadric tried his best. "It would mean he would renounce all law-making, and all taxation. He still collects taxes, where he can."

"The people resent it," said Sigeferth. "They have no love for Aethelred. Reduce their burden, and they will have love for you."

"Love? You English, you love the King who taxes you least."

"We love the King who protects us most," Sigeferth said.

"Protects you from who?" Sveyn demanded. "We know damn well that Aethelred won't march north. He won't protect your chickens from a fox."

"Edmund might," said Eadric. "I don't know if he wishes to expand the kingdom he will one day inherit. I do know that he's inclined to the idea that attack is the best form of defence."

"It will be easier for us to argue against him if we can call on a treaty signed by his father," said Sigeferth.

"You win loyal people and prosperous lands, with not a single sword drawn or arrow shot," Morkere added.

Sveyn's chin jutted forward, and his little beard bobbed like a wagtail as he thought. "There is one germ of an idea in this proposition. I shall post men on Watling Street, and along that line to the Nene which you will show me, Sigeferth. They will kill any tax collectors who cross it, in either direction, and your people will love me for it. Eadric, you have your chest of silver."

He had done his best to mollify Sveyn with the offer of the Five Berhs, but since Sveyn was unmoved by mere symbols of rule, it was true that it offered little benefit to him. The Five Berhs were all but torn from Saxon England, but they were evidently safe, for why would Sveyn lay waste lands he felt were his already? He doubtless saw the prospect of Edmund invading as nothing more than a kite flying over a distant hill. Sveyn had talked about Oxenford, Readingam, and Albans… the danger of another Great Heathen Army sweeping across Mercia was more real.

It was time to offer his gift, one that all kings respect. "We did not ask, how is your wife? Are your children well, and growing up brave and wise?"

Sveyn threw back his head and roared with laughter. "How easily you give up, Eadric! Yes, they are well. They flourish in Denmark."

Sveyn's eldest was his daughter Estrith, and he had two sons, Knut and Harald. Previous years had seen Knut sail the eastern sea to live in Jorvik; but never had Harald made the journey. Thus Sveyn's plans for his sons were as clear as mountain springwater.

"And how is your wife?" Sveyn said. "And your children? Oh, you have none, forgive me."

Eadric let that predictable barb glance off the chainmail of his smile. "Eadgyth is a picture of health, but deeply sad that she has not borne me children. God's will seems to be that I must grieve in that regard. But as you know, my ward Aelfgifu brings me as great a joy as any daughter."

"And hopefully a lot less vexation. Between ourselves…" he leaned over his beermug "…Estrith is a Valkyrie, and I pity the man who has to marry her."

"Ah, Aelfgifu is sweet, and bright. She has spirit enough to charm, but is no Valkyrie. And beauty! You may accuse me of bias, but for me she shines more brightly even than Lady Aelswyth. They are cousins, you know. They share the blood of a common grandmother – such a beauty she must have been! Edmund Atheling set his eyes on my Aelfgifu, and once set, could not tear them away."

"And so Eadric of Mercia burrows ever closer to England's crown," said Sveyn, with a knowing glance at the others at the table. Then he leaned closer to Nothman. "And what do you think of that?"

Eadric felt Nothman bristle. His mouth opened, but he had no reply. So Nothman wanted Aelfgifu. Of course he did.

Poor fellow. Eadric took Sweyn's attention from him. "And Knut? What kind of man has he grown into?"

"A boy to make his father proud. Strong as a battleaxe and twice as sharp. Perhaps next time we meet, I shall bring him."

"The rumour is that he is in Lindesege. It would be an honour to have met him today. But perhaps that would be premature."

It was now clear to all that Eadric was heading somewhere with this conversation. The other five men at the table fell silent. Eadric too stayed quiet.

It was Sveyn who lost patience first. "Why premature?"

"Because I wish to make a proposal that concerns him." He let his pause extend, but not so long that Sveyn would end it. "I offer you Aelfgifu to be Knut's wife."

The remnants of Sveyn's beard near fell off his chin. He was again silent for a long time. Nothman started as if to say something, but Leofric's grip to his arm was swift and firm.

Sigeferth, realising that Aelfgifu was the secret gift Eadric had spoken of, shook his head in wonder, and no little admiration.

Eadric knew that Sveyn was thinking about nobly born girls in Denmark, and what their marriage to his son might mean at home. Which alliance offered the greatest advantage? He was thinking about families in Svege too, and the Norselands, and – who knew? – Kiev and lands east. Whichever land gave Knut a wife, that land would give too a dowry of loyalty.

And he was thinking about Northumbria, and Jorvik where Aelfgifu was born, and Eadric's province which now claimed Aelfgifu of Northamtun. He was thinking about Mercia, and about England entire.

At last Sveyn looked straight at Eadric. "Is she arrowed? Is she is a maiden?"

17. Collier Trud

(Walt)

"I can't sleep sound now."

He had to force himself away from that place. All he owned now were the doll, his blanket, his clothes, his shoes, and the pouch with two sceatts that had stayed hidden under him. He didn't even dare try to buy anything at the next hamlet, fearing his coins would be snatched on sight, and the trade would be a beating. He skirted villages, though he looked from afar with a fox's eye at the chicken runs and the coops. How he longed for an egg, even a raw one. He wished he'd made the journey in spring when nests were occupied and eggs not yet hatched, when rabbit kits were stupid.

Pickings were meagre, and Walt felt himself weakening, walking more slowly, losing his will to find the north, but knowing he'd come too far to return to Croming. He tried making a snare with broken sticks and thread pulled from his blanket, but without his string and knife it was a frail trap that rabbits laughed at. He found fungi, but dared not eat it. With no hooks and net, his fishing was reduced to tickling, but after he'd stood in the cold water for hours and seen nothing troutlike and large enough to tickle, he resorted to using his shirt as a net. This way, he caught some minnows whose heads he bit off to use as crayfish bait. He caught three – though more escaped – and ate their thumb-sized nuggets of flesh raw. But he had no shirt to wear that night, and had to carry it damp in the morning, searching for some sun.

He had barely survived in the wild when he'd had his gear;

he knew that without it he was reduced to begging, for he was barely able to offer the lightest of labour. Only the comfort of having the two coins kept him going. He'd shortly have to risk showing one.

When he saw a distant wisp of smoke rising above the trees one morning, he walked through the forest to its source, uncaring what cruelty he might meet, if only it came with hot food. The smoke rose from a small circular hut in a clearing. It had the mound of a charcoal kiln alongside, and he walked to it hoping it was fired and he could sit near, and lay his shirt over it to dry. The kiln was cold.

Both hut and kiln were permanent structures, with walls of flint and clay. The hut's roof was thatched with thick reed, dark with age, patched and built up over the years until hut and roof looked like a big flattened mushroom. A bodged stool stood by the door, buckets, rakes and oak shovels leaned against the stout wall, and a nannygoat was tethered alongside, nibbling at the short grass in the radius of her tether post. The hut was surrounded by piles of cut timber, branches tightly stacked and overlain with a crude thatch of fern and bracken. He recognised cabbage, carrot and turnip greens growing in a small garden on the far side of the hut.

Walt called tentatively "Hello?"

The cloth at the entrance was peeled back, and an old woman stepped out. She had grey hair and a white face, and white hands too, but her clothes were black as soot. Best of all for Walt, she was fat.

"You sent to buy?" she said, and he had a sudden panic that the charcoal Petwin used to render down his tallow had come from that very kiln, that she was a friend to the candlers, and word had spread of a thief hereabouts. She would kick him back to perish in the forest.

He just shook his head.

"What's yer name?"

"Walt, son of Waltheof, from Northwold." He didn't want to remind himself where he was really from.

"Then why ain't you in Northwold?"

"Ain't nothin' for me there no more."

"Was you outlawed?"

To be placed outside the King's law was shaming, dangerous, and perilous to any soul in need of someone's trust. "I was never. I swear on Jesus' own wounds."

She regarded him silently. She wanted more.

"The Headman, he killed my father, and he came after me." It was nearly true.

"Why?"

"He said my father stole from him, but he didn't."

She merely pursed her lips and nodded. "Ain't much of you, Walt son of Waltheof."

Either she had chosen to believe him, or it didn't matter to her. His face brightened. "I can work. For a meal."

"Puh," she said. "Look at you. You need the meal first.

"Feed me right, I'll do three times as much tomorrow."

Her eyes were relaxing as they got used to the brighter light outside her hut. He saw her facial wrinkles were inlaid with black where soot was ground into her skin like a tattoo. "When'd you last eat?"

"Yesterday, except leaves."

"So you work better on a full stomach," she said. "Most do. Better feed you then." She ushered him into her home.

It was warm inside, so warm that he thought the fire built in a clay firepit must have been alight all night. Perhaps it never went out – colliers never went cold, as cobblers never went barefoot. Walt was soon as warm as he could remember. She showed him a hook on which to hang his wet shirt.

The walls and ceiling were black like her clothes, and all he could see of her were the white hands and pale face and hair.

The hut was festooned with tools hanging from walls and rafters, all black save the gleaming sharp edges of her hatchets and axes and knives. Bunches of dried herbs hung too, and smoked fish and meats. Her bed was a wooden platform softened by a flat mattress. She sat him on a second platform, and he realised that at one time a family had lived here. Was she the last of them?

She broke off a heel of bread and gave it to him with a thick slice of soft cheese and an apple. "I'm Trud," she allowed, before watching him down the breakfast in bites too big. She unhooked her dried meats and fish from the beams and pushed them through a knee-high door into a small pantry on the north side. Did she fear he'd steal them, or were they just now dried enough and wanting to be stored in a cooler place?

The bread swelled him, the cheese was sharp and goaty, and the apple's tang brought water to his mouth and eyes, but he didn't taste them so much as feel them in his mouth and his belly, planted there, giving him strength.

"Right. Time you pay for breakfast in blisters," she said.

She got him to walk with her through the forest, until she stopped and pointed out a sapling grown to the thickness of his lower leg. Together they felled it, and trimmed off its twigs and leaves. They went on, passing more saplings the same size, until she picked out another destined to become charcoal. They felled more, and he saw no reason why any one was better than the rest. She sent him up bigger trees with the axe to lop branches she pointed out, and he saw earlier cuts, old and healed, one or two per tree, and wondered how long she'd been doing this, and who taught her how much pollarding a tree might take. Her father, perhaps.

They walked on, dragging the boughs to a head-high shelter of bracken tied like brown fishscales onto a sloping frame. They added the fresh branches to the piles already started, and

Trud pulled out older seasoned branches, saying they'd return for them later. On they went, felling, pollarding, trimming, and finding another shelter where the green wood would season. Walt noticed that each shelter had three large rocks resting beside it.

The trackless forest all looked one to Walt, and he could not have found Trud's hut again should they be separated; but from the moss-side of trees and the occasional glimpses of sun through the canopy he thought they were meandering generally west.

They stopped to drink from a stream, and she pulled out a flatbread and a leaf parcel, which she opened to reveal a white ball of goatsmilk cheese. This she spread onto the bread, and they sat on stones, eating like reeves. Trud said "It good to get some higher branches down. I can only cut saplings these days now, but that's like flaying the forest's feet when all you want is a trim of its fingernails."

Sometime around mid-afternoon, Trud turned, and Walt's guess that they were retracing their steps was confirmed when they came to one of the shelters with its rock collection. The smaller of the three rocks was the size of a man's head; the larger two both had slight indents. Trud cradled one of the seasoned boughs in the indents so it bridged the rocks. She hefted the third stone above her head.

"Stand back," she ordered, before throwing the stone down onto the bough's unsupported middle, cracking it into two. "Easier than the axe," she said. Walt had to admire her strength – he doubted he could have lifted the stone. In this way she reduced the seasoned boughs and branches to three-foot lengths, which she bound into faggots to be carried on their backs in heavy bundles. Trud carried two; Walt could only manage one. She laughed. "Heavy? Don't worry, we can fetch the rest come morning."

By the time they brought the load home his legs were ready

to buckle, and his back and shoulders screamed for rest. His hands were blistered, his fingers had no grip.

They rested a while outside her doorway. "Five days for cut and collect," she said. "Two days for a burn. I don't have no Sunday. The lot you cut today won't be for burning for weeks, so's it can dry first."

He wondered at the lonely life of the collier. She was getting old, this Trud, and had no-one to whom to teach her craft.

She stood, and beckoned him to follow. They circled well beyond the perimeter of her clearing, and Walt saw she was patrolling the rabbit runs. Two dozen snares she'd set, for a catch of three adult rabbits. Twenty snare for decent fare. She smiled at him. "You my lucky boy, my charm," she said. "You not be hungry tonight."

She made a stew of one whole rabbit, with the other two skinned and hung from a rafter. She cut in carrot, turnip and cabbage from her garden, and rolled in dried chervil and sage from sprigs on the rafters, and a handful of dried mushrooms from a pot. Walt was a little concerned at seeing these go in, but assumed that she'd been eating them for years. She handed him a big wooden spoon. "I go out now for a bit. You stir this now and again till I get back."

He began to stir.

"No no!" she yelped. "Not widdershins! Don't you know nothing in Northwold? Never stir widdershins, or you stirs in the devil."

"What's widdershins?"

"When you looks at the sun, which way goes it across the sky?" She made an arc with her hand, answering her own question. "Widdershins is t'other way, not God's way."

Days he spent, working hard, eating well, and rebuilding his strength. She noticed that he was deaf in one ear, and when she saw him cupping it with his hand, she asked if it ached? It did, a hot throbbing as if that devil Dane had placed one of his demons' hearts inside his head, and now it was rooted and growing.

"Was you hit there?" she asked.

He told her about the attack on his village and how he'd been laid cold by a pagan. Trud could tell there was more to the story, but she probed no deeper. She made a salve, with oils and leaves from her various jars and pots, pulped in a bowl. She spooned it into his ear and tied a bandage around his head. "That'll draw out them imps the pagan let in, and then you'll hear again."

Visitors came, women with bags to buy her herbs and potions, and men with sacks to fill with charcoal. Some brought eggs or cheeses or meats in barter, some had coins, and some came to mend a tool or sell Trud a pot. They all knew her, and they all greeted her in friendly enough ways, but none stayed for food or long conversation. When Walt was alone with her, she talked more to herself than to him.

He slept warm and secure, curled up on his right side so that his head wouldn't weigh on his ear. That was when the nightmares started. They were like the visions he'd had when he'd eaten those strange mushrooms shortly after leaving Croming, that had raised dragons and helms and axes. But worse, for the fungal visions did not include his mother's dead face, nor Portheof's blackened body, nor Benna's doll and her blood, nor Jack's split skull. Nor had the mushrooms drawn up such terror as he felt now, seeing the axe rising above him, terror that he was about to die over and again with each blow, and through it all unable to rouse himself and run.

He was shaken awake by Trud. "It's not real no more Walt, it's your nightmare is all." She held his hand as he tried not to cry but just emitted a low keening wail, then when the whine turned to sniffs she boiled up a posset and ground some dried root onto it. "Valerian," she said. "For sleep." As Walt drank, she asked him to tell her what he dreamed. He couldn't, and she didn't press.

She gave him the drink every evening, and some nights it helped.

He didn't count the days he spent there, but it took them past two charcoal burns and a new moon. He went out every morning to re-set the snares along the rabbit runs. Some had to be relocated, because rabbits weren't entirely stupid. He knew of old that they smelled death at a successful snare site, and made new paths.

As he worked, he thought about his life. He wondered if he could stay and learn the woodsman's and the collier's trade. It was a lonely life, but he could cope with solitude. Trud would not be able to do this work forever. Some aspects, like pollarding, were already a struggle for her.

Or he could continue north. What was he going north for? A family he might not be able to find?

He'd been away checking and re-setting snares for a couple of hours, and was returning with two rabbits. He recognised the donkey cart by its new wheel, and recognised the skinny man by his wispy hair. Aside from the blacksmiths, Petwin the candler must be among Trud's best customers. Walt turned away, trying to disappear into the trees, but Trud had seen him, and she called "Walt, come here, fill these sacks."

Petwin turned. He kept his silence as Walt approached.

Walt handed the rabbits to Trud, and picked up a broad oak-bladed shovel leaning against the hut. Petwin held his sack open, and Walt shovelled charcoal to fill one sack until Trud, having hung the rabbits, said "Enough."

Petwin tied it and opened another.

As Walt filled it, Petwin looked levelly at Trud and spoke

low and slow. "We knows this 'un. He comes to us, we gives him work for a meal, but…" It was as if he was waiting for his wife to finish his thought. Walt could have stood in for her, because he knew what Petwin was about to say. "But we knows him for a thief. You don't want his likes here, Collier Trud."

Walt's hands shook, and he spilled the next load onto Petwin's feet. It wasn't a deliberate mistake, but he was pleased. He gripped the shovel harder. Until he controlled himself, until he was sure he wasn't going to swing it at the liar's head, he didn't dare speak.

"Stole candles. Maybe other things we hain't noticed yet."

Walt saved Petwin's skull by throwing down the shovel. "I never stole!" he yelled. "You cheated me, you put me out in the rain when you said-"

"We give you shelter," Petwin said. He turned again to Trud. "We give him shelter, like we say, and he steals from us. You want to get rid of him Collier Trud. He's no good."

"Ain't stole from me," Trud said, as Walt picked up the shovel to begin filling another sack.

"Ah but he will. He'll eat your larder bare and go on his way, but before he does, he'll slice you with your own knife and take your coins you got hid, and then where'll I get my fuel?"

"You're the thief," Walt accused. "You stole my work, and your village stole everything else."

"He lies too," Petwin said. "Tells a tale he's from Northwold, but he ain't. I asked the priest there when I went selling candles."

"Wasn't for me," Walt said, "you'd have no candles to sell."

"You sell all the way up to the coast?" Trud asked.

"Northwold ain't on the coast. He's an outlaw, Trud. He'll say he ain't, but he surely is."

"Three sacks do you?" was all Trud said.

Petwin opened a fourth sack to be filled, paid her, and took his fuel away on the cart. Trud disappeared indoors to hide the money before letting Walt in, as usual.

They weren't pollarding or fetching wood from the forest today, for they had a big stack of seasoned boughs ready for a burn. Walt was kept busy preparing the kiln, then tending the vegetable garden, and binding another layer of ferns onto the roof. Trud cooked another rabbit, and after they'd eaten she sat facing him.

It was plain that she had something to say, so he tried to get his words out first. "It's true I tried to take two pair of candles. I'd worked all day, and they said I could have somewhere to sleep, but they made me go outside, and the shelter they put me under didn't keep the rain off. I wasn't even going to take the candles, I just had to go back into their hut for my blanket, and I found them and thought they were fair payment."

"Why'd you lie?"

"I never lied!"

"Northwold?"

He hung his head. Why did I not say Croming, Walt thought? Because I was suspicious, and in the habit of hiding. Stupid, stupid.

"Where you from really?"

"A place called Croming. On the coast."

"And you ain't there why?"

He couldn't speak it. Trud just said "Bah," knowing it was the place of his nightmares. "Thing is," she said after a long silence, "I can't sleep sound now for what the candler told me. 'Cause you did steal."

"You've been kind to me, Trud. You've been fair. I'd never do-"

"Ah but you lie. And now I don't know, so I can't sleep. You got to go Walt. You been a help, but you got to go."

He was not angry. He did not feel cheated. Their understanding was terminated, that was all.

"I give you a bag of food to take. I'm sorry it's near night, but I been thinking all day. And at least you fed."

He nodded. Food for the road would help, but what he needed were replacements for everything he'd lost. "I want cord. I want a knife. A steel and flint. A net if you have one. I'll pay you for them."

"No net, not spare. Charcloth you can have. That and the rest, I give you, 'cept the knife."

The knife he'd have to buy. A knife demands respect, if it feels unvalued it will turn on both gifter and receiver.

One sceatt, and the trade was done. It was not much of a thing, with half its wooden handle gone and its blade sharpened down to little more than a short skewer. It could skin a coney, and the point could prong a carrot, but it had not the weight to chop bone, not even a rabbit's. She gave him a cloth to wrap it in, and he slipped it under his belt.

He didn't know how to say goodbye to the old woman. He felt moved to kiss Trud and thank her, but the thought that maybe she'd not been touched since she was a girl held him back. So he took his bag, his blanket and his waxed cloth, and said goodbye to her, to her food, her warm hut. He walked away with the knowledge that she had probably saved his life.

And it was Petwin who would have robbed him of it, and who now robbed him of Trud's refuge.

He was another fucking Dane. Walt's hatred became no longer visceral, as it had been, but cold and rational. Be they Viking raiders in dragonhead boats or candlers settled in English villages, Danes lied and robbed and killed and raped. They were the source of all evil in his world, and he would take revenge whenever and wherever he could.

He set off up the trail that Petwin had taken.

It was well after sunset by the time he reached the

spot where he'd been assaulted. He stepped off the track, out of sight of the village, to refine his plan. He wrapped the blanket around himself, and his eyes grew ever more sensitive as the night darkened. An hour and more after the last activity ceased and the last rush candle was extinguished, he made his way around the village to approach Petwin and Gro's hut from the rear.

There was the cart and the tethered donkey, the fireplace, and the cauldron under its feeble canopy. The four sacks of fresh charcoal would be inside the hut, Walt knew, but dry charcoal lay in the ashes under the cauldron, and more was stored below the hearth, ready for Petwin to stoke the furnace. Moving slowly and silently, Walt made a pile of charcoal on a shovel, and took it away from the hut so there was no chance of anyone hearing him strike his flint to spark the charcloth. The cloth caught, and he placed the charcoal twigs, then bigger lumps, over it, and blew until they glowed red.

As he approached the bowl of solid tallow, he didn't know what would happen. He only knew two things: that tallow burned easily, and needed a wick to control its burn; and that the cauldron of water was to melt it without allowing it to overheat. The first glowing charcoal lump rested for an instant on the tallow before subsiding into its own melt. But not all the way – the charcoal floated, and served as its own wick, and the tallow burned from it in a flame the width of his hand. The second piece did the same, and the third, and the pools of molten tallow merged, and suddenly the whole of the tallow bowl was a lake of living fire.

Walt stood back, flushed with its heat and astounded at its beauty. He could have stared at it all night, but he still had a mound of glowing charcoal on the shovel.

He went to the hut, raised the shovel, and tipped it onto the thatch. The charcoal nestled there, the reeds caught, and flames quickly spread up the pitch.

He wanted more. He wanted to turn the tallow out onto the ground, but the bowl was too heavy, and now, too hot. And more, he wanted to stab Petwin and Gro as they ran out of their door, but that was too risky, and his knife too light. And yet more, to set fire to the whole village, to stab the boys and the Headman as they fled their blazing cottages. But that was impossible.

Then it came to him that Petwin, Gro and the villagers were not the root of his plight. They had done him less harm that the Danes at Croming. And even those monsters weren't the source of the evil that had befallen his family. No, it all sprang from Elfhelm of Jorvik, who unjustly killed Walt's loyal father and forced his family to flee south, to where the Vikingr raided. Of those who must pay, Elfhelm should be first.

A loud crack of split stone told him that the glazed bowl had not survived being trapped between the hot burning tallow inside it, and the cauldron of cold water in which it sat.

Walt had to run now, so run he did. He was not running away any longer. Injustice would be met by justice, this he promised himself. His ear hurt with each step, but he was happier than he'd been for numberless days since last he was at home being pestered by Benna, punched by Portheof, sneered at by Djorka, and held by his mother.

18. The Bedpan

(Fleada)

"A little favour, if you please."

Fleada was disappointed. While Eadric took Eadgyth with him as far as Tamwerth, Aelfgifu was instructed to stay in Coventre. It was a shame, because Tamwerth was but a short trip to Lyccidfield, her favourite place, and Aelfgifu's too. Coventre had nothing at all to commend itself, with bare rooms, poor food, and draughty halls. But there was no arguing with Eadric's desire to keep his ward as safe as possible in the heart of Mercia. Tamwerth and Lyccidfield, he said, were too close to Sveyn. No, of course Sveyn will not turn on Mercia, nor harm my family in any event. But men at war, they sometimes will not be controlled. Why Eadric did not have an equal wish to protect Eadgyth was a mystery.

Coventre was certainly safe, and they were free to roam. The other novelty was that the daughter of Coventre's Thegn had offered to take them to a place she knew to the south, where land sloped gently down to the bank of the Avon river. Fleada had met Godgifu but once, and being three years younger and six inches shorter had found her both haughty and frightening. Now, seated on a stallion big enough to carry a man to battle, Godgifu looked more intimidating still. Her hair was the same chestnut colour as her horse, and her face nearly as long. With her high cheekbones, wide mouth and strong chin, Fleada supposed her handsome rather than beautiful, and wondered if the girl was the kind who would look ever better as she aged.

Fleada was fated to become as dumpy as her mother, she

knew, once she had a child or two.

Aelfgifu rode her pony Guelder. She called him a palfrey, so tall and elegant was he, not pony-like at all. Fleada was unsure of the distinction, but Aculf the stableboy said it was Aelfgifu's pride that stopped her hearing the word "pony" when he spoke it. More amusing to Fleada was Aelfgifu's choice to name the pony Guelder, for a rosebush, and for the fact that he was far less boy-like than he was pony-like.

Fleada's mount was definitely a pony, a stocky nameless Waelas fellow probably stolen in a raid across the Sabrin. But he could trot and canter and gallop, and although Fleada had no stirrups she didn't lag too far behind when Aelfgifu and Godgifu stretched their horses' legs across the flat lands beyond Coventre's walls. Hector and Paris trotted beside them, detoured to explore the rich smells of field and hedge, then bounded to catch up like the hunters they were.

When Godgifu took a notion to canter off ahead, Fleada asked her mistress if it was possible that they might never see Lyccidfield again.

"Of course we shall." Aelfgifu's mood bloomed like a fresh nosegay. "I love it there best too. We shall go soon, and we shall go to Hereford and Stafford and Wulfrunheaton and Weogorna and everywhere!"

Fleada smiled, but could not share Aelfgifu's optimistic outlook, for it was not the towns of Mercia she most wished to visit. "Do you think we shall ever see Jorvik again?"

"Why would I want to see Jorvik?" Aelfgifu spoke sharply, annoyed at having her posy so suddenly crushed. She heeled Guelder to a trot, and this time Fleada didn't try to catch up. She just called "I'm sorry," at Aelfgifu's back.

And she was. She'd put her own feelings above those of her mistress, and that was unforgiveable. For Aelfgifu, Jorvik was the site of her mother's and father's murders. The placename echoed cruelly in the hollows of an orphan's soul. For Fleada,

Jorvik had been a bustling focus in her life. She wasn't born there, but she'd gone many times to the market with her family to sell the honey and the cheeses that her village produced. Her father had convinced his villagers that just one person setting up a stall at the marketplace was better for them all than everyone going, competing for space and attention, and undercutting each other. So the village prospered, and Fleada was happy. Being chosen to be one of Aelfgifu's playmates in Jorvik, and thence the honour and opportunity of being her handmaid, these too were points for the place.

She was brought into Mercia. She loved her mistress, she did, but she loved her mother, her father and Ozzie and Nothryth too. She wondered if they still prospered, if they were in good health, if they missed her as she missed them.

Aelfgifu caught up with Godgifu, and Fleada struggled to keep the two older girls in sight until they reached the spot Godgifu had chosen. "My father's land," she said as she dismounted. "We shan't be seen here, and if we are, the ceorls all know me and will keep themselves scarce."

Fleada was sure they would.

They untethered their bags and unsaddled the horses, and let them wander to eat the lush meadow grasses and lap at the crystal clear river water. They put a cloth on the grass and spread out their breads and pies and apples and cheeses to share. Fleada carried bones for the dogs.

Godgifu produced a flask of wine and passed it around, showing no disdain when Fleada drank too. She asked about the feast in Lunden. "I wanted to go, but my father decided not to get mixed up in all the Witan's arguments and dealings. I think he feared he might have to choose a side."

Aelfgifu was affronted, or pretended to be. "His side is Mercia!"

"Surely it is," Godgifu replied. "That doesn't mean he wants to wave the Mercian Wyrm in the King's face."

The leg-less dragon was the symbol on all Eadric's banners.

"Why did you want to go?" Fleada asked.

"Why, to meet a thegns' son who isn't a Mercian," Godgifu said.

Aelfgifu snorted, and red wine came down her nose like thin blood. "Sorry," she said, wiping her mouth. "I think, Godgifu, that my Godfather can be trusted to keep Mercia safe. I think we are safer here than Wessex."

"There are rumours of Danes gathering less than two day's march east of here."

"Eadric is returning from seeing King Sveyn at this minute. He will have ensured we stay safe. If there is a force, it is going to march south. So much for marrying a southern thegn!"

Godgifu was silenced, and from the downturn of her mouth, didn't like it.

"If you want to marry a southerner," Aelfgifu said, "nothing less than a prince will do. You know I danced with Prince Edmund," she added, as if that was as common in her life as chatting with a stable-boy.

The downturn of Godgifu's mouth spread to her eyes.

Aelfgifu pressed home her advantage. "Oh yes. He is very handsome. Nothman and Leofric were so jealous, you could see green steam coming from their ears! You know the Hwiccans?"

"Of course," Godgifu snapped. "And I will wager you ten silver pieces that you and I will be sisters-in law before many years have passed."

"I would pay a hundred sceatts to avoid that," Aelfgifu cried. "A thousand!"

Godgifu glared at her, and instantly Aelfgifu was contrite. "Oh no! I didn't mean I would not want you as a sister! I meant, well, you are older than I am, so you'd marry

Nothman, leaving me with Leofric. He has lips of muttonfat and the eyes of a dead pig."

"I know!" Godgifu said. "But I'd still rather have him than Nothman, who has the fingers of a squid, and a brain to match." She shuddered.

Then, to Fleada's surprise, the girls started to laugh. She didn't know who started, but once the laughter was out, it couldn't stop, but ran from one to the other and back like a shuttle in a loom. When Aelfgifu confessed that Prince Edmund had kissed her, Godgifu was open-mouthed more in wonder than envy, or so it seemed to Fleada.

"Will you see him again?" Godgifu asked.

"What if I never do? What if he is destined to marry, I don't know, some Frankish princess?"

"Surely a marriage that brings Wessex and Mercia closer is what the King would want?"

"Doesn't Eadric and Eadgyth achieve that? Wouldn't his son marrying me just be a waste? What if Edmund falls in love? I could not bear to be left with Leofric."

"It's so unfair, isn't it." Godgifu leaned towards Aelfgifu and embraced her.

Are you two now friends, Fleada wanted to ask? Thank goodness.

The afternoon passed with lighter chatter and sticks thrown for the dogs. After Godgifu produced another flask of wine which she admitted she's been holding back for herself in case she'd wanted to leave early and make her own way home, they even took off their clothes and jumped into the river.

Fleada did not want to join this adventure, but she was told she had to. Godgifu again said this was her father's land, and the people hereabouts were all her father's ceorls. Aelfgifu said "There is nothing to be scared of," and Fleada saw that both were innocent of those already outlawed, or foreign, or mad, or desperate, or drunk. And what were their fathers' names worth after dark when ogres woke in the trees and nixies emerged dripping from the rivers? "Please let us not stay here too long," she asked.

She managed to ensure sure they got back to Coventre an hour before dusk, and it was as well that they did, for Nothman and Leofric rode into the market square while they were handing the ponies back to Aculf. Godgifu saw them from the dark of the stable, swiftly kissed her new friend, and took her horse out through the back door.

The brothers didn't come to the stables with their horses, so no questions needed answering as to where the girls had been. It wasn't their business, to be sure, but Nothman was liable to throw his weight around in Eadric's absence, and Leofric was the type to look for any tiny secret that might one day be useful.

Fleada watched and listened from behind Aelfgifu's seat as they ate. Leofric explained that they had ridden from Caestrfeld with Eadric, Sigeferth and Morkere, as far as Deoreby. Then Eadric had gone west to see Eadgyth where he left her in Tamworth, to return with her to Coventre soon.

He had invited them to break their journey to Weogorna here, because they had been travelling for the worst part of twelve days. With two more before they'd be home again, they were looking for good food, a big fire, and soft beds.

"Whatever you need, just ask, and if it is not forthcoming someone will have me to answer to," said Aelfgifu, her head held high.

Leofric thanked her politely, but Nothman was effusive. "We are humbled by your kindness," he said, "by your concern and your consideration. You treat us like princes."

Fleada wondered if Nothman was thinking of Prince Edmund. She wondered if Aelfgifu was.

"And how did you find Sweyn Forkbeard?" Aelfgifu asked. "Is he as fearsome as the stories say?"

She was proud of the way Aelfgifu ignored Nothman's insincerity. The man didn't know the meaning of the word humble. Look at him, petting Paris and Hector and feeding them scraps of meat as if he was their master.

"Here's what you need to know about Sveyn," he said. "First, his beard is not forked. Once, it was. But no longer."

"For why?"

"My guess is that it looked even wispier divided into two than it did left alone. Sveyn Wispbeard doesn't want anyone questioning his virility."

"The fact is, he's getting old," Leofric said. "That's what you need to know about him. He's even older than Aethelred."

"Is he dying?" Aelfgifu asked.

Fleada could not begin to guess what changes would come on his death, but knew they would be profound.

"He shows no sign of illness. A thin beard and receding hair, it comes to us all."

"Speak for yourself," said Nothman, laughing at Leofric, who smiled humourlessly. He must be used to Nothman's jibes.

"Is he too old to attack Mercia?" asked Aelfgiu.

"I don't think he is an enemy of Mercia," Leofric reassured her.

"Oh good. I do hope I can meet him before he dies."

"Perhaps you will," said Nothman, "Perhaps you will."

Was the glance that Leofric delivered to Nothman meaningful, Fleada wondered? It was as hard for her to read the brothers as it was easy for them to read each other.

Aelfgifu was still curious about Sveyn. "So he was pleased with the treasure Eadric took for him?"

"He wasn't pleased at all," said Leofric. "He was insulted. But his ire was at King Aethelred and Wessex, not at us."

"He was offered other advantages, shall we say," added Nothman. "So you needn't worry."

This time Leofric's glare was obvious.

Aelfgifu apologised for not having separate rooms for the brothers. "If we were in Lyccidfield, you would have your own rooms, I promise you. But Coventre is not grand."

"No matter," said Leofric. "We are brothers, after all."

"We'll even share when we're married," Nothman said. It sounded like a joke, but only Nothman laughed. "I try to get him to warm my bed, like your girl does for you, but he refuses. I even say 'Brother, I'll warm your bed if you warm mine' but he's still not interested."

"Because that's brainless," Leofric said. "We still have to get into a cold bed."

"Ah, but we'd have the reward of then getting into a warmed bed! He prefers hot ashes in a pan," Nothman said to Aelfgifu.

"We have those in place," she reassured him. "And the mattresses are kept aired."

"You are very kind." Leofric said. He said it coldly, but at least the words were right.

Aelfgifu had hot ashes too, and the dogs were lying on the bed, so Fleada's task of warming would be no trial. The girls put on the shifts they wore for sleep, and each passed her waters into the pot. Fleada put the lid on it, and hauled the dogs to the foot of the bed where, with luck, they'd stay. She blew out the candles save one reed candle spiked into a crock of sand, which could be allowed to burn quietly down.

The girls lay together in its tremulous light discussing the brothers. "I've decided I don't like Nothman after all," Aelfgifu confided. "He is handsome, and I would not turn down a kiss from him, but his jokes are tiresome."

"Leofric is cold."

"How do they stand each other?" Aelfgifu giggled.

"They will share, even after they marry."

"That's horrible, even as a jest."

"Some jests are truths too," Fleada said.

Aelfgifu was quiet for a moment, then she asked Fleada what she thought Eadric might have offered to Sveyn to soften the insult of Aethelred's inadequate gafol.

"I don't know how such men play their games. Perhaps it was land. What does Mercia have that Sveyn doesn't?"

"Apples?" said Aelfgifu, giggling again. "Good horses?"

The door opened. "Not apples. Not horses." It was Nothman's voice. "Not even land."

"What? Get out!" Aelfgifu wailed. "Fleada, get the ceorls."

"There's no need for that," Nothman said. "You don't want to see ceorls die in your room, do you?" A sound came, the unmistakeable sound of a sword being half drawn, and Fleada thought for an instant that Nothman had gone mad and wanted to slice them in their bed where they lay. But the sword was replaced, and his voice was mellifluous. "And for no reason. Gentle Fleada is all you need to keep you safe from me."

The dogs were no help, Fleada saw. They had lazily wagged their tails at the arrival of their friend, who came boldly to the bed and casually patted their sides and stroked their heads.

"You were listening at the door," Fleada said, outrage in her voice.

"I can't deny it," Nothman sang. "Well, I could. I could say I was looking for the place to make soil, but you wouldn't believe me."

"It's just-"

"Rude. I know. Listening, not making soil." He closed the door behind himself. "But it is interesting. You never know what you might find out."

"What did you find out?"

"You don't like my jests, for a start. Your maid thinks my brother cold. She's right, of course, and I admit, my humour isn't to everyone's taste. But my lady, I didn't mean that I never know what I might find out. I said 'you'. You never know what you might find out."

Aelfgifu was perplexed. "What I might find out?"

As indeed was Fleada, but Fleada wasn't mired in her curiosity. "There is nothing my lady needs to know that she needs to know tonight."

"But there is," Aelfgifu said to her. And to Nothman: "I want to know. Tell me. What might I learn?"

Her lady was not easy to help.

Nothman went to Aelfgifu's side of the bed. "I will tell you. But first, a little favour, if you please. I've seen you look at me, my sweet. I know that you like what you see."

"What favour?"

"Just a kiss. It's not so difficult. It's one of life's great pleasures, a kiss shared between a handsome man and a beautiful girl."

"I don't want a kiss."

"Oh but you do! I heard. Your own lips gave you away. They know what they want."

"She doesn't want a kiss," Fleada repeated.

"She does, more even than she knows. Aelfgifu, sweet lady, before your first honeycomb, did you know how much you wanted honey? Before your first ripe berry? Your first cream? I promise you, after your first kiss you will be happy to give all of those up for more."

How many girls had he offered such blandishments?

"And if I'm not? If I don't like it?"

"You keep your side of the barter, I'll keep mine. But you will love your kisses. Do not be fearful."

Fearful? He never saw her with Edmund!

"Just one kiss, then," she said.

"Then it must be long, and sweet, and unforgettable."

Nothman leaned over Aelgifu. Her arm came out from under the covers and curled around his neck. The kiss lingered, and continued, and Fleada sensed a small motion, the ripple of Aelfgifu's hips that she knew well enough. Nothman's hand was moving, it slid under the cover, it was moving onto Aelfgifu's breast. Where would squidfingers stop? When would she stop him? "My lady…" Fleada said.

The kiss continued.

"My lady."

Nothman raised his head. "Have you no delicacy? This is a private moment. You should no longer be here. I suggest-"

"No," Aelfgifu gasped, her voice a croak.

"No? Very well. She can stay. She does add a certain something, I will admit. Now where were we?"

He bent again, but this time Aelfgifu pushed him away. "You had something to tell me."

"Ahh, but more kissing first. Not for the barter, but because you so love the kiss."

"Tell me. Then I'll consider."

"That is fair. But my lady, it is chilly here, and I have not worn my day clothes. I am just in linens. Permit me to lie alongside you, where it is warm."

Aelfgifu sighed, though whether from resignation or desire, Fleada could not tell. She lifted the cover for him and shuffled to the middle of the bed. Fleada had to move to the far edge.

Nothman lay alongside Aelfgifu. "Ahh," he sighed, pulling the covers over himself, "You are so warm, so welcoming, so gracious."

"And you are so devious," said Aelfgifu. "Now speak, or I scream for the ceorls, and let what blood may flow, flow."

"Oh, blood may flow," said Nothman.

"Speak!"

Nothman emitted a long and heavy sigh. He sat up, and leaned back on the pillow. "I'm not sure you will welcome the news."

"For goodness sake," Aelfgifu snapped. "You obviously came here to tell me, not just to honeytalk your way onto my lips and into my bed."

This is more like my lady, thought Fleada. She understood Aelfgifu's painted veil of giddy girlishness, but she didn't like it.

"Ah, but if I had no desire for your lips, I would have waited until morning to talk."

"Now you've tasted them, speak."

"On one condition."

"Conditions! I think you are breaking our contract now. I think you should leave."

"Very well, no conditions. Just a humble request, that when Eadric tells you this, you feign surprise. It will serve you best, I think."

"And it will serve you best too."

"Granted. Thus, we share more than kisses."

"I will pretend ignorance."

"Does he see through you?"

Aelfgifu snorted, and Fleada thought: do you?

Nothman shuffled to a more upright position. "Very well. When we were face to face with King Sveyn-once-Forkbeard, Eadric doused the royal anger with an offer, an incomparable offer, that will endear him to Mercia and all the English in the north, and many in the south too. A gift, precious and unique."

"A gift?"

"And that gift, dear lady, is yourself."

"Me?"

"In marriage, to his son Knut. To be celebrated just as soon as the boy arrives from Denmark. I say 'boy'. He is a man, fearsome, cruel, and mean, by all accounts, and given to fits of temper that all about him fear."

"My God," whispered Aelfgifu.

"He will take you to Denmark, away from all you know and love, away from your home and your friends. Away from your trusted handmaid. Fleada? He will not want her there. Or if he does, it will be as his mistress. He is known as a voracious monster, defiling girls and casting them aside like a youth spits out apple pips."

Aelfgifu was shocked into silence.

"I cannot pretend to know what your ambitions are, or were…" Nothman said.

"I- I-"

"…But it is obvious to all where your destiny rightfully lies. You are surely not innocent of this."

Ambition and destiny, Fleada thought. Can they not be the same? What were Aelfgifu's thoughts, as she waited for him to speak again?

"When your godfather and guardian looks unlikely to have a natural child of his own, as he does, you become key to the future of Mercia. A union between Mercia and Hwicce would be universally welcomed."

"Meaning me, and you."

"Ah! Such delight to hear those words. For I would happily devote myself to you were you a miller's daughter or a shepherdess."

"Mercia as a dowry would not go amiss, I feel."

"Mercia as a dowry would mean as little to me as a baked bun or a single cobnut. Were we united, to keep you happy I would even work on the quality of my jokes. If you wish, each time I felt the urge to jest, I would offer a sweet kiss instead."

Aelfgifu shook her head, though whether this was annoyance at his continuing unabashed honeytalk, or dismay at the thought of Knut, Fleada couldn't tell. Nor could she ask. She wanted time alone with her mistress. She felt Aelfgifu needed time alone with her.

"Is this a proposal of marriage, Nothman son of Ledwyn Ealdorman of Hwicce?"

"I had never thought of pledging troth in bed alongside my beloved and her handmaid, wearing my nightgarments. But yes, it is."

"If Eadric has promised me to Sveyn for his son, he will never permit it. So pledge all you like. You'll have to run away with me to Hereford, but then you'll face your father's ire. Eadric will find another lord to take over Mercia when he's gone. Not you."

"Your brother, perhaps…" Fleada was unable to resist interjecting. Her trust in Nothman's protestations of love was like an unlit reed candle, and she was certain Aelfgifu's faith was equally slender.

"There may be another way to save you from Knut." Nothman spoke slowly, tentatively, as if he'd just this moment conceived an infant notion not yet shaped to maturity… which Fleada suspected he'd been nurturing all through that long ride back from Caestrfeld. "Yes, I do believe there is."

"Then share it," Aelfgifu said, and her terse tone told Fleada that she agreed: Nothman had this all worked out in advance.

"Sveyn insists his son must marry a maid. A virgin. Agree to our betrothal, dear Aelfgifu, and seal it tonight. Then Sveyn will refuse Eadric. And you will be free."

"From him. From Knut. Not from you."

"Ah, but your tongue becomes a blade that stabs my heart! You would be no more free of me than I would be free of you, for marriage is God's sacrament between man and woman, it is for life, and it is for love. We shall be indentured to each other, and together, both free. All it takes is for you to surrender your most lovely treasure to me…"

Fleada sincerely hoped that when the time came for the surrender of her own most lovely treasure, she wouldn't have to endure all these words. She hoped it would be with someone who made her laugh, not one who felt such an absurd need to flatter and cajole. Edmund had made Aelfgifu laugh. Was he now out of reach? Would Eadric insist that she be Knut's, whom Nothman painted in such brutish shades?

For all its gilded falsity, was Nothman offering her a lifeline?

"Come, my flower. It must be now, for Eadric will be here tomorrow, and his carving will be complete." His mouth was at her ear, his hand was on her breast again. He was kissing her cheek, her neck, her shoulder. How she loved such kisses. His leg rose to lie across hers. His face rose too, and he kissed her lips again. "This sweetness I give you, my love, for ever." Another kiss. "Delight, not despair. Tenderness, not tears." His hand moved lower, her hips flowed again, her breathing quickened.

Fleada's body responded too, and her thoughts mingled and were hard to capture. Her mistress must be in greater turmoil.

Nothman lay over her. "Fleada, it is time. My lady and I must be alone. But you will always have a place in my house, be assured."

Fleada would not move at his instruction, only her mistress's.

Aelfgifu's arms were around him. Fleada waited for her to push him away as she'd pushed Edmund, but her body seemed to be making a different choice. The bed cover fell aside. Nothman was groping to raise her shift. There will be blood.

Fleada realised: he planned all along to have her whatever she said. That was why he'd made so much fuss of the two dogs back at the meal.

"Fleada, go!" Nothman ordered. "Tell her," he said to

Aelfgifu in an equally sharp voice.

She rolled from the bed and looked back at Aelfgifu who squirmed under Nothman's weight. For all her intimacy with her mistress, she could not read now whether Aelfgifu danced in desire or desperation.

But she could read Nothman. One big hand trapped Aelfgifu's slim wrists above her head while the other groped down between her legs. His black-haired knee pressed itself along her smooth-skinned thigh.

How would a man who forced himself like this ever be the loving husband of his promises? Whatever kind of monster Knut might be, was Nothman better?

Fleada went to the reed candle burning low, and plucked it from the sand like a flower. Cupping the flame, she walked around the bed to where Nothman lay on top of Aelfgifu. She knelt. Nothman, interested only in consummating his ravishment, ignored her.

The hem of his undershirt hung over the bed's edge. It took a few seconds to ignite, but she held the candle in place until the linen was truly caught, and the flames grew, and spread upwards. Aelfgifu saw them, and she bucked violently, taking Nothman by surprise. She scrambled from under him.

When he saw the flames he leaped from the bed, but they followed him, and his movement only allowed the fire to climb all the way up his linens. The dogs sprang from the bed and stood back, hackles up and growling, frightened of the flames. Nothman slapped at the tongues of fire, his beard singed to nothing, and he screamed and hopped until Fleada lifted the bedpan and poured two maidens' worth of piss over him, then wrapped a blanket around the unextinguished folds of his smock. Aelfgifu threw a sheepskin over the mattress before its feathers caught.

Fleada unwrapped him, and they saw his wet clothes stuck to his limp manhood. The dogs yipped and ran in excited circles, and Nothman fled the room, dripping, charred and bare-arsed.

The two girls stood there in silence. For two seconds. Then they squealed, and rolled onto the bed, and held themselves and each other, and laughed and laughed until it hurt. Hector and Paris leaped up to lick their faces, and two tails beat the air.

19. The Traitor's Wife

(Godwin)

"Valkyrie!."

"GO! Do as my son says!"

"Gather your valuables and your livestock," called Godwin. He knew they would not leave without the former, and he knew equally that they'd need the latter. "Take food for a day, and blankets. Any animals you can lead. You have one quarter of one hour, and the village must be empty."

"NOW GO!" screamed Saehild again, and the villagers fled. Put men armed and trained behind her, and Brihtric would have stood no chance. She had but boys and women. "Cenwig, why are you still standing there?" his mother demanded. The youth turned.

Godwin called after him. "Cenwig, you must gallop. The villages south may have less time." Cenwig might run into Brihtric's men coming up the Cicaestr road, but he'd surely have the sense to get off the road. Men on foot would not catch him.

Only Brother Snell was left. "I'll not leave my church."

Snell was the one person who might be safe. "Then go to the southern end of the village, and if you see anyone approach who you don't recognise, run back screaming 'Mercians!'"

"Is it as bad as you say?"

"Worse. Trust me, Brother." In his life, and especially in recent years, Godwin had talked with Snell more than with any other man, even his father. And Snell listened. The priest nodded and turned to walk through the village.

Godwin turned to his mother. "We must go too."

She gave him the same look that she'd given him all his life, the same dragon's stare she gave the village.

"Mother, Brihtric will raze us. There's nothing we can do. Comtyn is no berh, it can't be defended."

He knew she would not be moved.

"Saewin!" she called, but Saewin was right behind her. She looked down. "Get your woollen mantle and a blanket and bag, and do what Godwin tells you."

Godwin stuffed food from the pantry into his own bag. When Saewin came with hers, he told her to rope two goats. He went outside, where already people were plodding into the street with capes over their shoulders, sacks filled with complaining chickens on their backs, goats on ropes and pigs led by the nose, and some prodding a cow ahead of them. They were old men and women, they were mothers and children. The few younger men were crippled or feeble. Perhaps that was just as well, for the strong and the bold might want to resist. They'd be outnumbered, outfought, and the village would burn just the same.

Gret came to him, carrying a hemp bag. "You didn't say hello," she pouted.

"There was no time," he said. "Hello," he said, equally sharply.

"Aren't you pleased to see me?"

He was pleased to see her, for she was a pleasing sight, with her big eyes and thick hair the colour of night. Wasn't it obvious he'd be pleased? Why did she demand he tell her? Couldn't she see there were more important things for him to deal with? "One day, maybe, but right now, I wish I didn't have to." He was offending her, but she had other imperatives today, even if she did not fully recognise them. "Now go with your mother."

"Where to?"

"You have uncles in Elstead, no?"

"Where will you go?"

"Gret, just go! Don't return until it's safe." She turned back to her mother looking as if her wedding had just been called off.

"Where will we go?" said Saewin.

He was the Thegn's son. Any headman in any nearby village would offer space for himself and Sae, but only until word spread of the Thegn's treason, and then they'd cast him out. Brihtric would ensure that everyone knew. He might even put a reward out for the Thegn's son. Who better to make an example of? Godwin doubted that abandoning his father at Brimclif would count for much against the message Brihtric and the King could send by beheading the traitor's son. Those same headmen, how many would not hand him over for reward and favour, or merely to keep their own village safe? How many would protect Saewin?

The answer to Saewin's question was: as far away as possible. "For now, we go to Elsted, with Gret." That would please them both. "Then I shall take you to Liss Abbey."

"I don't want to be a nun."

"Just for a while, Rabbit."

He began the walk north. At Comtyn's bounds, he turned and looked back at his home, still expecting to see the Scorham men march in, or palls of smoke from Walderton, Ashling or Bosham against the pink clouds of sunset. How far had Cenwig got? Would the southern villages believe him?

Where were Cudbert, Sel, Eg and Odylia? What would they walk into when they arrived?

His mother emerged from beyond their house with a face that was going nowhere.

He shook his head at the sickness now in the pit of his stomach. He looked for Gret's thick mop of black hair, called her name, and she came to him at a run. "Gret, please, I need you to look after Sae. If it comes to it, take her to Liss Abbey." This time he kissed her, on the lips, and he felt her softness and warmth pressed to him, and he held her tight, feeling her reluctance to let him go. He gently pushed her back. "I can't come. I know I can rely on you." He watched her, waiting for argument, but she gave none. A kiss, a hug, and a favour humbly asked. Was that all it took to make a girl feel special, and compliant?

Saewin looked from her brother to her mother. She ran up and held herself to him like a limpet. "Don't," she whimpered. "Please don't."

Don't what? Don't stay? Don't let mother stay? Don't die?

He prised her free "I'll follow with mother. It will be all right."

Tear-filled eyes accused him of lying.

"Rabbit, I promise." He turned away. He could feel Gret's and Sae's eyes on his back like four burning coals. He shook the coals off, returned to his mother, and did not look over his shoulder. My last promise ever, he thought. Certain to be broken.

As darkness fell, they took turns sitting by the open door, watching for torches in the night, listening for Snell's call. The Brother had stationed himself at the southern end of the village, and was wrapped in a blanket against the night air.

Godwin told his mother that Saewin was with Gret, and she'd be taken to Liss if the worst happened. His mother made no answer. There was no point trying to converse.

She broke her silence only twice. The first time, she said "We'll never see the fiery bastard again, you and I. And what has he left you with? The King will take his hundreds."

The King seizing Wulfnoth's estates would not appease Brihtric. The King giving them to Brihtric might.

"We have a village about to be no more. All you will have is your sister and your sword and your horse, and I'm not even sure about the horse."

She had not counted herself in that small list of things Wulfnoth bequeathed him.

The second time she spoke, it was to ask Godwin why he had not left with the villagers.

Because even your most terrible fury cannot withstand fifty men, he wanted to tell her. Because maybe I can somehow find a way to deflect you, or them, so even if Comtyn cannot be saved, perhaps you can. And he wanted to say "Because this is my place." But was it? Even if Comtyn somehow survived, Godwin felt he deserved no inheritance. Someone had to pay for his father's crime, and surely it was he.

All he said was "Why do you stay?" He was sure she'd say nothing, but he was wrong.

"I am half-niece of Aelfric, Ealdorman of Wessex. I do not run. I will not be turned from my home."

So his inheritance was not just from his father. For that he was glad.

Then he fell asleep, and woke to find his mother sleeping too, with the day dawning fresh and bright. He'd not heard the cockerels, but one of their own cows was lowing in the field nearby, wanting to be milked. He went to her with a bucket, so they could have creamy porridge for a breakfast. Another cow mooed, and another, but he couldn't relieve all their remaining herd.

They had not yet finished the porridge when Brother Snell came running, his habit flapping, from the end of the village. "Someone's coming!"

A horse whinnied, but there was no movement. Both Godwin and his mother silently reached for the bawdricks on belts, and the swords leaning against the wall. But before they had knotted them on, a single horse walked into the village with a short limping gait. It was a cob the colour of peat, and was riderless. Godwin clicked his tongue, and Linden lifted her head and plodded unsteadily towards them. Something stuck out from her shoulder like a twig growing straight, with three leaves of chicken feather. Another was in her side, and another through her neck. Three more shafts sprouted from her hindquarters.

So somewhere between here and Bosham lay Cenwig, fallen, growing arrows of his own. He didn't know the danger. Godwin should have been the one to spread the warning. Instead he'd sent Cenwig to his death.

He took the horse into the shade and gave her water. The arrows had gone deep into the muscle, but the bleeding was not severe, and when he washed the wounds, he saw that the punctures were narrow – the arrowheads were likely round bodkins, not cutting flatheads. He gentled her as best he could, and pulled out the shallowest of the arrows. He was right. The others would come out and not tear more of her. The arrow through her neck he would cut, and pull out forwards. He wished Ferley was still here for his way with horses, and Heja, for her poultices.

His mother stood in the house doorway with her arms folded, brooding silently over what was now her village.

"I hope Cenwig got to Bosham and all," he said. "I hope when the Mercians saw him, he was on his way back."

"You hope his death had purpose." Snell said. "Even if he failed, Comtyn is proud of him."

Brother Snell returned to his post, and they stood guard all morning. Only cats, chickens and flies moved.

Then villagers returned, one, two, three. More would follow. They said they wanted to see if their homes were safe. Could they come back now? Godwin showed them Linden, and said that she had returned without Cenwig. At last they believed him. "Take the remaining cows, and go. Take ours. They need milking." The villagers hurried away as fast as they could herd the stock.

Out of the blue, Saehild spoke. "He knew no duty."

It took Godwin seconds to realise she was talking of his father.

"He thieved land. He bought cheap when people were on hard times. He set rents high. Then he was stupidly generous, so people loved him. When he wasn't laughing he was fighting just to amuse the devil. He was a Viking. If England had more like him, we'd not be so fearful."

"We'd not be England," Godwin said. "Why did you marry him?" It was something he never thought he'd dare ask.

"If I hadn't, you'd not be here," she said sharply. Then she pulled a face like stubbed toe, which was as close to a smile as she'd get. "Because he was the man I'd be, if I was a man. So you'd better watch for yourself, because whatever's in us… well, none of it went to Rabbit, that's for sure."

Yes. And this was her day. She guarded Comtyn against Brihtric's fifty men not out of duty or honour, but to entertain Satan.

And Godwin chose to be at her side.

It was past afternoon that the black plume of smoke appeared, rising and bent to the east by the wind. It could only have come from Walderton. Brihtric was burning the villages that had unknowingly betrayed him, one by one. Bosham, Hambrook, Walderton. What special reprisal had he for Comtyn?

A black bearded figure, puffed and sweating, came into the village. Not from the south, but from the east, so unseen by Snell. It was Cudbert. He stooped, resting his hands on his knees, gasping as he spoke. "Wald- Wald-"

"We see," Saehild said.

"Get your breath, Cudbert. Where were the Walderton folk?"

"Gone. 'Twas mostly empty. You did it, Godwin! You got there in time!"

Cenwig got there in time. If I'd travelled quicker, Godwin thought, Cenwig might not have run into Brihtric.

"Are Alric and Agtha safe?"

"Yes. Gone to the Hartings." Agtha was Cudbert's dead wife's sister, Alric his nephew. After Sel, they were the only family he had. "And Sel, Eg, and the girl? Are they safe?"

Cudbert hung his head, as if ashamed. "I told them, go north."

"Good," said Godwin. "Means they'll find Agtha in Harting."

"I told them, and I tried to bloody beat them away. But they wouldn't go. I had to leave them, to run here." Cudbert lifted his head. "Brihtric's men are looting the bits of Walderton they haven't torched. Then they will come. We saw from the trees."

"And Bosham?"

"We didn't come on the road. Never saw them all together, but I think half went to south to Bosham and Hambrook."

"How many in Walderton?

"About two dozen. Hard to tell, with them running around, and the smoke."

Half of forty-eight. That made sense.

Saehild stood. She settled her swordbelt about her hips and pulled higher the chainmail she'd been wearing all day, then wrapped her cloak of woad-dyed wool about her shoulders. She fastened it with a brooch, an heirloom of value not for its metal – brass in need of a polish – but for the intricacy of its design: two snakes entwined and biting each other.

Saehild drew her sword and strode to the centre of the village.

Godwin started after her, and Cudbert after him, both with swords drawn.

"No," she ordered without turning. "You two to stay well behind me. Run when you must. Godwin, look after your sister."

He kept walking with Cudbert.

She turned. "And you, Cudbert, you need to look after your son."

"So do you, lady."

"No. It's you who has to keep your oath to protect Godwin. I need to look after my home, and my people's homes. So, obey."

Cudbert was more obedient than Godwin, and he put his hand on Godwin's shoulder. They watched her walk a few yards ahead, then stop. Cudbert pulled Godwin reluctantly back, halfway towards the house. "If we have to run, be like a chased hare."

If?

Comtyn was silent but for a skylark and some oblivious chickens clucking from a run somewhere behind a house.

The pall of smoke, the last of Walderton, paled and thinned.

How long does it take to loot a village, raze it, and walk with the spoils the next couple of miles to Comtyn?

Snell was still stationed to look down the road. He rose, took a step forward to inspect whatever he'd seen, and hurried to them. "They come." He stood alongside Saehild, but she motioned him away, so he retreated halfway towards his chapel.

A movement. Three figures appeared, running into Comtyn. Not Brihtric's men, but Eagbert, pulling at Selferth's arm as Sel staggered as fast as he could, exhausted and sweating, outpaced even by Odylia. "They are just behind us!" Eg called.

Cudbert stepped towards them. "Get out of the village. Selferth, you can't run further, you have to go now!"

Sel shook his head.

Godwin said "Do as he says, Sel. Get beyond my house. There are horses. Barely fit, but all we have. Odylia, you too. One of the horses needs care. You can do that? You can, I saw you with your brother. So go! Mount up and make ready to run. Don't wait for us."

Odylia went, but still Sel and Eg stood.

Cudbert said "I command you!"

Sel didn't even shake his head, he just stared back.

"Saddle Whitebeam," Saehild ordered. "And bring him to me."

Eg followed Odylia at a trot, but Sel remained rooted.

Godwin shouted "Fuck you, Sel! Just go!"

It was an outrage against friendship, but it worked. Reluctantly, Sel turned.

Cudbert looked at Godwin. "Why does my own son obey you but not me?"

Sweat shone on Godwin's face and dampened his armpits, though the sun was weak.

Eg came with Whitebeam, leading him to Saehild. He locked his fingers into a stirrup, to help her mount. She stilled Whitebeam with a pat to his neck, then sat motionless and stately, facing the danger.

Brother Snell called "Look!"

A horseman rode into the village ahead of a crowd of raucous men who no longer marched in ranks. They had clearly found Walderton's store of wine. All had swords, and a few had bows. Two, the fattest and least fit, carried torches that shimmered in the daylight and gave off black smoke. Their waggon trundled to a stop behind them, piled high with loot: full sacks, pots, and furs.

Jeers went up when they saw Saehild, sitting regally on her

white stallion in her mail hauberk. "Valkyrie!" one shouted, and another warned "Beware Boudicca!" A third called "Amazon! Show the boys your tit."

The leader stopped and held up his hand. Dark hair protruded from under his helm, and a black moustache spread wide under his noseguard. Godwin wondered why he wore a helmet – if he thought it made him look fearsome, he was wrong. Coming into an empty village, it made him look fearful. Was this Brihtric, brother of Eadric Streona?

"Who comes armed uninvited into Comtyn?" Saehild shouted, and the jeers grew louder.

"Ah, this rathome is Comtyn," the man said from beneath his moustache. "Whose name is shamed by the very man who was once its Thegn. It is nice to have a welcome, even a rude one. The other villages were empty. We found the boy who gave them warning…"

The archers among the men raised their bows and cheered themselves.

"…but I never got to ask him how he knew we were coming."

The cheering hushed.

"I am Brihtric, Ealdorman of Mercia…" More cheers. "…and commander of the King's fleet. Who is the crone who can barely carry the weight of the chainmail she wears like a shroud?"

"I am Saehild, daughter of Ecfrith of Wintancaestr, and until the King or Ealdorman Aelfric my uncle appoints another Thegn, I am Headwoman of Comtyn and Walderton."

"Stand down, or you will be the head-less woman of Comtyn and Walderton." He was playing to his men, and gave them time to laugh before turning back to her. "The King has a fury at Wulfnoth. Your husband, yes?"

"Renounced."

Brihtric laughed, and turned to shout to the men "So no-one in his family knows anything at all of loyalty." They cheered him. "It will not save you or your festering hamlet."

Brihtric said something to the man beside him, some senior husceorl, who motioned with his arm, and the two with the lit torches stepped forward.

"You have no authority for this," Saehild shouted.

"But I do. I have the King's authority. I am commander of the fleet, appointed by Aethelred himself."

"I see no boats. We are not at sea. Ealdorman Aelfric would not let Mercians attack a Wessex village."

"Ealdorman Aelfric is not here."

Another man on horseback appeared behind Brihtric, with a dozen more riders behind. Reinforcements, as if Brihtric needed aid. They must have been following him on the road from Scorham. Brihtric either didn't hear them, or he expected them, for he took no notice.

"Start," the husceorl ordered.

"No! Stop!" Godwin shouted.

"Keep quiet, you, at least until your balls have dropped." And twenty-four men laughed.

Godwin and Saehild could only look on helplessly as the pair carrying torches went to the edge of the village, and thrust their flames into the thatch of one cottage, front and back, ensuring it had caught, before moving on to the next. The younger stepped aside to apply his flame to one of the beehive skeps. Waxy from being handled, it caught swiftly. As confused bees swarmed angrily into the air, honey and wax flooded over the platform and onto the ground. The man jumped back from the bees before any stung him, but the bees saved their sisters' hives.

Comtyn needed its guardian, and quickly, but the giant Bevis slept on in his barrow.

Godwin searched his head for something he could offer to

Brihtric, and remembered Hemming's oath to his father. "I will leave my home to serve you, if you leave the village unharmed."

"Let me guess," Brihtric sneered. "If the woman in mail is the traitor's wife, then you are the traitor's son."

Godwin could only set his jaw more firmly, and that sufficed for Brihtric. "We already know that treachery is in your family's blood. The only reason to take you would be as a hostage, to make your father return with the boats he stole. But plainly he has no regard for you, your mother, or the village he was sworn to lead and protect. You have no value to anyone." He turned to face his troop. "What do you think, men? Should I just exact the punishment here and now, that I'd have to do in a few months after his father fails to give himself up to save this lout's paltry life?"

The men cheered an affirmative. The new arrivals on horseback looked on silently.

"Bring him here!"

Four men stepped forward. Saehild drew her sword. Whitebeam lifted his hooves and set them down again, ready to skip where directed. Cudbert drew his sword, and the men halted, unsure what to do now they faced resistance. The rings of Saehild's chainmail rattled, and the men were suddenly aware they had no such protection.

Brihtric swept his arms forward, left then right, and the men fanned out on either side so that Seahild was at the centre of a horseshoe. Fourteen drew swords, and eight notched arrows.

She turned her head and muttered over her shoulder to Godwin. "If you fight, you die. Do not fight."

How could he do other?

Brihtric's men held their swords two-handed, most of them pointing at Cudbert whom they feared most. The archers raised their bows, awaiting a signal to attack. The pair with torches stopped their work to watch events.

"I would have done as the Romans did," Brihtric called. "Executed one man in ten from each village, for crimes against the King. But I'll be content with the traitor's wife, the traitor's son, and this bear standing with them."

"I can tell you how twenty boats made fools of fifty faster ones," Godwin shouted. It was a weak offer, and he knew it.

"Tell me how to command a storm," Brihtric snarled. "And I might be interested." He noticed the men with torches standing still. "Did I tell you to stop?"

The resumed setting Comtyn ablaze.

"Your boats sailed into a trap," Godwin shouted, stepping forward. "They knew nothing of fighting at sea. If they couldn't beat my father, how will they match the Danes?"

He saw Brihtric fighting to control his fury. He probably felt he was being mocked. This wasn't the way to deal with a man like Brihtric. There was a lesson here, though it was unlikely he'd live to act on it.

"And your proud father returned to boast of this to you?"

"No. I saw it happen."

"What's your name, boy?"

"Godwin. Godwin of Comtyn." He'd never say "Son of Wulfnoth" again.

Brihtric's eyes narrowed. "And somehow you got here before me, to warn your village to flee. Well Godwin Wulfnothson, master of seafaring tactics, you too should have fled, and taken your mother with you. The King will be grateful you did not, and Ealdorman Aelfric will be quiet."

The leader of the newly arrived horsemen lifted his helm, revealing a strong, angular face with a beard trimmed to a point. He spoke. "Unfortunately, Brihtric, neither are true." He was calm and confident. In fact, he looked amused, and Godwin thought it a strange and dangerous manner to use against so powerful a lord as Brihtric of Mercia.

Now Brihtric turned, and was clearly surprised at who he saw. "Edmund!" he said.

The man called Edmund smiled. "Lord Brihtric." He stood high in his stirrups, and held his sword aloft. "Hold!" he shouted. "I am Edmund Atheling, called the Ironside. King Aethelred's order is rescinded. Halt what you do. Put down your swords, lower your bows. And you two, lower those torches."

All that remained unlit were Godwin's own house, the mead hall, the huts at Comtyn's north end, some beehives, and the chapel that Brother Snell guarded with his cross.

"Brihtric," Edmund said. "This is not your land. These are not your people to judge and punish."

"It was my boats sunk, my crews drowned."

"The King's boats, and Ealdorman Aelfric's people. The only thing of yours that's suffered is your pride."

He walked his horse forward, past Brihtric, past Seahild, and stopped before Godwin. "So you were in the sea battle?"

"I watched it from cliffs."

"And you realised that Brihtric would want reprisals, and you got here in, what, less than four days, to warn your people."

Godwin nodded.

"And yet you did not run away with them."

"Even though I bloody told him to," Saehild said.

"And you then are Saehild? You should have gone to your place in Wintacaestr."

"My place is here."

"You have nothing here." Edmund raised his voice for all to hear. "You are no longer a thegn's wife, and you are banished to an Abbey for your husband's crime." He looked at the two men standing next to the largest house in the village. "Burn it," he said. "And the hall."

They went to Godwin's home, and held their torches under the thatched eaves. Once the blaze was unstoppable they took them on, thrust them into the hall's thatch, and left them there.

Edmund looked again at Godwin. "You offered to serve Brihtric. He spurned you. So you shall serve me, and redeem a fraction of what your father lost us."

Godwin bowed. He was alive. His mother was alive. Cudbert, Sel, Eg and Odylia too. He hadn't run. His pride was alive. Bevis has come.

"Follow me," Edmund said, and walked his horse through the village towards the Winctancaestr road.

Godwin went after him, then turned back to wait for his mother. Edmund's troop were walking their horses past Brihtric's men, who gathered around their leader. He leaned down from his horse to speak to his archers.

"Mother!" Godwin cried, and Seahild turned to him.

Five of the first six arrows hit her. Three sharp bodkins pierced the chainmail as they were designed to do, biting into her back. One sank into her right thigh, near the top, and one sank deep into the unprotected soft flesh of her upper arm. She made no sound, but lurched forward in her saddle, and twisted to stare at Brihtric.

Two other archers took more time, and aimed with care. She would have seen their arrows flying at her too fast to avoid.

One went into her left breast, and whether the hauberk stopped it hitting her heart was unknowable, but blood flooded through the mail like berry juice through linen. The other arrow entered her throat just off centre, and emerged from the back of her neck.

More arrows, and more red pouring bright and copious from her skin, her mouth and her nose. Saehild gasped and choked, drowning, and gently toppled from Whitebeam's back. She hit the ground with a thud and the brief tinkle of a thousand chainmail rings.

Godwin tried to run to her, but Edmund's horsemen blocked his way. Saehild tried to rise. Brihtric give an order to the four she had intimidated. Their swords descended, and their blades crushed her skull and severed all connection between head and body.

Brihtric stared at Edmund. He didn't have to speak his challenge.

Edmund stared back. "No more," was all he said, before turning away. All Godwin saw as Edmund's men forced him to follow was one of the Mercians stooping with a seax to slice his mother's brooch from the fabric of her cloak.

Whitebeam was led away towards Brihtric.

Cudbert, Sel and Eg would not be harmed.

Nor would Godwin. But he was bereaved of mother, father, friends, home, and everything save his horse, his sword, and a vow that one day he'd be revenged upon Brihtric of Mercia.

Historical note, places, and words

Warning: this note contains spoilers, so I recommend not reading it until you've finished the story.

I am a novelist, not a historian, and this is a novel, not a history.

The tale is told to sustain narrative flow, to heighten drama, and to create distinctive characters; and I'm not above blurring the line between attested history, legend, valid speculation, and pure invention.

Purists may complain, but I follow a tradition of playing with facts and taking advantage of the many blank pages in the historical record. I hesitate to place myself alongside literary gods, but Homer built myth and legend into his story of the fall of Troy. Shakespeare played with known history. Malory built on a legend of Arthur that may or may not have had a living seed. Don't get me started on the Bible.

Invention happens still, as with different presentations of the ages of the two Boleyn sisters. And Hollywood's mythmaking, shortcuts and calumnies are biblical in extent.

This saga is hung onto known events of the eleventh century up to 1066. Key events surely happened, described in short sentences in the Anglo-Saxon Chronicles and elsewhere. Like the gospels, different authors chose to retell different parts of the story, and told them slightly differently. The Chronicles give no analysis, and only commonplace speculations about cause and effect. Unlike the gospels, there are no quotes, and little moralising.

Another major historical source is the *Encomium Emmae*, written about and for Queen Emma by a Flemish monk. In its favour, it was composed within her lifetime; but it is a hagiography that can hardly be considered objective.

Other elements of the history have been exaggerated by chroniclers writing decades or even centuries later, giving modern historians endless ambiguities and contradictions over which to argue; and giving novelists acres of blank canvas on which if not to paint, at least to write in colour.

These events almost certainly happened: the marriage settlement with Emma following Aethelred's failed invasion of Cotentin; the St Brice's Day massacre; a dispute – we know not what – between Wulfnoth and Brihtric; the theft of Aethelred's boats and the loss of more boats in a storm; the numerous and escalating gafol payments (subsequently known as Danegeld); and Aelfgifu's marriage to Knut.

Most of these occurred over the years between 1009 and 1013, but I have compressed the timescale greatly to sustain the novel's flow. Some historical figures have been excised for simplicity. So, sorry Aethelstan, Edmund's older brother, who actually died within this period, but does not appear to have played a dynamic part in the history.

The major nobles, bishops and leaders existed. Stigand too is a real figure, but the adventures of his early years here are speculation, reverse engineered from some historians' conjectures about his later ones.

Some names have been changed to reduce but sadly not eliminate "Russian Novel Syndrome", whereby too many long and unfamiliar names make it hard to keep track of who is whom. This is especially problematic with aristocratic ladies whose names mostly start Ead- (meaning wealth) or Ael- (meaning elf – Aelfgifu means "gift from the elves"). The elves left at least three notable gifts in the era, but I've had to give them different names. Sometimes it is convenient to Latinise them, but there are still too many Ediths, Ealdgyths, Eadgyths, Eadgifus and the like. Changing one or another to Aelswyth only helps a little. Leofwyne of Hwicce and Morcar of the Five Berhs have become Ledwyn and Morkere to distinguish them from characters who will appear later. I hope the family lists will help.

Of their natures and personalities, we have very little to go on. Aethelred is known as the Unready, from unraed, meaning ill-advised (not unprepared, although he was that too). I've not gone against the common view that he was a ditherer. Eadric was later called Streona, the grasper, which is a clue. He has been named on lists of the worst Englishmen ever. Who doesn't love a good villain? Edward was famously pious; and Emma was certainly a manipulator.

The characters who aren't nobles, the Walts, the Fleadas, the Cudberts, and assorted headmen, thegns, ceorls, priests and peasants, are to a man, woman and child, necessarily invented.

As to Godwin, the main protagonist, although his early years are not documented, "the traitor's son" appellation is not controversial. He rose from that ignoble beginning to gain power equal to, if not exceeding, the King's. His son actually became King. He must have been a man of formidable ability, but to the delight of any author, history does not speak of Godwin the man, so I am free to recreate this mighty but neglected figure.

Place names

English place names and their spellings have changed over history. It is hard to accurately guess when one version mentioned, say, in a 10th century Anglo Saxon Charter, became another version in the Domesday book. I've tried to follow some indication from the records, but I've also used artistic licence. I've regularised most of the spellings of -caster, -caestre, -chester and so on, with a Latin-flavoured -caestr; and -borough, -bergh, -burgh to an admittedly cod early English -berh.

Some placenames, like Rye, appear to have survived unaltered through the centuries. I haven't wilfully changed these, although the recognisable form looks incongruously modern (Rye actually gets its name from old English Atter Ie, meaning 'on the island', thence Rie, until by the 11th century it had become Rye. The name of the wider area of Rameslege, which includes estates pledged to Normandy, is all but disused, but part of it is still known as Rye Foreign.)

I speculate that anyone in those times who was educated enough to have any geographical knowledge of continental Europe would use Latin forms, like Danuvius for the Danube, and the Germania Sea for our North Sea. English commoners more probably knew it as the East Sea; and the Danes, as the West Sea.

With a couple of exceptions, Norman towns seem to have had their current names, but for some I've found a Danish root. We will visit them in later volumes.

English towns, shires and provinces

Arun Dell	Arundel, West Sussex
Bernicia	The northern part of Northumbria, including modern Northumberland, Tyne & Wear, and County Durham
Bremesgrave	Bromsgrove, Worcestershire
Caestr	Chester
Caestrfeld	Chesterfield, Nottinghamshire
Cantenberh	Canterbury, Kent
Cantware	Kent
Cernwealas	Cornwall
Cicaestr	Chichester, Sussex
Coelmaersford	Chelmsford, Essex
Comtyn	Compton, Sussex
Coventre	Coventry, Worcestershire

Cranboka	Cranbrook, Kent
Croming	Cromer, Norfolk
Defenas	Devon
Dofras	Dover, Kent
Eassex	Essex
Escancaestr	Exeter, Devon
Gegnesberh	Gainsborough, Lincolnshire
Glocaestr	Gloucester
Hrofcaestr	Rochester, Kent
Jorvik	York
Ledecaestr	Leicester
Lincylene	Lincoln
Lindesege	Lindsay, approximately modern Lincolnshire
Lunden	London
Lyccidfeld	Lichfield, Staffordshire
Meddestane	Maidstone, Kent
Northamtun	Northampton
Oxenford	Oxford
Plymentyn	Plymton, Devon
Readingam	Reading, Berksire
Rameslege	Lands west and north of Rye, East Sussex
Sanwic	Sandwich, Kent
Snotengaham	Nottingham
Somorsaet	Somerset
Soussex	Sussex
Stamsford	Stamford, Lincolnshire
Suthamtun	Southampton, Hampshire
Suthrige	Surrey
Swanawic	Swanage, Dorsetshire
Tamwerth	Tamworth, Staffordshire
Tenrige	Tandridge, Surrey
Tilberh	Tilbury, Essex
Ulwic	Woolwich, Kent

Weogorna	Worcester
Wiltun	Wilton, Wiltshire
Wintancaestr	Winchester, Hampshire
Wulfrunheaton	Wolverhampton, West Midlands

Geographical features

Ciltern Hills	Chiltern Hills
Germania Sea, West/East Sea	North Sea
Pen Hills	Pennines
Sabrin	River Severn
Tamys	River Thames
Trehynt	River Trent
Wihtware	Isle of Wight
Wrikin	The Wrekin, a steep isolated hill rising above the Shropshire Plain

Outside England

Byzantium	Istanbul (also known in the Middle Ages as Constantinople)
Cotentin	Peninsula in west Normandy, between Cherbourg and Mont St Michel
Deppa	Dieppe
Eirinn	Ireland
Flandra	Flanders
Huniflet	Honfleur
Sveoren	Sweden
Waelas	Wales

Glossary of selected old English words

Barghest	Evil dog monster believed to roam the north at night.
Berh	Fortified town.
Braies	Baggy shorts of linen or wool worn as underwear
Byrnie	Chainmail armour, shorter than a hauberk.
Ceorl	Free man (pr. "churl").
Cild	Honorific title that predated "Sir" (pr. "child" or possibly "chilled").
Cofgode	House-imp, a mischievous creature that haunts households
Collier	Charcoal maker.
Cullions/culions	Old French / English slang for testicles
Dokkse	Mistress or lover ("doxy").
Firouzeh	From the old Persian name for turquoise.
Fyrd	Saxon army.
Glaive	A short sword-like blade on a spear's haft.
Hauberk	Thigh or knee-length coat of chainmail.
Husceorl	Member of a king's, ealdorman's or thegn's troop of personal guards.
Leech	Doctor.
Lem	Penis (old Danish, root of the word 'limb').
Merel	Stone or carved piece used in the game of nine men's morris.
Pintle	Penis.
Reeve	Senior administrator and tax-collector.
Scachis	Chess.
Sceatt	Silver coin. A half sceatt was literally the coin cut in half. In fact silver sceatts were replaced by silver pennies before the 11th

	century, but I have stuck with sceatt because to modern ears "penny" would imply lower value.
Scire	Shire (the post of scire-reeve later became the sheriff).
Seidh	Folkloric shamanistic system of magic (pronounced sithe – yes, George Lucas nicked it for the dark-side Jedi).
Seax	Small dagger.
Shaftment	Unit of measurement: width of the palm plus length of thumb.
Sheith	Sheath or scabbard; euphemism for vagina.
Slow fever	Thyphoid.
Stade	Landing place.
Teorse	Boss at centre of a shield; a euphemism for penis.
Thegn	Formally appointed local leader.
Thuw	Slave.
Widdershins	Anticlockwise – literally 'other direction, (to the sun).
Witangemot / Witan	Gathering of nobles with the King. The Witan had the power to approve, and hence appoint, a new King.

Some key characters

Godwin, and his circle

From the village of Comtyn:

Godwin Wulfnothson
Wulfnoth Cild, Thegn of Comtyn, Godwin's father
Saehild, his mother
Saewin, his younger sister
Eagbert ('Eg') and Selferth ('Sel'), his friends
Cudbert, a ceorl, Sel's father
Gret, Godwin's girlfriend
Brother Snell, priest.

From nearby Bosham, on the coast:

Ham, a boat's captain
Arni, Ham's son
Odylia, his daughter
Hemming, a Danish boatbuilder

Nobles of Wessex

Aelfric, Ealdorman and Chief Thegn of east Wessex
Athelmar, Ealdorman of west Wessex
Ecfrith, Godwin's grandfather, Saehild's father

Soussex:

Gewis, Headman of the village of Brimclif

The English Royals, their servants and ceorls

King Aethelred ('The Unraed')
Children by his first wife:
Prince Edmund ('Ironside'), eldest son
Princess Eadgyth, married to Eadric of Mercia
Princess Wulfhild, married to Ulfcytel of East Anglia
Princess Aelfrith, living at Wherwell Abbey

Princess Ecfrida
Cynethe, Ecfrida's handmaid
Queen Emma of Normandy, Aethlered's second wife, sister of Norman Duke Richard II
Arsindis, Emma's maid
Emma's children:
Prince Edward, Emma's first son
Fulton, Edward's friend and companion
Theodric, Edward's guard
Prince Alfred, Emma's second son
Wilf, Alfred's friend and companion
Wendel, Alfred's guard, Wilf's father
Princess Goda, Emma's youngest
Hendi, Goda's friend and companion

Ellin, household maid
Wilmaer, the Royal Reeve
Ercenbert, Edmund's first husceorl
Deorleaf 'The Mown', Ercenbert's deputy
Father Trebert, priest serving Edmund's fyrd

Mercia

Eadric Streona, Ealdorman of Mercia
Terning, Eadric's Reeve
Marton and Dudric, Eadric's personal husceorls
Thyra, Eadric's dokkse
Brihtric, his brother
Aelfgifu, Eadric's ward, orphan daughter of Elfhelm of Jorvik
Fleada, Aelfgifu's handmaid
Nothman and Leofric, sons of Ledwyn, Ealdorman of Hwicce

East Anglia

Waltheof, shepherd boy of Croming
Ulfcytel Snillingr, Ealdorman of East Anglia
Wulfhild, his wife (Aethelred's daughter)
Father Stigand, Ulfcytel's emissary

Northumbria

Uhtred, Ealdorman of Northumbria
Ule of Stowe, a village headman's son

The Five Berhs

Sigeferth, Ealdorman of three of the Five Berhs
Aelswyth, Sigeferth's wife
Morkere, Sigeferth's younger brother, Ealdorman of two of the Five Berhs

The Danes

King Sveyn ('Forkbeard')
Prince Knut, his elder son
Prince Harald, his younger son

Clerics

Wulfstan, Archbishop of Jorvik and Weogorna
Aelfheah, Archbishop of Cantenberh
Cardinal Elfmar, head of Cantenberh Abbey

The Normans

Duke Richard II of Normandy ('The Good', 'The Pious'), Emma's brother
Judith of Brittany, his wife
Gunnor, his mother
Richard and Robert, his sons
Adeliza, Eleanore and Mathilde, his daughters

ACKNOWLEDGEMENTS

Many words of gratitude are due to many people. I'd particularly like to thank readers Jackie Carter and Sus Coupland, and editor Louise Buckley, whose sound advice I didn't always take.

I should also mention staff and volunteers at the West Stowe Anglo-Saxon Village, near Bury St Edmunds, for their insights into the Anglo-Saxon lifestyle. The Sutton Hoo museum near Woodbridge was equally inspiring. The Jorvik Centre in York, and the 878AD Centre in Winchester provided some irreplaceable visual insights into the period. All are highly recommended.

I could list the many books and articles I've read that have informed the narrative and the descriptions. I shall refrain, not because they are too many to mention, but to spare the authors complicity in my many departures, deliberate and accidental, from their writings. I'm grateful to them all.

But I will mention Academia.edu, which holds a mine of scholarly and accessible articles on the period. And Wikipedia. We can laugh at its errors, but it is a shortcut to information on, well, just about anything. If you use it at all frequently, please make a donation to keep this global resource, this wonder of the modern world, free, well moderated, and ever more reliable.

A Traitor's Son – Volume Two

The book you hold is Volume I of *A Traitor's Son*. Volume Two follows seamlessly: Godwin's story picks up at the very moment we left it here, still in Comtyn.

The two were originally written as one longer novel, but it expanded in the writing and became too long for practical purposes. I divided it at what seemed to be a natural break for most of the main characters. The downside is that the arcs of the stories make more sense over both volumes. The pacing builds, and most of the main characters achieve some kind of resolution by the end of Volume Two. (Not too much, as the tale picks up again in Part Two of The Crown and The Arrow saga, *The Thegn*, in which more storylines converge.)

What I'm saying is, if you enjoyed this novel, you'll get even more out of the follow-ups.

And, please rate and review it on Amazon. Thanks.

If you'd like to see more of my discoveries and thoughts about lives and events of 11th century England, have a look at **www.geoffcarthy.substack.com** (free)

For updates, and news about the forthcoming books in The Crown and The Arrow series, please sign up for an occasional newsletter on **www.geoffcarthy.substack.com**

Subscribe – it's free! – and I'll send you an exclusive fun freebie: a deleted chapter from *A Traitor's Son*.

Geoff Carthy, 2025

Printed in Dunstable, United Kingdom

64539355R00163